NO SANC

MW00330949

Lee Hall Delfausse

Thanks for helping me (Lia) on this journey.

the PeppertreePress, LLC
Sarasota, Florida

Copyright © 2022 Lee Hall Delfausse.

All rights reserved. Published by the Peppertree Press, LLC. the Peppertree Press and associated logos are trademarks of the Peppertree Press, LLC. No part of this publication may be reproduced, stored in a retrieval system, transmitted in any form or by any means, electronic, mechanical, photocopying, recording, or otherwise, without prior written permission of the publisher and author/illustrator. Graphic design and Illustration by: James Knake. For information regarding permission, call 941.922-2662 or contact us at our website:

www.peppertreepublishing.com or write to: the Peppertree Press, LLC.

Attention: Publisher 715 N. Washington Blvd., Suite B, Sarasota, Florida 34236

ISBN: 978-1-61493-825-5

Library of Congress: 2022908395

Printed: May, 2022

We will not cease from exploration, and the end of all our exploring will be to arrive where we started and know the place for the first time.

T. S. Eliot

I learned this, at least, by my experiment; that if one advances confidently in the direction of one's dreams, and endeavors to live the life which one has imagined, one will meet with success unexpected in common hours.

Henry David Thoreau

We must walk on earth, a foot in the physical and a foot in the spiritual.

Lia Erickson

Dedication

If it takes a village to raise a child, then it certainly takes a bevy of friends to publish a book. My sincere thanks go first to my husband, Peter, who encourages my writing and speaking about the role of sports in women's lives.

Every writer needs a group of friends who will read the first draft and give honest and difficult opinions. My thanks to Susie Tompkins, Susie Winthrop, Rosi Fortna, Jim Martin, and Lil Peltz-Petow.

Finally, I'm proud to acknowledge my family: Sarah Olsen Blaisdell, Ollie Olsen, and Pierre Delfausse, who have listened, all their lives, to my stories about skiing on the World Cup tour.

List of other book titles and short stories by Lee Hall Delfausse

Short Stories

Oedipus

Orfie and Elise

Snowbound

Aftermath

Hungry

Novel: Snow Sanctuary

CHAPTER 1

The Supreme Court

I fall to my knees. Struggling to crawl, hand-over-hand like a baby, I surmount the last four steps of the US Supreme Court building, my palms burning on the hot, white Vermont marble, my eyes stinging from my salt-sweat, all the while wishing I were back in my cool Vermont. The National Mall is my training ground for the US Ski Team, the steps my snow-covered mountain, while I'm here working and rehabbing my ankle.

The five-pound weight on my left ankle snags on the last step. I stop to lift my foot and look up, meeting the frozen eyes of a marble lady draped in Grecian robes, juggling a tiny child in her right hand. Below me, a crowd of hippie protesters, adorned with colorful headbands, torn jeans, and masks chants, "No more war!"

Gasping, I feel a hand grab my waist, pull me to my feet, and over the last step. My roommate, Terry, dressed in jeans, tee shirt, goggles, and a black bandana across her nose, spurs me on, "Come on, Lia, you've made it. You've beaten your record of twenty-five minutes, running down the Mall."

A young man in Army fatigues and a yellow bandana over his face pushes toward me, yelling, "Go away, protester. I'm sick of your kind!"

Terry steps between us, "No violence, please. Leave her alone." Looking confused and concerned as if she's seen a ghost, Terry comforts me, "I've got this." She gives the man a gut punch. He strikes back with a blow to my head.

Terry pushes him down the steps, "You Weathermen—you're turning our peaceful protests into violence. You just want to stir up trouble."

Turning back up the steps to me, he yells, "I'll get you yet!"

Meanwhile I'm relieved that she wants to help me. For the last two months I've struggled alone, trying to escape the memories of my ski injury and the trauma of some predatory US Ski Team coaches. Just two months have passed since I flew back to the States from the World Cup race in Maribor, Yugoslavia, to have my fractured ankle reconstructed. During those months I've worked hard to regain my strength, so I could rejoin my teammates on next year's 1972 Olympic team.

After my surgery, I found no interesting job opportunities in Vermont, so I decided to try my luck in the nation's capital. I planned to stay with my Aunt Nancy, my father's sister, where I could get a job, have an adventure, and strengthen my ankle. Little did I know that I'd get involved with the anti-Vietnam War movement.

I first met Terry during one of my after-work training runs when she, too, was running along the Mall. She has a job with the CIA and often travels between Vietnam and America. Her career as a secretary began three years after college at UC Berkeley. On our runs, she quickly became my friend, especially when she learned that I'm a member of the US World Cup Ski Team.

Terry and I now share an apartment on the northwest side of DC. She was also the one who found me a job in the billing department at Doctor's Hospital. My work consists of gathering the accounts for patients who've died during the night, collating them, and then presenting them to grieving family members. Although I'm only nineteen, I find the job easy and very repetitive—yet incredibly sad—but at least I have an income. After all, I do want to be self-sufficient and not have to depend on my father.

When interviewing for the position in May, I didn't tell my employer about my desire to return to the ski team or possibly go to UC Berkeley. If I had, I probably wouldn't have been hired. The next few months will determine which path I'll choose.

The crowd at the top of the steps is now cheering for me. "One more step. You can do it." Terry's arm around my waist supports my tired legs—my broken ankle has swollen to twice its usual size. A gentle breeze at my back lifts me.

At the top, I look back over the Capitol Building and down the Mall to the Washington Monument. There are hundreds of protesters lining the steps of the Congressional Building and even more on the Mall. Tents border the grassy strip, resembling an entrenchment of advancing soldiers.

The sun is setting behind the dome of the Supreme Court, casting a ray of light on the Statue of Justice. Exhilarated, I'm growing more confident that through hard work, it is possible for me to control my destiny.

A woman surges forward from the crowd to help, shouting, "Lia, Lia Erickson, what are you doing here?" I look up to see Greta, a German woman whom I'd met on the train to Bad Gastein, while I was in Europe during the World Cup races. Her gnarly, gray hair has been cut shorter and a cotton pantsuit had replaced her ankle-length, woolen skirt.

I gasp, "Greta, this is amazing! Are you here protesting the Vietnam War?"

She laughs, "Now, Lia, you know I've devoted my life to peace, as well as to women's rights. You know I believe that the struggle to end the war is part of our fight for women's rights. Women need to have a voice in government, for sure!" She pauses as if remembering the horrors she'd told me about her life in Dresden, Germany, during World War II. Looking up into the eyes of the Statue of Justice, she continues, "Perhaps if we elect more women to government, then, just maybe, women can help prevent these horrible wars."

"Oh, yes, of course, I remember. You told me on the train that the next great cause in the States should be women's rights."

"So, Ms. Racer, why are you here in Washington? Why are you running up the steps to justice?" She smiles as if this were an inside joke.

I follow her eyes to the marble statue and sigh, "It's a long story. Why don't you come back to my apartment tonight and have supper with my roommate, Terry, and me?"

At this point, Terry steps out from behind me, heads toward Greta, and extends her hand. The two look into each other's eyes without saying a word, nodding as if they know each other.

Greta, still holding Terry's hand, says, "Okay, Lia, sounds good to me. What's your address?" She winks at Terry.

I look to Terry for confirmation, "Corner of Sixth and Northeast I Street. You know, just off Constitutional Avenue. See you at 7:00 tonight." I collapse on the top step, look up into the orange sun, and marvel at all the coincidences.

CHAPTER 2

Unexpected Meeting

Greta arrives at our apartment at exactly 6:30 that evening, just after Terry and I had picked up some spaghetti and a salad from the corner market. She enters through the back door and goes right to the living room couch, as if she's done this many times. I follow her, incredulous that she doesn't even exchange the usual pleasantries with me.

Terry greets her, carrying two glasses of red wine, "Nice to see you again. It's been a while." She sets down the glasses, then winks, putting her hands together in the form of a prayer, her fingers touching before making a strange move. The base of her palms separates, and her index finger drops across to form an "A." Greta does the same.

Taking a chair across from the two of them, I glance from Terry to Greta, then Greta to Terry, back and forth as fast as a hummingbird looking for extra pollen, my eyes asking for explanation.

Finally, Greta turns to Terry, nodding, "Well, Terry, I think we need to tell our friend, Lia, a few things." Terry smiles, saying nothing. She just puts her hands forward, as if offering Greta the opportunity. Under her oversized eyeglasses, Terry's enigmatic smile tells me nothing.

Standing tall in her pantsuit, Greta's German accent becomes more pronounced, just as I remember it from the train ride to Bad Gastein. "Okay, Lia. I need to tell you how Terry and I met." I roll my eyes, prepared for anything. She continues, "Vell, ve met three months ago at a protest here in Vashington. Some National Guardsmen had beaten Terry so severely that she had fallen to the ground, unconscious. Fortunately, I had some cold water that I rubbed on her forehead to revive her. Ja, I dragged her away from the crowd before the police could arrest her."

I shake my head, disgusted, "How nasty! Is this what happens during

9

protests?"

Terry interrupts, "Actually, it's often worse, especially when the guardsmen use tear gas to disperse the crowds. Once the cloud of gas covers the area, the protesters are forced to drop to the ground, allowing the soldiers to kick them as they crawl away. Sometimes even the Weathermen add to the insults—you know, a lot like the one who attacked you." She wags her finger at me, "You never know who is on what side."

Now I'm really confused and ask, "Who are the Weathermen?"

Greta continues, "Oh, you are so naïve. I guess you didn't learn much ven you vere on the ski team. Your coaches must have sheltered you from the real vorld happenings, ah … so you could focus."

I interrupt angrily, "Don't talk to me about coaches, those rotten creeps." Standing up, I stomp my feet to emphasize my point, "They never protected me, especially because they were the problem." An image of head coach John Boast attacking me in Maribor rattles around in my head.

Attempting to placate me, she motions that I return to my chair as she adds, "Okay, okay, calm down. Anyvay, you'll learn more about the protest movement if you go to Berkeley."

I put up my hands to stop her. "Wait a minute. How did you know I'm thinking of going to Berkeley?"

Greta laughs and pushes her gray hair back from her face, "Remember, Terry and I are friends." She looks to Terry to see whether she should tell me more. "Okay, so the Veathermen are a group of wery radical-militarist civilians who like to foment unrest, even chaos. As chaos-makers, they like taking advantage of students, causing more conflict between them and the National Guardsmen."

At this point, I ask for more background information. Terry explains that students have grown terribly angry about being drafted and sent to Vietnam. Frustrated, they have few options for avoiding the war, other than deserting to Canada, joining the Peace Corps, or declaring Conscientious Objections (becoming a CO).

She adds, despairingly, "It used to be that if you were in college, you couldn't be drafted, but Nixon changed that in 1969. Now even being in college doesn't ensure a young man won't be drafted. Ja? Last year on the first of December, the Selective Service National Headquarters here had a random drawing that assigns a number to each day of the year. If you were born on that day, you would receive a draft number and then your state would decide when you would go into the Service. No male born between 1944 and 1950 could be exempt unless he was disabled or a CO." She pauses to see if I'm following her point. "So now, even the rich kids—the Ivy League college kids—are being drafted. It's no longer a war for the poor, colored, and uneducated."

Naively, I ask, "Wow, is that the whole reason for the protests?" I pause, seeing Terry and Greta nodding to each other. Angry, I continue, "Do you think they'll ever draft women?"

Greta jumps to her feet, splashing red wine on her pants, "How foolish vould that be? If they do, vomen, who make up 51 percent of the population, would vote the government out of office. That is, if vomen could learn how to unite."

Her comment reminds me of what my ski teammate, Becky, had said when we all finally agreed to report the corrupt US Ski Team coaches to the authorities. "Snowflakes are such ephemeral things but look what they can do when they stick together." By joining forces, Becky, Carla, and I actually did manage to have two predatory coaches removed and sent back to the States to face the consequences.

Unfortunately, I've yet to hear what happened to them. Nothing's been said—the two coaches just disappeared. A new coach, Dave Hanson, was hired to lead the team to the 1972 Olympics. My thoughts turn to my friends, Becky and Carla, who are skiing and training right now at Monmouth Mountain in California.

Terry pokes me, "Hey, you, sometimes you get way too quiet." Then she turns to Greta to discuss the plans for the big protest on the following day, the first of May. She explains that the group will meet at the Washington Monument and walk down the Mall to the steps of the Capitol Building. There they will meet some anti-war Vietnam vets, including John Kerry. The vets will take their medals, their purple hearts, and silver stars, and throw them at the entrance steps, chanting, "No more war, no more war!"

Terry turns on her TV to check the news about the protests. Walter Cronkite announces that day's demonstrations, "Today, over 15,000 soldiers and police are gathering to handle the 30,000 protesters who are expected at the Capitol Building tomorrow. This will be the largest mass gathering to date. John Kerry, who spoke in front of the Senate Foreign Relations committee on April 22, will lead the veterans." Terry gets up to turn off the TV, saying, "We did it! We made the national news again!"

I gasp at the numbers and count myself lucky that I wasn't arrested today while running down the Mall. I worry, *How will my father feel if I end up in jail? Will I be allowed to be on the US Olympic Team if I were arrested in Washington?*

I sense that Greta and Terry have been planning these events for a while. I ask cautiously, "So how involved are you two in these protests?" No one says a word, so I quickly change the subject, "Hey, Terry, how often do you return to the States from Vietnam as a CIA secretary?" In a challenging, concerned voice, I add, "Aren't you worried to be seen with these protesters?"

Terry answers, "Not really, because I go dressed as a hippie and wear a mask. No one can recognize me, even if they take my picture."

A knock on the door startles us, so we immediately stop talking. Terry puts her finger to her lips and indicates with her other hand that we should move to the kitchen. I tiptoe out, letting my hand rest on Greta's shoulder. After we're out of sight, Terry opens the door and demands, "Who are you? Why do you have guns?" Then she yells, "What do you want?"

CHAPTER 3

Secrets Revealed

A stern voice answers, "I'm Lieutenant Callahan of the Metropolitan Police." Footsteps enter the room as he continues, "Miss, are you okay?"

Terry's footsteps retreat. She stammers, "Wh ... what the ... ?" and then she just stops.

"Sorry to startle you. Please relax. Your neighbor reported a commotion in your apartment. We know some protesters were headed this way and we want to make sure you're okay."

"Excuse me. Back off, please! Seriously, you're telling me that there was a commotion in my apartment and protesters are here?"

The officer, sensing that Terry knows her rights, steps back, "Not exactly. We're just worried you might be in trouble. A neighbor reported a problem."

Now indignant, Terry answers, knowing that she has the upper hand, "Excuse me, but could you please put your gun away and tell me the name of my neighbor and his address? I want to speak to him."

I hear him retreating, "Uh, relax. I'm not sure. I'll have to check with my captain ... " His nervous voice trails off.

"If you don't know, then you've no right to be in here questioning me. By the way, do you have probable cause to be here?"

Attempting to take control again, he answers, "Uh, calm down, Miss. We're only trying to help. The protest movement seems to be getting out of hand. Before I go, could you give me your name, your phone number, and the address here?"

A camera shutter clicks, a flash bounces off the wall. Terry screams, "Enough! Leave! I'm fine." She slams the door and gives it a kick.

I wait as though I'm counting down for the start of a ski race before stepping into the hallway. Greta stumbles into my back, causing both of us to slip on the wooden floor in front of Terry.

No one says a word until we hear the police car's engine start up.

Frightened, I mutter, "What … what's happening? I feel as if I'm in a police state with cops barging into an apartment for no reason."

Terry looks at Greta and then back to me before answering, "Well, Lia, everything is not as it seems. Here in Washington, President Nixon is growing more paranoid about student protesters." She points to the couch, "Have a seat."

Confused, I shake my head and settle down on her blue velvet couch.

Removing her glasses, Terry continues, "Have you been reading *The Washington Post?*"

I look at Greta who's smiling and nodding her head. Uncertain, I respond, "Not really, I haven't been too invested in the news—especially the war movement."

"Well, the CIA knows that there are government spies in Vietnam, who are bringing back the real news about the war. Facts comparing how many Viet Cong are killed to how many Americans are killed or wounded. Also, President Nixon knows someone is leaking the truth about the bombings in Cambodia and Laos. You must know that he lies to the American people when he says that we're not bombing those countries."

She stops to see if I understand any of this, and continues, "You know, the war is going badly for the American government. In fact, the military hates to admit it, but we're losing. Nixon says he just wants to sign a peace treaty at the Paris Peace Accords and get out. On the other hand, he doesn't want to be the first president to lose a war." She looks to Greta and stops, not sure whether to say more.

I stand up and step forward, throwing my hands into the air, "So are you going to tell me more? What's going on here?"

Greta leaps up, runs her fingers through her gray hair, and gently pushes me back down. "You're not ready to know more at this point. Ve don't want to get you too involved … " she hesitates, " … yet." She looks around the room and whispers, "The situation can be dangerous for those in the know. As far as I'm concerned, the cops could've just planted a listening device in this apartment." She scans the room, sparsely furnished with ragged, white cotton drapes, two side tables holding my American literature books, a blue couch, and three chairs strewn across a green shag rug.

After dinner, Terry and Greta are reticent to tell me more about the protest movement.

Instead, Terry asks me about my first meeting with Greta in Austria on my train ride to a World Cup race. Both want to know more about my years on the ski team, especially about the cabal of predatory coaches.

My memories start leaking out, thoughts that I've repressed that feel like a grammatical error in my development.

CHAPTER 4

Doctor's Hospital

The next morning, catching the 7 am bus, I'm happy to return to my simple job at Doctor's Hospital. Certainly, collating bills about patients who passed away in the night seems easier than figuring out who's spying and who's lying about Vietnam. The bus ride, filled with a mix of Afro-Americans, Asian-Americans, and young white-collar interns, resembles a mini-UN.

Only two patients died last night at the hospital, all over the age of eighty. To me, this seems the natural way of life and death, in comparison to the one thousand young US soldiers who died this year in Vietnam. I greet Karen, my morning coworker, who answers the phones and directs visitors to rooms of their relatives.

Karen is a heavy, red-haired older woman who's worked here for twenty years. She has taken me under her wing. She, too, extends sympathy to the bereaved family members, while accepting the older deaths as a natural progression.

We avoid the topic of Vietnam as much as possible because she seems to be deeply pro-war and pro-Nixon. Her husband, an Army veteran, served in the Korean War, so she unconvincingly argues that America must be the protector of democracies around the world and that the communists want to win the cold war by toppling elected governments, one by one. Just like my father, she describes the domino effect—once one country falls to the communists, the next will go.

I wish she'd listened to John Kerry's speech to the Senate Foreign Relations committee. He's a veteran who argues that we're the invading army. The Vietnamese simply want to live a quiet life, under *any* government, work in their rice paddies, and raise their children in peace. We're the enemies, alongside the corrupt, American-supported South Vietnamese government under President Thieu. Furthermore, we're losing American lives in a war that's already been lost in the hearts and minds not only of the South Vietnamese people, but in the minds of my generation at home.

I've tried to tell her about my friend, Bill, who'd left college because the US Ski Team coach, John Boast, had promised him a spot on the team. Boast told him he could help him avoid the draft. However, when Bill was suddenly dropped by the coach because he'd begun ROTC in college, he was immediately drafted into the Army, sent to Vietnam, and killed within two months. I'll never forgive Coach Boast for his duplicity.

Karen shows a little sympathy about his death. However, she continues to argue that military service should be mandatory for all American males as a rite of their passage.

I used the argument of my new friend, Greta, to try and convince her that women should also be drafted. For sure, this would end these useless wars, because women, in even greater numbers, would join the protest movement. No sensible woman would tolerate the destruction of families.

This morning I avoid discussing last night's invasion into my apartment, but instead busy myself gathering Louise Goldberg's hospital files. I ask Karen, "By the way, do you remember that sweet old lady who came into the hospital with pneumonia? The one who said she saw me running on the steps of the Supreme Court building?"

"Of course, she had the cutest smile and a million questions for you. Didn't she ask if you were going to be part of the first of May protest movement?"

"Uh huh, and she berated me for not knowing more about the largest demonstration of the year. She told me that her grandson had been killed in Vietnam three years ago and that she could no longer support the war effort."

"I remember how angry she was. Didn't you go to her room to visit?"

"Yup, I did, and we both commiserated about the unnecessary deaths in a war that still hasn't been declared a war by the US Congress. She told me that Congress has called it a conflict or 'an extended military engagement.' "

Karen, concerned about the direction of this conversation, changes the subject. "So why are you asking me about Louise?"

"Well, on one of my visits to her, she gave me a folder. She died last night and now I have it." I show her the manila envelope.

17

"Interesting … so what's in the folder?" Karen moved closer to me, reaching to take it or maybe see the cover on the package.

"Hold on. It's sealed. I haven't looked inside, and I don't feel like sharing it until I get a moment to myself."

Karen backed off, saying, "Okay, okay, I'm sorry. I know you liked her. However, do remember she was eighty years old."

I nod and turn my head so that Karen can't see my tears. I gather all the bills for Ms. Goldberg, which include the ICU, medications, doctor visits, pulmonary tests, and even transportation to the morgue. When I run the final bill, it totals $3,000 for just two days of dying. Medicare covers about fifty percent of her bill, fortunately. I quietly thank President Lyndon Johnson for approving this health benefit to seniors back in 1965.

I hand the bill to Karen who immediately puts it down and says, "We don't have to do anything with this bill."

"Why?"

"Because she's the mother of the president of the Hospital Board."

"So, what does that mean?"

"Have you never heard of professional courtesy?"

"Nope." I grab the folder and wander into the employees' lounge. The darkness makes me stumble until I find the light switch on the wall. I lay the manila folder on the table and caress Mrs. Goldberg's handwriting. She had labeled the folder: PERSONAL: FOR LIA ERICKSON ONLY.

Karen pokes her head in and asks, "Are you okay? You look troubled."

"I'm okay, thanks. But I need about ten minutes to see what she wants to tell me."

I wait until I hear Karen's departing footsteps and the sound of the reception door closing before I turn the envelope over and lift the flap. Inside I find a pile of handwritten papers, perhaps forty in all. Each is dated, the first going back to the beginning of April 1971, which is when I started working at the hospital. On top of the raft of papers is a note from Louise.

> *Lia, please take care of these papers. I know I can trust you to keep them secure. Every week, since my grandson, Dan, was killed in Vietnam, I have been checking the statistics of war deaths and casualties. These numbers do not jibe with the official toll coming from the Pentagon.*
>
> *I have a friend in the CIA who has been passing on information about the deaths, the battles, the corruption in President Thieu's government, and the bombing of Laos and Cambodia. My friend will be contacting you.*
>
> *Please hide this folder in a special place as the FBI is trying to track down all informers.*
>
> Αντιγόνη

I don't understand this signature. Is it a secret code? I choose not to read more until I get back to my apartment, because I don't trust Karen. Cautiously, I carry the folder back to my desk, slide it into my backpack, and make sure that I won't lose sight of the bag all day. I'm growing more curious about a possible spy network at the hospital and wonder, *Is it just coincidence that I met Mrs. Goldberg on the steps of the Capitol Building? And wasn't it Terry who directed me to Doctor's Hospital for a job?* A shiver runs up my spine. Paranoia sets in.

A scream from outside breaks my reverie and immediately two hospital staff rush past the front desk, pushing a gurney. As the outside doors open, I hear a woman's plea, "I don't want to die, I don't want to die." Karen jumps up from the front desk and runs into the hallway while I follow her, forgetting about my backpack.

A small, twenty-something woman lies on the ground, blood welling around her nose and head. Her arms are twisted around her head and her left leg bends out at a right angle. The two hospital aides throw a sheet over her to protect her from the curious crowd gathering on the sidewalk. I hold the hospital door open to help another aide carrying a backboard.

Carefully, the aides roll her onto the board and then lift her onto the gurney. She starts to scream again, "Oh, the pain. Please don't let me die!" The sirens of a DC police car drown out her words, and an officer jumps into the crowd, pushing the onlookers back from the sidewalk. I'm shocked at the crassness the leering crowd.

A bleached-blonde woman points at the injured girl and says, "Such a fool! I saw her jump from the third-floor ledge. Of course, she'll die."

A tall crew cut man in a seersucker suit asks, "Do you think she just wants attention?"

A child crawls between the legs of two men just to get a closer look and laughs, "Dad, does she think she's superwoman?"

The wrapped body, bound like a butterfly cocoon, is wheeled through the hospital lobby and into the unlit employees' lounge. Because this is a private hospital, there's no emergency room. The woman's muffled cries continue until an aide takes a respirator to her. Now I can only hear the susurrations of the machine, stamped out by a white-coated doctor who demands, "Take her to Operating Room 3 and call immediately for a blood transfusion."

The gurney turns into the elevator and the snap of the metal door reverberates in my ear, reminding me of my own journey into the operating room in Maribor, my foot twisted at an unnatural angle after my accident in the slalom race. I say a silent prayer for the woman, hoping that she'll live.

Tears well up in my eyes and my mind races, *Why would someone so young want to die—or was she pushed?* Karen grabs my arm and leads me back to my desk, leaving her hand on my shoulder. My tears turn into sobs and then gasps. I find myself out of breath. Memories of all the trauma I've seen in the past year cycle in my head: Guy's half-eaten face, dead in his cabin at Monmouth; Damien's crushed skull at Sugarloaf after his fall; the twisted body of my teammate Wren lying at the bottom of the downhill bump in Vail; Carla's body half-covered in the avalanche.

I ask Karen to leave and give me some quiet. She pats me on the back, making my sweaty white cotton blouse stick to my skin. I reach under my desk to pull out the backpack, hoping to find some answers in the papers Louise left me.

The pack is gone.

CHAPTER 5

Intrigue

Down on my knees, I crawl around my desk, searching under the drawers, behind the curtain, in the closet, inside the filing cabinet and still no backpack. In the process, I bump my head, scratch my back, and bang my injured ankle against the desk leg, all for naught. In just ten minutes, Louise's papers have disappeared.

Karen, her red hair disheveled, enters, incredulous to find me on the floor. "Lia, what're you doing down there? We must take care of clients who're checking out." Her concern grows when she sees my expression.

"I'm upset because I can't find my backpack. You know, the one that Louise gave me."

"Not to worry. I grabbed it and put it under my desk. You know, I'm curious about what she gave you."

Already feeling that my little job in Washington had become a part of something more complicated, I grill Karen. "Hey, I looked inside and saw numerous papers with statistics about deaths in Vietnam. There were maps of Cambodia and Laos, and even details about American bases. Louise wanted me to keep these secure until I was contacted by an unknown person—I'm scared, Karen."

Karen sits down on the floor next to me. She looks me in the eye and says, "Okay, tonight we'll go back to your apartment, and I'll tell you what's happening. I wish I could speak here, but others may be listening."

Later that I day, I learn more about the young woman, Manuela Sanchez, who jumped and died. A sixty-year-old woman has come to the hospital to identify her body and to accept the bill. In preparation, I've collated the charges from the operating room and blood transfusion, all totaling $1500, the cost of just two hours in the hospital.

Meekly, the woman approaches the counter. Her black-gray hair is pulled into a bun beneath her scarf. "Hello, I Manuela Sanchez' grandmother. I her only family, except her five-year-old daughter. Por favor, please tell me what happened."

Wiping her tears, she continues in a heavy Spanish accent, "What I need to do?" No one has prepared me for this moment. It's one thing to give a bill to a family of an older patient, but for this unexpected tragic death, I'm speechless.

Karen reaches over the counter and touches the woman's wrinkled hand. "I'm so sorry for your loss. Do you want to come into the back office and talk?"

The grandmother nods.

Karen motions for me to follow them. "Please come with us, Lia. I'll send someone else to cover the front desk."

Settling into the backroom where a couch sits facing two chairs, I wait for the older woman to choose her seat first. She picks the wooden chair with mesh and lowers herself slowly, as if she has a bad back. She lifts her skirt in a grandmotherly fashion, but before she can say anything, tears begin trailing down her cheeks.

Karen places a box of Kleenex next to her and then takes the chair opposite. She's very methodical—obviously she's done this painful interrogation many times. We wait for the woman to speak.

Blowing her nose into a tissue, the woman begins to talk, "Manuela was my granddaughter. Two days ago, she learned her husband, Carlos, had been killed in Vietnam. She couldn't take the stress. She tell me she go to a hospital, get some medicine. I no idea where she go."

Karen nods, affirming she understands.

The woman continues, struggling for words, "Manuela, she struggle for months. She worry about Carlos. He join army because he want to be American citizen. Both here illegally." She looks at me and then at Karen. "Is it okay I tell this?"

Karen slides to the edge of her chair and says softly, "Of course, we don't have to tell anyone about this—at least, not right now."

The woman continues, "I no can accept a bill from you. I live on welfare. I legal citizen, but I no have job." She throws her hands in the air. "I know not what to do."

Karen slowly sits back, puts her hand to her mouth and looks to me to make sure that I'm following this protocol carefully. "Now, Ms. ... I'm sorry I didn't get your name. Please do not worry." The grandmother's sobs mask the rest of Karen's words. Drawing her chair closer to the woman, Karen repeats herself, "Not to worry. Can you give me some identification, your address, and your phone number? The hospital has funds to help you."

"My name, Mariana Menendez. Here my Social Security card."

Karen takes the ID card and leaves me in the room with Mariana. I go over to hug her, letting her lean her head against my shoulder while she trembles. I've felt so helpless, just like when I was caught in an avalanche in Grindelwald and watched my friend Carla tumble past me in a wave of snow.

Karen returns with some paperwork, places a clipboard on Mariana's lap, and asks, "Could you just please fill out the relevant information and we will be in touch with you? Do you have any family members we can call to come get you?"

Mariana nods, "Yes, please call my brother at ... ," she stops. Then, continuing hesitantly, "No, he not legal here." She puts her face in her hands and mumbles, "I catch a bus home."

I return to the front desk, realizing how inexperienced I am and how I must trust that Karen knows how to handle such situations. I find myself growing angrier at this war—the nightmare that has promised so little and taken so much. After changing from my work clothes into my US Ski Team jogging outfit (my way of gaining control again), I peek in to tell Karen that I am leaving for the day. "I'll meet you at my apartment tonight. Can you bring the backpack?"

Karen laughs sarcastically, "Of course, and it won't leave my control."

CHAPTER 6

March on Washington

Outside, a light rain splashes against the concrete, forming puddles next to the curb. I misjudge my jump over the water and like a kid again, I soak my sneakers and pants. Dashing toward the Mall, at every corner I run into overturned cars forming roadblocks behind which protesting students taunt the National Guardsmen. The streets are a war zone where I dodge soldiers wearing steel helmets, flak jackets, and gas masks, brandishing rifles with bayonets and slinging ammunition pouches. I worry that some soldiers might have live ammunition.

Crowds of young hippies, dressed in jeans and fatigue jackets, mask themselves with wet handkerchiefs and chant, "No more war!" while they are pushed toward the grass on the Mall. The strip is so packed with Weathermen, women, protestors, placards, dogs, trash bags, tents, and horses that I can't figure out who's an enemy and who's a friend.

I decide to detour to the west. Police sirens reverberate around the buildings like an out-of-tune symphony. Firecrackers or gunshots punctuate the noise. Panicked, I run toward the Lincoln Memorial, where a band starts playing my favorite Bob Dylan protest song, *Blowin' in the Wind.*

Something big is happening here. Buses continue to arrive filled with more hippies. A police officer on horseback charges me, yelling, "Get away from the monument." I stumble back as the horse pushes past me and heads up to the steps of the Lincoln Memorial, pooping on the white marble. With his bayonet, the officer smashes a sign reading, "Don't like the bombings in America? You should see Vietnam." A hippie, sporting a torn American flag, falls down the steps, only to be trampled by the horse. The horse lets out a noisy, noxious fart. No one goes to pick up the hippie. As I turn to help or at least check on the young boy, a bleeding, flower-crowned girl rushes by me, crying, "Get away from here! They're trying to arrest all of us. Go!"

I turn away, covering my ears, and duck to avoid a Chinook helicopter whirling only meters over my head before it lands on a patch of nearby grass. More combat-ready soldiers disgorge from the open door. A fog of tear gas clouds my sight. I gag, put my hand over my nose, and fall to the ground.

Crawling slowly, I remain below the veil of tear gas. A man dressed in torn jeans and a military jacket starts to kick me, yelling, "Get back up. Go fight. I'm a Weatherman and we want to take down the DC police." Lying flat on the ground, I cover my head with my hands, while his metal-toed boot continues to jab my ribs. I throw up. I'm not sure who he is or on what side he's on. I don't know which way to go. The Lincoln Monument hosts its own civil war.

I hear a car door open and a commanding voice yells, "Get in! This is turning into chaos!"

I hear a scuffle and someone yelling, "Get away from here! We don't need the Weathermen's help. You're hurting our cause. Hey, put the gun down! Just go!"

A hand circles my arm and helps me to my knees toward an old Volkswagen bus. With a sigh, I collapse on the back seat.

My unknown savior tilts his head in the back window, announcing, "Wow, you were lucky not to get arrested. There are over 30,000 protesters gathering for tomorrow's May Day rally. We need your help."

I rub my bleary eyes while the man moves around to the driver's seat. This man-boy, with a head of dark, thick hair and prominent chin, starts honking the horn, puts the van in gear, and yells, "Vietnam Veterans against the War. Clear away." He's wearing a dull green camouflage military shirt and pants, and I catch a glimpse of the badges on his left breast when he turns to me, saying in a Boston Brahmin accent, "I'm glad we found you. Did you know that the FBI has been watching you ever since they saw you go into Terry's house?"

I throw up my hands, "Who are you? What the heck's going on?"

A voice from the passenger's seat, one I recognize, calmly says, "So welcome to the fight, Lia. I followed you from the hospital because I figured you would be caught up in this."

I blink, choke, and answer, "Karen, I'm so confused."

"Not to worry. I have the backpack and John … oh, you don't recognize him. Meet John Kerry. He'll leave us at Terry's apartment." She reaches toward my forehead, "Are you okay? Your head's bleeding." She hands me a towel which I wrapped around my throbbing forehead.

*   *   *   *

Karen helps me into my apartment, while Terry brings out a pot of hot tea as if she knew I'd be coming. Crashing on her couch, I lay my head on a pillow, and close my eyes.

Karen begins to explain to Terry about Louise's backpack, the death of the girl at the hospital, and my decision to run back to the apartment.

Terry becomes upset. "What was the name of the young girl? How did she die?"

Karen hesitates before saying, "Manuela Sanchez. The authorities say she jumped from the third floor. She was distressed over her husband's death in Vietnam."

Without acknowledging the tragedy, Terry closes her eyes and whispers, "Do you think she had come to the hospital to get something?"

Karen shakes her head, "Not sure what you mean?"

I start to pull the events together and say, "Well, I'd just received a backpack belonging to Louise Goldberg."

Terry breaks in, asking, "Where is it?' She starts pacing. "Enough right now. Tell me about the movement. What's happening on the Mall?"

Karen holds up her hand. "Slow down. I'm getting to that. Lia ran into the protesters at the Lincoln Memorial. Already the Metropolitan Police have cordoned off the monuments and are beating the protesters. Helicopters are dropping tear gas, so the protesters are releasing balloons tethered by cables to deter the copters."

"Jeez," responds Terry, "We knew this would get bad. Do you think Nixon will revoke our marching permit?"

Karen stammers, "He … he probably already has. This will give him the right to arrest anyone. We're not safe." She goes to the front window, pulls the curtains, and locks the front door.

Frustrated, I challenge them both, "Okay, tell me what's going on. I feel as if I'm a pawn in someone else's game."

Terry takes control. "Calm down. We'll explain."

Greta steps out from the kitchen, smiling, "So Lia, you're now part of the movement. Do you have the backpack?"

I shake my head and look at Karen, "Do you have it?"

"Yup," Karen responds and hands it to Greta. "So here are the documents you've been waiting for. I checked them out and they list all the deaths and casualties in Vietnam during the past month. They describe the bombings in Cambodia and Laos along the Ho Chi Minh trail—even the exact dates. The Nixon administration has been lying to us on a daily basis. More soldiers have died than the Pentagon has told us. And, as we suspected, the American army isn't winning."

Terry says, "Can I see? Where did these come from?"

Karen pauses, looking around to see whether she should share the information. "A woman called Louise gave it to Lia, just before she died in the hospital."

Terry jolts up, "Did you say Louise? Louise Goldberg?"

Karen affirms with a nod.

Terry shakes her head saying, "I'm the one who collated these. They were supposed to go to the Students for a Democratic Society for distribution to the leaders of the March. I gave them to Louise, a trusted friend who coordinated our protest activities at the hospital. She knew who to give them to." She shakes her head and looks at Karen with a stare that could cut through ice. "She must have worried about spies at the hospital."

Karen, brushing her dyed-red hair out of her eyes, gets up with a huff and leaves, not even looking back.

CHAPTER 7

Decisions

Terry and Greta sit me down and grab two chairs opposite me. Terry, looking very professional in a pantsuit, strokes her short brown hair. The radio in the kitchen blares news about the protest and repeats parts of John Kerry's speech to the Senate Foreign Relations committee, ending with, "Who will be the last man to die in Vietnam?"

Greta looks dour and shakes her head before saying, "Okay, Lia, do you remember the train ride to Bad Gastein when I told you that Martin Luther King once said, 'The arc of the moral universe is long, but it bends toward justice.'?"

"Of course, you said I had to help, and you even encouraged me to stand up for myself against the coaches," I answer, shaking my shoulder-length blonde hair away from my eyes.

"Well, did you?"

"Yes, and those coaches were removed—or so I was told."

"Okay, don't get huffy. I'm glad you did that."

"So, what has this to do with what's going on here?"

"Remember, I told you that I've been speaking to student groups about the Vietnam War and women's rights?

"Of course. But what has this to do with me?"

"Well, since that train ride, I've become more involved with the students' protest movement against the war—the SDS, Students for a Democratic Society. Terry tells me that you're considering going to University of California at Berkeley this fall."

"Okay, I'm pretty certain I'll do that, because my ankle isn't strong enough for me to put on skis yet—not at least for four more months. I can do a semester at Berkeley, and then go to Europe to try out for the Olympic team."

Greta smiles and looks to Terry. She confirms, "See, I told you she could help us in Berkeley."

Now I'm confused and demand, "Help you! Help you how?"

Terry stands up, puts on her glasses, and cautions, "Don't get so demanding. We'll tell you what's happening." Walking over to the front door, she checks the lock and goes into the kitchen to turn up the radio. Returning to the living room, she pulls her chair closer to me and waves to Greta to do the same.

Terry starts with a whisper, "To the point, you do know that I work for the CIA in Vietnam? I nod my head. Well, every month I return to the Washington office to report to my boss about the situation in Saigon."

"Okay, okay, but what does this have to do with me?"

Terry pauses, glances around the room, and slides her wooden chair so close to me that our knees butt. "Greta thinks that you could become my contact in California when I bring the reports back. My last contact person was just arrested."

I'm growing nervous but curious. "Reports? What reports?" I ask.

She pauses and checks the room. Over the noise of the radio, a clock is ticking. Terry puts her hand up to stop my talking, continuing, "Don't get ahead of me. I can't tell you everything now, because you need to get to Berkeley and establish yourself with the campus newspaper and the SDS … you know, the Students for a Democratic Society … before I can share more."

Remembering the backpack, I shuffle my feet, asking, "Does this have to do with the information in the backpack?"

Terry hesitates, "Well, let's say that could be part of what's happening."

The sound of a bomb exploding outside stops our conversation, and then I hear screams. The protesters must be surrounding the Capitol and the Supreme Court Building. Tear gas wafts into the apartment even though all the doors and windows are closed. Picking up the backpack, Terry grabs my hand and leads me into the kitchen. Greta follows at a distance like a bodyguard. Next to the refrigerator stands a paneled wooden door that looks like a kitchen cabinet.

Terry pulls out a chain, fumbles for a key and unlocks the six-foot door. She grabs a flashlight out of her jacket pocket and shines it down the stairs. A musty, moldy smell makes me sneeze. Terry puts her finger to her nose and points for me to go first. I shake my head and put up my hand, indicating that I'm scared and don't want to go.

Greta pulls me aside, saying, "Hey, I didn't think you were ever one to be scared. You told me you always felt invincible. What's changed?"

Stepping back, I answer, "Only in the mountains do I feel safe. I'm not a city person. In fact, I'm afraid of the cities—of crowds. I hate the noise. In the mountains, I know what to expect—avalanches, cold, crevasses, tree wells, fumaroles."

Greta laughs, "Well, Miss Know-It-All, you've much to learn if you plan to go to Berkeley. Do you know how big San Francisco is?"

Pausing, confused, I frown. "Of course, but how can I refuse the scholarship the ski team offered. Plus, I can always return to Monmouth Mountain for some training, you know, with my friends on weekends. It's only a five-hour drive. I'll definitely go over Thanksgiving."

A pounding on the front door startles the three of us and Terry pushes me toward Greta who's started down the stairs. Terry looks back up the stairs, shines the light on the paneled door, twists the lock from the inside, and then returns, cautiously tiptoeing down the stairs. A rat squeals and runs across the floor. I squat on the concrete pad and whisper to Greta, "What's going on?"

She turns toward me, placing her hand on my shoulder. "I'm not sure, but I'm afraid that the police may be back. Now that we have the backpack, and if they've gotten a search warrant, they can come in and search for it. Who knows what they know?"

Terry leaves us standing in the dark and goes into a corner where there's a large bookcase against the wall. She beckons to Greta and me to come help her. Edging my fingers around one side, I feel it move. Terry, lifting from the other side, forces the bookcase forward.

Dust blows into my face, causing me to spit. Terry squeezes behind the bookcase toward a metal vault that's camouflaged by the gray wall. She grabs her keychain again, opens the vault, and shoves the backpack in. I'm scared yet excited—this is right out of a Poe short story. My heart starts pounding when I hear footsteps overhead. Terry turns off the light and indicates that I shouldn't move, not even to try putting the bookcase back. Silence.

Someone turns the radio off and a deep male voice, although muffled, demands, "Is anyone here? Police! There's been a bombing outside the building. Please evacuate!" I hold my breath until I'm forced to take slow, deep breaths.

Although it seems like an hour, just five minutes passes. At last, two sets of feet tromp into the kitchen, then out the back door. Terry indicates that we shouldn't move. The officers may have left a person behind to see if we'll come out of hiding. Ten minutes, fifteen pass, though I'm not exactly sure how many since I can't check my watch.

Slowly, Terry begins to edge toward the stairs, waves her hand, indicating that we should follow her. She slips off her shoes and carefully steps up each stair, toe first, making sure that the wooden boards won't squeak before setting her foot down. She turns her flashlight to the door, puts her ear against the keyhole and listens. Carefully, she slides the key in, noiselessly turns it. Pushing the door open, she peeks into the kitchen and whispers, "Hello, is anyone here?" She waits for an answer, then steps onto the linoleum and asks once again, "I said, is anyone here?"

She turns back to Greta and me and beckons us forward. Following her example, we slide our shoes off and creep up the staircase. I hit a board that's loose and it groans. I stop to see whether I should continue. Terry waves me on. "It looks like the coast is clear."

Upstairs, Terry checks each room, behind each chair and curtain, and even upstairs in the bedrooms, and finally comes back to us. She takes a few deep breaths, turns on the radio, grabs a piece of paper, and starts scribbling.

She holds up the paper:

Don't talk until we can get someone to check for recording devices. The Nixon administration is trying to identify and arrest the leaders of the student protest movement. We are part of it. They may know that.

Αντιγόνη

I mouth the words and then point to the last word that resembles a signature. Terry smirks and whispers, "Later." She presses her palms together and then makes an "A" with her index finger. "It's time for you to get out of here and go back to Vermont."

CHAPTER 8

Return Home

My bags are packed, so once again I'm a vagabond, but this time I'm headed home. My new friend and collaborator, Greta, escorts me to the train station to catch the first express train to New York City, then to Boston, and finally a local train to Waterbury, Vermont. She's given me a gift of two hundred dollars. I'm scared because I don't know if I've been reported to the FBI as a spy.

Greta puts her arm over my shoulder in a motherly fashion, saying, "I wish we didn't have to ask you to leave so abruptly, but we sense that the FBI has infiltrated Doctor's Hospital."

She looks down the track at the arriving train, sleek silver cars flash red from the reflection of the neon lights, a scene right out of a spy novel. The noise forces her to lean closer to my ear to continue, "I don't trust Karen. She seems to pop up in places I've never expected. Doctor's Hospital has been our staging area for the Washington protests for over a year. Someone seems to know this."

Puzzled, I ask, "Wow, I really like her. I can't believe this." Then I remember our conversations about her husband and the domino effect. "You could be right. She seems to be playing both sides,"

Greta nods affirmatively. I put my hand to my mouth in surprise, questioning, "Do you think Terry could be in trouble with the CIA?" A voice over the intercom stops me and then I add, "Could her life be in danger?"

"Leave that idea. Right now, I'm worried. I know that the FBI is paying the Capitol police to dress as protesting students, take pictures, and then arrest the demonstrators. I'm just worried they could have identified Terry."

I look up and down the train platform to see if anyone is observing us, even listening to our conversation, or taking our picture. I shiver, realizing I'm living a real spy story. I know that I've got much to lose if I'm caught, especially my place on the

Olympic Team and my scholarship to Berkeley. A hot breeze pushes me backwards, ninety-degree heat distilled from the concrete floor.

Looking down, wanting to hear the answer, I ask, "What could they do to Terry or you?"

Greta shakes her head, "I'm more worried about the safety of the movement. Karen is the one who helped us set up Doctor's Hospital to use as the headquarters for the Washington protests. The location is so convenient. She probably knows about Goldberg's role as disseminators of the information regarding the deaths, casualties, and bombings in Cambodia and Laos, including the maps and troop locations. I'm not sure whether she knows that Terry is the one bringing the information back from Vietnam and that I'm the one who is collating it and passing the facts on to the protesters."

A train blasts its whistle and slows down in front of us. The updraft brushes my cheek along with some dirt. A few blank faces stare out the windows. A small boy presses his hands on the glass as if trying to touch me. A soldier with a head bandage leans his face against the transparent barrier. The aluminum-bullet express pulls to a stop three bays ahead, so I know this isn't my ride.

I continue my questioning once the noise has ceased. "If I can't trust Karen, who can I trust?" As a silence ensues, I shake my head and ask her, "Do you know what really happened to Manuela? Did she jump out of grief or was she pushed?" I pause again, worried that I'm in over my head, wishing I hadn't asked that question.

Greta ignores my inquiries, closes her eyes, and repeats, "Remember the arc of the moral universe needs help to bend toward justice."

"I remember. You told me that in Innsbruck."

"Well, Lia, at this time, to be safe, we've closed down the operation at Doctor's Hospital. Too many police are investigating, and Terry no longer reports to the Goldbergs. She's set up other receiving agents in the city." Greta stops, looks around again, and beckons me toward a corner of the station. She continues, "Terry trusts you. She wants to use you when you get to Berkeley as a liaison with the students and the SDS. As you know, Berkeley has been a hot spot for the protests, because California is where the soldiers depart for Vietnam and where their bodies are returned ... " She hesitates, shaking her head in disgust, " ... in coffins."

Growing angry, I push my hands out toward her, "Wait a minute! I'm not going to Berkeley until September. I've got much to do before—you know that."

"Of course, and Terry needs time to set up her new chain on the West Coast. She'll find you when the time is right." Shifting her purse, she grabs my arm and leads me back toward the track. She asks, "On a happier note, what do you plan to do when you get back to Vermont?"

I explain that my father has arranged for me to work in the fire tower on Scrag Mountain, three thousand feet above my house. I'll live in the tower cabin, watch for fires during the day, and write in my free time. The pay, $2.60 an hour, will allow me to save enough money to take the train across Canada in August, hike in the Wind River Range with my friend, Rob Attlefellner, and then drive with him to Berkeley.

I add that during my time in Vermont, I'll be running the two miles up to the cabin at least three times a week, carrying supplies and food. This exercise will help me get in shape for my possible bid for the Olympic Team in December. The new coach of the team has promised to save me a spot on the team since my FIS points rank me number two in the country in slalom and giant slalom. Of course, this all hinges on whether I can stay in shape while studying at Berkeley.

We exchange little more than the usual pleasantries until my train arrives. When it stops, I can see our reflections in the window. My blonde hair has knotted in a nest on top, and her gray hair has blown back around her neck. I turn to Greta, sorrow in my heart, and whisper, "I remember when we first met, and you gave me the courage to confront the predatory coaches on the ski team. Now once again, you're giving me courage to do what is right … protest the war. I'll do this for Bill who died in the Vietnam muck."

I hesitate and stomp my feet in frustration. "This war must end." I'm amazed at my own anger and continue, "Okay, so I'll help you with the students in Berkeley." I pick up my fiberglass suitcase and backpack, bound up the train steps, turn back, and add, "I'll help bend the arc, but I'll not break any laws. Bye for now."

Greta waves, gives me the "A" sign, and turns, covering her mouth with her scarf.

CHAPTER 9

Home

"Welcome home," says my dad, enveloping me in his arms when I step off at the Waterbury, Vermont, station. I'm home, safe, away from all the intrigue, even feeling loved. At times like this I wish my mother were here, too, but if she were, I'd worry about what kind of mood she'd be in or whether she'd approve of all my wanderings.

Our white cape house sits close to the Common Road. Two twisted sugar maples, like sentries, guard my dirt driveway. Looking up into the one on the left, I spot the sickle that lies embedded, nearly eight feet up. The bark has grown around the tip, leaving just the curved metal blade; the wooden handle long has since rotted away. My father tells me that it has remained there since the year, 1942, witness to the last defiant act of the former owner's son, who threw the sickle here just before he left for World War II. No one was allowed to touch it before his return.

The gray, gnarled bark has swollen around the holes of missing lower branches, fashioning a perpetual Munch-like scream. A chipmunk jumps down and skitters to his hole. I'm beginning to understand what returning home can do for one's sense of worth: a haven in which to remember a childhood, a place to assess future choices. Now I'm home where my memories flash like an old family slideshow.

Our Labrador dog, Sheba, greets me with her unbridled enthusiasm, not showing any anger that I've been gone almost two months. After unpacking in my small bedroom, cheered by my many colorful books, I check out my father's study. He still has his wedding photo on the desk, in addition to a black and white picture of my mom holding me as a two-year-old. Her smile haunts me to this day, so joyful and carefree, with no sign of her later alcoholism and depression. In the hallway, the photos of my ancestors speak to each other like ghosts from the past. *I wonder what would they say about my choices?*

To return to happy memories, I decide to climb Scrag Mountain, my childhood retreat. There's no trail up this side, but for years, I've memorized my forest route.

I choose to go solo, without Sheba or my father, wanting to bask in the quiet of the natural world, to relive ten years of hiking and to rediscover my trees, my cliffs, my dreams, and my innocence.

Up through the pasture I go, passing our spring surrounded by red staghorn sumacs and cross into the orchard where our apples are ripening. A Macintosh apple hangs low, tempting me, so I snag it and take a bite of the bitter, hard flesh. Then I throw it toward the stream where it can become a new tree. When I stop to pick a bouquet of black-eyed Susans, goldenrod, and Queen Anne's lace, two black and white oreo-heifers, almost full-size, thunder towards me, heads lowered, heels kicking. I'm forced to jump a stone wall and crawl under the barbed-wire fence. I lie in the unmown grass, laughing at the snorting noses that reek of wet grass, and taunt them, "Good fences make good neighbors."

Back on my feet, I brush off the nettles while singing a rendition of Frost's poem "The Pasture," by Randall Thompson. It was a song my high school chorus director, Ms. Loring, taught us:

> *I'm going out to clean the pasture spring*
>
> *I'll only stop to rake the leaves away*
>
> *(And wait to watch the water clear, I may):*
>
> *I shan't be gone long—you come too.*

I'm going to fetch the little calf

That's standing by the mother.

It's so young

It totters when she licks it with her tongue

I shan't be gone long—you come too.

Following a logging road stitched to the mountainside, I stop at the granite cellar-hole of an old farmhouse whose inhabitants probably deserted during the 1929 Depression, perhaps dreaming of the fertile California farmlands. A large pine tree stands sentry in the middle, revealing the age of the ruins, forty-plus years.

A sugar house, its metal roof collapsing from the snow loads, sits next to a grove of maples. Inside, the tin sap buckets, neatly stacked next to the metal boiler, await the farmer's return.

In the back, two untended gravestones tell of the family's sorrows. I kneel to pull the leaves and grass away to find the names of Edward and Alice Joslin. They were twins who were born in 1913 and died in 1918 at the age of five. Sadly, one died twenty-five days after the other. These were two children who could have passed away from the Spanish influenza, as my father used to tell me.

I scamper around a large witness tree marking the boundary of the National Forest, and up a dark stream-thread. The water courses down the mountain, rests in stepped terraces, throbs over falls, and jumps around logs and rounded boulders. Its preternatural flow comes from an underground aquifer, touted to be the largest in Vermont.

I decide to run up the middle of the brook, ricocheting while trying to land on the flattest rocks, often getting my hiking boots wet. My moves are as quick as a dragonfly collecting bugs, flitting, hovering. Each step takes me farther from my past fears, yet, unfortunately, I still worry about my future. *Do I really want to become part of the most divisive protest movement in America?*

With each stride, I grow more emboldened, confident, remembering that

I'd recently risked everything by reporting two predatory ski team coaches. In the same vein, I recall the two race podiums I'd stood on last winter as the best skier in America.

Midway, I stop to lie on my back and look up into the maple trees, their branches corkscrewing toward the sky, while their three-pointed leaves store sugars for the long winter. I think, *I'm like them, building reserves for the upcoming winter.*

Farther up, the stream explodes over a thirty-foot granite cliff. Truck-size boulders park at the bottom. I cup some water and let it trickle down my throat. Holding my breath, I listen for the overtones harmonizing with the undertones of the falling water. Looking up, I remember every foothold, every crack like pages in a book. Although I'm usually afraid of heights unless I have my skis on, here I don't worry about failing or falling.

I clamber ant-like, making my four appendages act as six by using my knees and always balancing on—at the minimum—three solid purchases. The feel of these ledges resides not in my brain, but in the senses of my hands.

In the middle of the climb, at a two-foot quartz outcropping as white as a snowdrift, I sit and rest. For a moment I feel both in the world, yet out of it, basking in the joy of the quiet. Here, resting still as the yellow chanterelles around me, I'm timeless, and only a slant of light sifting through the canopy tells me that it's past noon.

This climb reminds me of my recent struggles up the marble Supreme Court steps where I met Greta. *Wow, has my life taken a new direction since that day.* A robin's trill calls me to my feet. I still have a mile to go.

Carefully, I start pulling myself up, clutching the rough-scaled white pines, clawing the seventy-degree slope. My feet slip on an avalanche of pine needles. I must make sure that my grip on the next tree or sapling is secure. I'm literally doing pull-ups over the last ten feet, but having done this for years, it's rote. I have no fear. Over time, the old-growth pines haven't moved—they've just grown fatter. Their dense overstory makes for little undergrowth. On this old mountain, just like the pines, I'm safe—no predatory coaches, no police, no National Guardsmen, no one to cut me down.

Now my ankle starts to throb. I move over to a narrow cleft where the rocks give me more purchase. The pain, a slight ache, soon becomes a knife-like jab. I slow down, reprimanding myself that I've returned home to strengthen my ankle, not to re-injure it.

Once over the steep flank, I descend into a ravine that separates the front face from the final rise. Here is the well-worn trail from Palmer Road that the Boy Scouts cleared, the same group who built the rustic ranger cabin that'll be my refuge for two weeks. Mud-rimmed puddles bear the wet prints of animals: the pointed-toed coyote, the padded-fingered fox, the cloven-hooved deer, the dainty-clawed squirrel, and the webbed-footed beaver. I kneel and place my palm in a large bear print, recalling the grizzly attack on my teammates and me when we were hiking in the Sierras. I close my eyes and whisper my father's favorite quote by Wendell Berry:

> I go and lie down where the wood drake
>
> rests in his beauty on the water, and the great heron feeds.
>
> I come into the peace of wild things
>
> who do not tax their lives with forethought of grief.

A dragonfly zigs across the water, landing gently on my nose. A squirrel scolds, telling me that I'm the stranger, so I press my tongue against my front teeth and 'tisk' back, letting him know he'll see more of me. A ruffled grouse thumps, warning his family of my presence. A woodpecker taps a code on the tree. As I rise, the rank muck sucks at my feet.

On the final scramble up the ice-polished granite, I reach for a small balsam fir, its sweet fragrance clogging my nose. My foot slips and my nose bumps against a clump of moss. I gasp, as I spit out the soft fuzz that tastes like bitter dandelion greens and scrape the mud from my chin. A rock cracks loose and bounds down the slope. I rest in the earthy smell of decaying leaves and damp earth.

After three more turns in the trail, the cabin's roof appears over the treetops, and a light-lance from the aluminum panels blinds me. Smoke rises from the stovepipe and circles into the clouds where stiff-winged hawks wheel effortlessly. Not expecting to find anyone, but as a precaution, I announce my presence.

"Hello."

A bass voice answers, "I've been expecting you, Lia Ewickson."

Startled and a little scared, I see no one, but answer, "What? Did you say … that you knew I was coming?"

"Your fatha called me to tell me you'd be up as soon as you wetuwned." The voice has a hard time pronouncing his "R's", a little like Elmer Fudd in the Bugs Bunny cartoons.

As I walk toward the front door, I see a bearded six-foot boy-man step out. He holds out his large hand, turning to hide his left sleeve that hangs like a limp sock. A smile creases his sooty face as he continues, "He phoned me this mowning that this hike would be the fiwst thing you'd do."

"Wait a minute. Back up. How do you know my father? And how did he call you?" I feel unnerved, as if I've been watched all the way up the mountain.

"Oh, Lia, you don't recognize me, do you?" He laughs, "Yet, you look just the same as I remember, muscular, blonde, and resolute."

"Sorry, no." I squint, trying to find something I can identify in his face.

He points to a wire strung on a pole. "Okay, well first, I have a phone line up heya. Important for calling in fiyas." He laughs, "Oh, yes, and by the way, I'm Henwy or as you used to call me in high school, Henwy David." Laughing, he sits down on the doorstep and points to a rock outcropping across from him, indicating that I should take my seat. Pressed into the hard stone, I wiggle my butt until I can find a comfortable depression.

Looking hard into his eyes, I recognize the handsome, yet sad loner in high school who'd never joined any group. I ask, "Hey, I thought you were in Vietnam. Weren't you drafted last year?"

"Well, look at me. Do I look like I can do much good in Vietnam?" He lowers his head in dejection.

I try not to stare at his limp left sleeve, but he grabs the cloth and yanks on it, saying," I guess when you were over in Euwope, having fun and wacing, you didn't heaya about my injuwy. This past Januawy an IED exploded near Da

Nang and I lost half my awm. I weturned, got some wehabilitation, went on disability, and found a tempowawy job with the Fowest Sewice this summah." His mechanical tone lets me know that he's not completely accepted his fate.

Swallowing hard, I sympathize, "Oh, how horrible. I'm so sorry."

"Well, yes and no." He pulls on his beard. "Wemember, I always loved being alone in the mountains. You weya the only one who didn't pick on me in high school when I wefused to join sports teams and clubs, but instead just wandahed in the Green Mountains every aftahnoon. So now, I get paid to live high up heaya. To be by myself." He smirks.

"Oh, I see. But then, why did my father tell me that I'd be working alone for two weeks?" I shake my head in bewilderment. "He didn't mention that I'd be joining you."

"No silly. Just you heya. I have to weturn to the VA in White Wivah Junction for two weeks to clean up a slight infection in my stump and then hopefully get a pwosthetic ahm." He laughs as if making a private joke, "He asked me if you could be my weplacement. He thought that you'd like it up heya."

I stand up, walk carefully across the stones toward him, lean over and give him a hug. He smells of smoke, unwashed armpits, and beer. His beard scratches my cheek. "Oh, Henry, I can't imagine what you've been through."

I stammer, feeling awkward. "Oh, for sure, you're a hero to me for going to the war. I'm so happy to help you out."

Pulling back, I see a red scar running up the left side of his face to his eyebrow, most of it hidden by his beard. He instinctively reaches over with his right hand to cover the wound.

"Same heya, I'm happy to be able to help you out as you wehabilitate your ankle and make it to the … ah … Olympics." Looking at my ankle, he suppresses a chuckle, "I guess you could say we'ya both wounded wawiwors."

"Oh, you've no idea how true this is. I've had my own private hell while on the ski team."

"Do you want to talk about it?"

"I'm not ready yet, except to say that over in Europe, I had to deal with two … what is the word … pernicious coaches."

"You were always one with words, but I don't know what you mean. In fact, if I wecall wight, you wead the dictionawy covah to covah yah sophomoah yeaya." He shakes his head in wonder. "If it whymes with vicious, I think I've a sense of what it means."

I nod in affirmation, "Close—it means having a harmful effect in a gradual or subtle way."

He lowers his voice in deference, "Oh, I see. So, what happened to them?"

"I don't even know. It's as if the problems were swept under the rug. No one's talking—in fact I still feel as if I'm the guilty party for reporting them."

"I'm not suah what you mean. Anyway, this is the pewfect place to we-coop and find youahself again. I know you'll love living heya on Scwag. You weya always a naychah fweak like me. Let me show you the wopes. I must leave …" He stops and stutters, "I… I must leave in two days to go fowah with my tw … tweetment." He can barely pronounce the word.

"Well, then walk me through my responsibilities."

To assert himself, he stands up, using his good arm to lift his heavy body. Beckoning for me to follow him, he scrambles up a narrow trail toward the erector-set tower that perches over a cliff. A staircase spirals inside, weaving around the metal stanchions before leveling out every ten feet.

As I climb, following Henry, I find myself growing nauseous, my heart pounding, especially when I look between the steps. On the western side, where no trees grow, the view opens up to the ridge of the Green Mountains: the tops of Mt. Abraham, Mt. Lincoln, Mt. Ellen, General Stark Mountain, Burnt Rock, Camel's Hump, and to the far north, Mt. Mansfield, Jay Peak, and into Canada.

Rounding the last turn, to the east I see Mt. Washington, Mt. Lafayette, Mt. Monroe, and the rest of White Mountains. To slow my heart rate, I take a deep breath; the pure Vermont air renews me—no smell of car exhausts, gunpowder, or tear gas.

At the top Henry puts up his hand to stop me, grabs a key, unlocks the hatch door, and pushes it with his one hand, all while bracing his knee against a step. The clang of the door on the metal floor, causes me to grab the railing in panic.

Crawling through the opening, I pull myself up into the ten-by-ten-foot glass room. There are three chairs to one side and a table in the middle. I cautiously walk around and touch the windows while I enjoy the unobstructed views. The afternoon sun blinds me.

He sits down, observing me. "Youah pwobably wondewing why theya awe thwee chaiyas?"

"I hadn't thought about it."

"Well, remember in *Walden*, you know by Henwy David Thoweau. He had thwee chaiyas: one for solitude, the second for fwiendship, and the thiwd for society."

"Got it. So clever. So, which am I?" I jest, giggling.

A topographic map of Vermont, with two moveable pointers, rests on the waist-high table in the middle of the room. Tracing the latitude and longitude coordinates, I ask if I can adjust the pencil-like pointers to identify the location of my village, 44.1926 degrees N and 72.7798 degrees W.

CHAPTER 10

My Responsibilities

Henry, watching me intently, lets me soak in the view before speaking again. The wind, moaning like a banshee, continues to pound on the windows, reminding me that we're at least forty feet in the air. The tower sways, I lose my balance, and fall into Henry.

"Not to worry, Lia. This towah has been heya twough two huwicanes and numwous lightning stowms. It's well-gwounded." Over the wind, it's hard to understand him.

I spread my legs for balance, "Okay, but do I have to climb up here if it gets really bad?"

"Of course not. In fact, see this journal heya? You don't even have to spend all day heya. All you have to do is scan the howizon evwy half-hour and wite what you see or don't see." He pauses and laughs, "Obviously, if it's waining, you can stay in the cabin or even hike down."

I open the log to see his record—he has meticulously recorded the day, the time, a brief description of the valleys, and any unidentified smoke. Most of the entries cite controlled fires that have already been approved by the fire wardens. In Vermont, a farmer can't have a brush fire without getting a permit. His writing is neat yet dramatic, printed with strong crosses on the *Ts* and large circles over his *Is*.

Underneath the log lies another notebook. Lifting it, I ask, "What's this?"

"Oh, you cuwious one, that's my pewsonal jouwnal. I like to wecord my thoughts, uh, even my poems, and often my stowies about the animals while I'm up heya." With downcast eyes, he continues, "Ya know that people who have journals get to live life twice."

I take a deep breath, sensing what he's saying, and ask demurely, "May I open it?"

"Sure, in fact, wead the poem in the beginning because it expwesses how I feel about this place. It's by Wendell Bewwy."

I only have to read the first two words to know the poem: "When despair ..." I stop and look at him and whisper, "*The Peace of Wild Things*. I love this poem."

"Well then, you'll love your time heya. Youah day will go like this: wake up with the sunwise over the White Mountains, listen for the last call of the hoot owl, and walk to the spwing to get some fresh watah." He smiles and looks out. "If you wemain silent for a moment, you will heyah the fiwst chiwping of the songbirds."

"Sounds Thoreauesque. Will I run into any animals?"

"Usually, a poowcupine will be finishing his evening wowunds, so you might heya him dwagging his spiny tail over the wocks. He's hahmless. I think he lives undah the cabin. All otheahs will have finished theya nightly haunts." He hesitates before adding, "Oh, yes, theya's a beaya and heya cub who sometimes come awound in the mowning to check if I've thwown any gahbage into the pit by the outhouse. Just wait foya heya to finish heya wowunds."

A little unnerved, gulping, I ask, "Okay, then what?"

"You'll want to light the wood-bowning stove foah a little wamth and to heat the watah fowa youya coffee. I use instant coffee with powdahed milk and sugah. Then, I use the west foya my oatmeal. I'll leave you my maple sywup for sweetening."

"Sounds easy. What time do I have to be in the tower?"

"I twy to get theya awound 7:00 as that's when the towns wake up. You'll need to cwank the phone thwee times to alewt the fiya wahden in the next town, you know, the one on Hungah Mountain, that you ah up theya. He'll wespond with fouya cwanks or even a call."

"What do I write in the log?"

"Just follow my example. The time. You do have a watch, don't you?"

"Yup," I lie because I'd left my watch at my house.

Okay, and so your day begins. I hope you like to wite or do something else by yourself. The eight houahs can go slowly up heyae. I wead a lot, too."

"Not a problem for me. I love to journal, and I have much to write about, especially my experiences on the US World Cup Ski Team. I'm thinking of turning these stories into a novel."

"Good. Then, awound 4:30, you can end the day and enjoy a hike or stawt dinnah. I twy to get all my choahs and dinnah done befoah the sun sets at awound 9:00."

I'm beginning to like the idea of this solitude, so I ask, "Can I expect visitors to the tower? And if so, what should I do?"

"Mostly on weekends. Sometimes they come duwing the weekday, usually around noon. The policy of the US Fowest Sewvice is to let them into the towah with you, but not into the cabin. We don't want people to think they can use the cabin as a campsite."

"Will I be safe here?"

"Theya's never been a pwoblem. Most people who hike are natuah lovahs like us. But then again you are the fiwst giwl that I know of who has done this job. I suggest that you call your fawher occasionally, uh, so he doesn't wowy about you."

I nod but feel a little concerned. He notices my worry, and prods me, "Do you have a gun?"

My jaw drops and I shake my head. "Nope and I've never even shot one."

"Oh, I see. Would you like to leahn?"

Pausing and remembering that, on a Sierra hike, Coach McElvey once protected my teammates and me from a bear by using a gun, I answer guardedly, "Maybe."

"Okay, so I'll tell you what. I have a pistol and I'll show you how to use it. I'll leave it heya for youah pwotection from both the animals and anything else that fwightens you."

"I like that idea. I'm up for new experiences and who knows when I might need a gun."

I'm thinking about the time the police broke into Terry's apartment. *What if they hadn't been police?*

"You look wowied. Don't. It's vewy safe." He picks up some binoculars, scans the horizon, jots in the log, and points that it's time to go. As we climb down the stairs, I'm feeling more comfortable with the height and the singing-wind in the girders.

Henry leads me to the cabin, stamping his feet twice before entering, where he teaches me how to jerk open the iron stove door, how to unstop the sink drain, how to fill the wash basin, and how to sweep the floors so that the dirt doesn't catch in the cracks. I'm amazed at how adept he is with his one arm. He moves methodically with the pride of a nouveau-riche person showing off his mansion.

He lifts the mildew-stained mattress on the top bunk, being careful not to disturb his sleeping bag on the bottom, and cautiously pulls out a silver pistol, making sure to point it to the floor.

"One can never be too caahful. I do keep the pistol loaded, so if I need it, I can use it quickly." He motions for me to follow him outside. A crow skims through the balsams, weaving as if it had radar, just missing my head. Henry screams, "Duck," and flattens himself on the rock. Standing back up, he tries to jest, "Oh, sowy, a habit I leawned in 'Nam. Amewican planes, our F100D Sabah jets, used to scweach low thwough the jungle, avoiding the flak from the enemy fiyah, while they dwopped their napalm bombs. My platoon would always duck for cover."

Unnerved by his behavior, I cautiously follow him down the path toward the outhouse, a flimsy structure hanging over the ledge. Stopping at the outcropping, he asks me to stand behind him while he spreads his legs, crouches, flips off the safety, and aims the gun at three beer cans that balance against a cliff.

I cover my ears and watch as each can explodes into the air like popcorn. He grins and says, "Now you twy it."

Setting the gun on a log, he strides over to the cans, picks each one up, and again balances it against the cliff. Coming back toward me, he stumbles. With only one arm, he can't stop his fall, so he hits the rocky ground with his knee. I rush over to help him, but he pushes me away, "Hey, I don't need youah help or anyone's." A tear forms in his eye. "When I get my pwosthesis, I'll be bettah at balancing myself. Just imagine yourself, twying to wace a downhill course with just one ski pole."

He walks up behind me and hands me the gun. "Just do as I did, and you'll be fine."

I spread my legs, crouch, raise the gun with both hands, and pull the trigger three times. Nothing happens.

He laughs, "Okay, I guess you didn't notice that I set the safety again."

With that, I release the latch and fire three more times. Not one aluminum can moves. I snarl, "Darn, I guess I'll need to practice."

'You'll have plenty of time foah that. Just don't waste too many bullets."

The tops of the White Mountains are now lit with a pink alpine glow. I awkwardly announce that I need to leave so that I can get back before dark.

He yells to me as I start down, "I won't see you again, Lia. I'll be gone befoya you get back up. I'll leave the keys undah the dooya step." There's a tone of vulnerability in his words that reverberate in my mind—a sadness or possibly a warning?

CHAPTER 11

Nothing Gold Can Stay

As I look back, my two weeks in the cabin passed quickly, because I was doing just what I wanted—being cloistered on a mountaintop with none of the world's busyness, mostly from the news, the TV or the gossip.

I spent my first few days running the two miles up and down the Palmer Road trail, lugging food, a sleeping bag, books, clothes, and writing utensils. Fortunately, the cabin was well-stocked with matches, candles, and firewood. For these luxuries, I always gave thanks to Henry, especially during my nightly meditations.

The boulder-strewn run helped me get in shape. My time improved from one hour uphill to forty-five minutes, and the downhill from forty minutes to thirty. My legs grew stronger, and my agility continued to develop into racing form, especially the proprioception in my weak ankle, which is my body's ability to sense movement, action, and location. However, the pins that hold the ankle bone together still chafe on my hiking boot, creating a perpetual blister, a pain with which I just had to live.

I discovered a pile of Henry's books in a box under the bed. I immersed myself in his collection of mountaineering books: *Lost Horizon* by James Hilton, *We Die Alone* by David Howarth, *Annapurna* by Maurice Herzog, and *The Conquest of Everest* by Sir John Hunt.

To supplement these, he had stored an anthology of American writers, including Emerson, Thoreau, Berry, Frost, and Muir, as well as political nature-writers such as Rachel Carson's book *Silent Spring* and Euell Gibbons' autobiography *Stalking the Wild Asparagus*. Thoreau's works and Emerson's poems were the same ones I'd taken with me to Europe while on the ski team. How synchronous. A worn copy of *Moby Dick* lay hidden at the bottom. One evening, as I lifted it out, the book opened to a wrinkled page with an underlined exhortation by Ahab, "All visible objects, men, are but as pasteboard masks." I had no idea what Ahab meant, but it gave me a sense of foreboding, worry, even doom.

While rereading the quote, a piece of paper slipped out onto the floor with a poem copied in Henry's handwriting.

> *We shall not cease from exploration*
>
> *And the end of our exploring*
>
> *Will be to arrive where we started*
>
> *And know it for the first time.*

I worried about what Henry was now feeling, especially his experiences in Vietnam. Certainly his amputated arm had changed him, turning him into a more morose, introspective person.

Because of all his books, I decided to limit the number of my own books that I carried up. Instead, I brought three of my European travel journals. I planned to use them as a springboard for my novel. I also brought my well-worn copy of *King Lear*, the same copy that my teammates and I had read when we were snowed in. How I loved Shakespeare's language, especially his wit. Memorizing lines from the play helped pass the hours in the tower. It was also fun to quote them to the few visitors, strangers who must have thought I was a bit eccentric.

Blow, winds, and crack your cheeks! Rage! Blow!

You cataracts and hurricanes, spout,

Till you have drench'd our steeples, drown'd the cocks!

By letting my hair grow and wearing ragged blue jeans, I became Jane Fonda of the tower, an image that added to my aloofness.

I loved these seamless, simple days during which I didn't have to talk to anyone. My routine gave me purpose, as well as taught me that living in the moment can be restorative. The routine of the essential—rising with the sun, lighting the fire, watching the fog lift from the valley floor, carrying and heating the water, climbing the tower, recording the fires, writing my novel, wandering the forest, chronicling the new flowers, listening for the animals, cooking my dinner, and reading—none of this silent sameness became monotonous. I often thought of Thoreau's words, *"I went to the woods because I wanted to live deliberately, to front only the essential facts of life, and see if I could not learn what it had to teach, and not, when I came to die, discover that I had not lived."*

The daily inconveniences of no showers, no fresh vegetables, and no clean clothes became just that—temporary frustrations that I learned to accept, just as I had learned to tolerate the sub-zero cold when skiing—nothing to fret over.

I tried some creative writing and after an awe-inspiring sunrise over the White Mountains in New Hampshire, I scribbled a poem to remember the moment.

Squinting at the sunrise

An orange glow peeks

Surrounded by a green aura

An oval awakening

Encircled by a black ring

Blinding rays blast the earth

The earth shakes off its dark overcoat

Warming to the life-giving force.

A new day. I'm alive.

Each day I found my thoughts growing further from the Olympic team, as well as the disappointments of the US Ski Team. In the same vein, the emotional tether of my memories of Washington, DC, my worries about the Vietnam War, and my friends being drafted, started to dissolve like mist into the sky.

The more I wrote about my experiences on the ski team, the more I began to recall the happy times—the times of singing with Wren before her accident; of powder skiing with Becky, Stephanie, and Carla in Switzerland; and of snuggling by the fire with my boyfriend, Bill; of watching Brandy play the fool in *King Lear*; and listening to the wise words of Coach McElvey on our hikes in the Sierras. I decided to call my novel *Snow Sanctuary*, because living high in the mountains, ironically, made me feel safe.

My only bad experience in the cabin came when a black bear and her cub clawed at the door, forcing me to fire the gun out the window to frighten her. After that, she never ventured close. The squirrels came every morning, chattering for crackers, and a raccoon actually learned how to eat out of my hand.

During my breaks, I loved to lie down, absolutely still, on a bed of velvety moss near a rocky outcropping, and let my presence fade into the soft ground, hoping the animals would resume their routines. A small rivulet would tinkle next to my rock-bed like wind chimes. Peaceful, I became a rosa rugosa blossoming under the sun—I wanted for nothing.

I was happy.

In my mind I could float off into the sky, becoming just another hawk soaring. I lost the commotion by getting rid of the motion.

At another time, high in the tower, after I'd learned to control my fear of climbing up, during an early foggy morning when the wind blew hard and the stanchions swayed, I opened a window, leaned out, and imagined I was Ishmael, resting against the iron railing of the Pequod's masthead while I sailed across the cloud-sea. I became an adventurer, exhilarated yet scared. The clouds, a surging sea of fog-swells, circled just below the highest peaks whose rocky outcroppings breached like the snouts of breathing whales.

Feeling empowered and finally owning my own story, I yelled into the void, *Call me Lia, controller of my own destiny, explorer, World Cup skier, writer, conqueror of worlds!* At such times, I'd lamented that I hadn't read more novels or short stories about female adventurers—characters who could inspire me.

My human visitors, mostly young married couples or boy scouts, climbed up searching for exercise and solitude. I avoided telling them much about myself, as I really didn't want to relive the last year, at least not until I'd figured it out myself.

My nights offered me time to read until my candle-lantern burned down. When the moon rose in the east, the crescent gave my room a bluish glow. Sipping tea, I'd steep myself in the elixir of the Transcendental writers. Then, I'd wander to the outcropping, marvel at the mackerel clouds, and watch the barn lights come on below. My neighbors, the Barnards, the Euriches, and the Neills, were finishing milking the cows and cleaning the stalls. Using binoculars, I could even spot the three streetlights that lit the covered bridge spanning my Mad River.

Across the valley, I could see the ridge of Mad River Glen where I'd learned to ski. I imagined myself to be the goddess Athena, watching over her community, proud and protective.

Nothing blissful can last and I knew at the end of the month, I'd be packing for my next adventure: a train ride across Canada, all the way to Vancouver where I'd meet my Navy friend Rob Attlefellner, join him for a hike in Wyoming's Wind River Mountains, and then drive together to Berkeley, California, to start my college courses.

Right now, on my last day in the cabin, I draft a note to Henry.

August 1, 1971

Dear Henry,

Please keep in touch, as I worry about you and your arm. My time here on Scrag has helped me to recharge and find my purpose again.

You know that in December, I'll have to decide whether to join the ski team in Europe or continue with my college. For sure, my FIS points are good enough for me to qualify for the Olympic team. All I have to do is show the coaches that I'm healed and eager.

My teammates, Becky, Wren, and Carla want me to come back to Monmouth.

With thanks, Lia

P.S. I've found the peace of wild things.

I recopy the letter three times, making sure that my handwriting is neat, before folding and placing the last one on top of his boxed books. As I start to close the container, I see an envelope stuffed along the side, a small paper that had escaped my attention during my two weeks here.

Worrying that this might be personal, I step back, but then my curiosity takes over. I pull out the card written in Henry's neat handwriting: *To Lia.* Inside are the words from a Frost poem:

> *Nature's first green is gold,*
>
> *Her hardest hue to hold.*
>
> *Her early leaf's a flower,*
>
> *But only so an hour,*
>
> *Then leaf subsides to leaf.*
>
> *So Eden sank to grief*
>
> *So dawn goes down to day.*
>
> *Nothing gold can stay.*

At the bottom left, in tiny letters, he wrote,

Live for me, my friend.

Goodbye, *Henry*

CHAPTER 12

Across the Continent

So here I am, staking out my claim to a Canadian Pacific Vista Dome seat, chugging west across the continent, wandering through the farmlands of Quebec, pulsing along the rivers and lakes of Ontario, whistling through the cities of Manitoba, and bathing under the northern lights of Saskatchewan.

Trains have always fascinated me, so for my return to the West, I've decided to ride the beast across Canada. My dad drove me to Montréal where I caught the through-train to Vancouver. I chose this route for three reasons: I've never been to Canada, the fare is cheaper than the train across the US (only forty-five dollars), and there aren't many stops.

However, this also means that I have to sit up all the way. My seatmates rotate, depending on the cities where we stop. Sometimes I have a Chinese immigrant who speaks no English—other times, I might visit with a college student, or a family who's relocating. Trains attract every type of person, except the wealthy who choose to fly to avoid the riffraff. I guess that's what I am.

My favorite times are when no one sits beside me, I close my eyes and feel the warm sun melting into my blonde hair, a gentle, other-worldly massage. Or I can spend hours reading and writing. I've brought three of Henry's books: *The Conquest of Everest, Annapurna,* and *We Die Alone,* hoping to learn more about mountaineering in anticipation of my two-week hike in the Wind Rivers with Rob. Of course, I also try to journal every day to build memories of the people I meet.

My ticket doesn't allow me a berth at night. However, a porter often wakes me, usually at 1 a.m., and lets me use an empty bed. Being able to stretch out and rest my head on a pillow is my newest luxury. The porter, an Asian man in his forties, always saves my Vista Dome seat, so I can return to the same spot in the morning. Occasionally, he brings me a cup of coffee and some bread from the dining car.

At the major cities, the train stops for an hour to refuel, to load food for the restaurant, and to change staff. I discover during the longer stops that I can dash into the Hudson Bay Company for all the supplies I need. The store is like Sears and Roebuck in the States, selling every necessity, especially for the explorers of the wild: snowshoes, traps, guns, tents, wool blankets, and cooking pots and pans. Unlike Sears though, the store also has a fresh-food section. I fill up on apples, oranges, peanut butter, jelly, and bread.

*   *   *   *

After three days, I get to Calgary where the train leaves the plains and winds its way through the Rockies—no more cities, just raw nature.

I think often about my good-bye to my father, a difficult time because he had just started to open up to me. He asked more about the coaches after I told him about their lies, their bribes, and their assaults on me. He actually cried, saying, "Lia, I let you down. I didn't listen to you when you called me from Europe to talk about your concerns. How sorry I am."

He promised me that he'd try to find out what happened to these two malevolent coaches, John Boast and Dan Ryan, and he also offered to be more supportive if I should return to the US Ski Team. Best of all, he hugged me and actually said, "I love you," for the first time since Mom died in a car crash when I was ten. After her death, he'd shut down all his emotions.

On my last day in Waitsfield, to commemorate my visit with him and celebrate my next adventure, we carried a balsam fir down from the top of Scrag and planted it in front of my white house. The Canadian Rockies, the continuation of our Rocky Mountains, form the backbone of the continent. The perpetual-snow covered peaks rise to 12,000 feet, the rivers run a milky turquoise, the lakes align in necklaces of translucent pearls, the spruces grow tall and straight, and the bridges span carved canyons, while the tunnels extend thousands of feet.

When the train stops for two hours at the Chateau Lake Louise in Banff, the penultimate respite, I decide to splurge—eat lunch in the formal dining room and call my father. Embarrassed that I don't have a skirt, I don my cleanest slacks and a silk top, my only extravagance for the trip. The porter promises to hold my seat in the Vista Dome and watch over my backpack while I'm gone.

For one hour, I can pretend to be a tourist, not a vagabond, relaxing with all the money and time I need. The hotel, built in 1911, offers plate-glass views of the blue-green Lake Louise, a color created by the rock-flour silt suspended in the glacial melt.

Entering the formal dining room, I pass photos of celebrities who've enjoyed this classy lodge, including Marilyn Monroe, Alfred Hitchcock, Queen Elizabeth, and Prince Rainier. The waiter nods in deference and takes me to a table overlooking the water toward Mount Victoria. How I've missed the towering peaks of the Sierras and Europe. For the first time since leaving the team in Maribor, Yugoslavia, I realize my real joy is being high in the snow-covered mountains, especially where no trees can grow.

After a decadent lunch of hamburger, salad, and fries, I ask for a hotel phone. My waiter points to a red British-style phone booth next to the main counter. Even though there is a two-hour time difference from Vermont, I hope that my father has returned from church. I need to ask him to wire some money to the Western Union office in Vancouver, because I've spent most of my one hundred dollars on the train.

The operator has trouble understanding that I want to make a collect call to the States, so I hang up and go to the concierge.

"Excuse me, but could you help me make a collect call to the States?" I ask, beginning to panic, because I'm a stranger here with no support from my teammates or a coach. For the first time in my life, I'm on my own, vulnerable. Even in Washington, DC, I had my aunt and my friends. If I were in the mountains, I'd be fine, but here I feel so inexperienced, so naïve. The concierge dials for me. "Oh, yes, to Waitsfield, Vermont. Collect to a Mr. Stan Erickson." Impatiently, he hands me the phone.

After four rings, my father's concerned voice comes on, "Lia, Lia, are you okay? Why are you calling? Where are you?"

His panic makes my heart race faster. A knot forms in my stomach and the hamburger begins to push back up my throat. I hold the phone closer to my ear before responding, "I'm okay. The train is in Banff and I'm at the Château on the lake."

"Oh, good, so tell me, how's the trip going?"

"I'm beginning to feel lonely, away from everyone. I miss home and you."

"That's natural. You've never been totally on your own like this before. You've always traveled with a team or with family."

"Yup, and I'm getting concerned that I don't have enough money to get to Berkeley. I've never had to be so responsible for money, food, and travel." I start talking faster and my voice goes up an octave.

"Calm down. I'll call the Western Union office at the Vancouver train station and wire you some money. It'll be waiting for your arrival. Okay?"

"Oh, thanks, Dad. I think I've got enough to get there. Have you talked to my friend, Rob Attlefellner, to make sure he'll meet my train?"

My father hesitates. He hasn't been happy about my hiking plans in the Wind River Range. "Uh, Lia, he calls me every day to find out whether your train is on time. He assures me he's an experienced mountaineer and that the two of you will be fine on your hike across the Rocky Mountains." His voice drops, "You did say that he'd been in the navy and is very responsible."

"Oh, yes, and if you go to my bureau drawer in my bedroom, you'll find all the letters he wrote me. I told you I'd met him in Grindelwald when I was racing there. Remember, he was the one who encouraged me to stay with the team and focus on my racing. I'd been so discouraged about the corrupt coaches." I pause to hear my father's reaction and then continue, "He has stayed in touch since then. You know, as a friend."

"I'm so glad for you. Also, before I forget, I sent your extra clothes to Aunt Susie's in San Francisco. You need to stop by there before you head to college."

"Got it. I think Rob can take me there. By the way, I didn't know you'd been in touch with Aunt Susie. I thought you had stopped talking to her after my mother died."

"Well, Lia, I figured if you were going to college in Berkeley, even though your mother had had a fight with Aunt Susie, I thought it might be time to patch up family relations."

"Thanks, Dad. I look forward to meeting her." I hug the phone, thinking about my mother and her sister not talking for all those years.

The train whistle blows three times, announcing that the Express is ready to board. "Oh, no, I must go, but I'll call from Vancouver. My train's leaving now. What a fun journey this has been … everyone has been very nice to me."

"Oh, Lia, before you go, you need to know one thing. I'm … I'm not sure how to tell you this."

I don't like the hesitancy in his voice. "What? Go ahead."

"Well, remember Henry David from the fire tower."

"Why, of course. What about him?"

"Well, he didn't get his prosthesis, so he returned to the tower. The Veteran's Administration claimed he needed another operation." He stammers, "The … the infection had gone into his upper arm." I don't like his use of the past tense. "They put him on a heavy dose of antibiotics again."

"Oh, dear. When will he get the operation?"

There's a silence on the other end, so I have to yell, "Dad, can you hear me?"

"There won't be another operation … " His pause is so long that I thought I'd lost him again. "Henry returned to the tower and shot himself."

I drop the phone and fall to the floor like a dead sparrow. The train whistle blasts twice. I pick up the phone and cry, "Oh, no! Dad, he was such a wounded warrior—we called each other wounded warriors."

"I know … I know. I'll talk to you at your next stop. I love you." I hold the phone to my ear, hoping to hear the words again, but all I can think of are Henry's last words to me, "Live for me, my friend." *Did he know then what he had planned to do?*

As I stand up, a cloud comes over the summit of Mount Victoria—the lake becomes a black morass.

CHAPTER 13

A New Friend

Trying to beat the other pilgrims back to get on board to reclaim my seat, I grab my shoulder bag and sprint toward the last car. Everyone else is required to board from the front. However, my porter-friend promised he'd meet me at the caboose to let me in before the others.

Our plan works perfectly except that when I reach my Vista Dome seat, there's a young hippie boy in my place by the window. His brown hair is unkempt, his chin sprouts immature blond tufts, and his possum-ears stick out. What catches my attention most are the bags under his eyes.

Seeing my expression, he stands up and steps into the aisle. "Oh, sorry, but the porter told me to sit here. I didn't know he'd saved this seat for you." He bends over and reaches down. "Sorry, I put your knapsack on the floor."

"No problem. You can have the seat next to me. I'm used to others sitting there. In fact, I've met some interesting people this way. Each person has told me their story, you know, like the pilgrims in *The Canterbury Tales*."

He bows, sits next to me, and quotes in an old-English accent, " 'Whan that Aprill with his shoures soote.' Well, I hope you'll find me as fascinating as those other pilgrims." His awkward grin tells me he's hiding something.

Amazed, I knit my eyebrows, wondering what he knows about me and about my obsession with English lit. Not to be outdone, I respond quickly, " 'The droghte of March hath perced to the roote.' " He shifts trying to find a rebuttal, but I continue, "When did you study Chaucer?"

"In college, just like every other well-educated English literature scholar. I majored in English literature at Dartmouth. We had to memorize the first fifteen lines of the prologue to be able to understand Middle English. And you?"

"Well, I had a demanding English teacher in high school who wanted us to learn the roots of the English language." I laugh self-consciously, not sure whether he wants to talk more or not.

He looks out the window, and after an intolerable silence, he says, wistfully, "Well, I guess I'm on my own pilgrimage to places unknown."

A long silence ensues as I watch the others boarding—a routine similar to checking out new classmates in a high school line, wondering: *who'll be friendly? Who'll be talkative? What are their stories, and where are they going?*

Finally, I decide to break the ice. "So, you're new here. I've been on the train since Montreal."

"Well, I guess you could say I'm new. I came via Washington, DC on the Union Pacific Railroad through the States. There's only one place I could safely cross the Canadian border."

"What do you mean ... safely?"

Not sure whether to continue, he hesitates, looks out the window, and says, "It's a long story."

"Try me. For sure we have time."

"First, are you an American?"

"Yup, born and raised in Vermont." I raise my chin in pride.

"Do you know much about what's happening in the States right now?"

I nod my head slightly. "Not sure what you mean."

"Do you follow the Vietnam War?"

"A little." I begin fidgeting with my backpack that still rests on my knees, knowing I've told a white lie.

He takes a deep breath as if bracing himself for a jump off a cliff into a deep pool of water. "Let's back up. How do you feel about the war?"

This interrogation scares me because I've just been in Washington with Greta, who had taught me to be discreet about my knowledge of the war and the protest movement. Cautiously, I respond, "Well, I've heard terrible things about what the American soldiers are doing to the villages in South Vietnam." I look out the window, not sure how much to tell him.

"Well, do you know anything about the draft dodgers who've chosen to leave the States instead of going into the war?" He looks directly into my eyes, trying to see what I'm thinking.

"Of course! In fact, I had a friend who was drafted and thought about fleeing to Canada." I close my eyes and try to remember my last image of my boyfriend, Bill Emerson, before he left Monmouth to accept his deployment. "Instead, he chose to obey his father, joined the army, and was sent to Vietnam." Trying to avoid breaking down, I swallow and slowly say, "He was dead two months later."

My new friend puts his head in his hands and starts shaking. "I'm so sorry. This war is so horrible. Let me tell you what I'm doing here in Canada. I trust you." He looks around to see if anyone is listening and leans closer to me. "I'm an army soldier, too. But I'm a wanted man in the States. Just before being sent to Vietnam, I went AWOL, you know, Absent Without Leave. I went to Washington to join the protest movement with John Kerry. My sergeant heard about my desertion and sent orders for my arrest."

He pauses to gauge my reaction. I nod to assure him. "The police found me near the Washington Monument, just as I was getting ready to burn my draft card. When the officers started putting handcuffs on me, an older woman with a scarf over her head came out of the crowd, led me past the Capitol police officers, and asked the protesters to surround her and me. Then she spirited me into a parked station wagon."

"Wow, I think you and I were there at the same time."

"What? What do you mean?" He seems more relaxed.

"I was there on the first of May and got caught up in the march on Washington, too."

Both of us look out the window, realizing that maybe there's some destiny that has brought us together at this time. I let my eyes wander up to the mountain peaks that hang over our fast-moving train. The track has developed more curves as the train crawls up the Continental Divide, snaking along a cascading river. Like a living, breathing dragon, the engine groans over the bridges and screeches through the tunnels, while our car sways side to side. I fall against my seatmate's shoulder.

After this awkward silence, I continue, "Oh, by the way, my name is Lia."

"I wish I could tell you mine, but then you'd be complicit in my draft-dodging. Just call me Will."

I gasp, noting that the coincidences are mounting up like building blocks.

"Okay, but back to why you crossed the border below Calgary."

"A long story short. Do you remember reading about the underground railroad during the Civil War?"

"Yes, but what does this have to do with now?"

"Well, we have a similar escape route for Vietnam draft dodgers, except that we really do use the railroad. The military police have closed the borders on both coasts, so a group has formed to help us get into Canada at the Lethbridge border ... just north of Great Falls, Montana. I was able to enter Canada by hiding in a tourist's car. Because I was already under military arrest, I got top priority over other protesters. A group called Antigone helped me."

I did a double take on hearing him refer to Greta's protest group. "Wow, so you were smuggled from Washington DC to here."

"Yup, and it all started with a woman called Greta."

At this point, I grab my head and gulp, almost gagging on my own inhale. Paranoid, I look up and down the car to see if I'm being watched. "Are you serious? A woman named Greta. Can you describe her?"

"Of course, she'll always be my savior. Let's see, she has medium-gray hair, a stocky build, and very round cheeks. What I remember most is her German accent."

"Tell me more. How'd you get on this train and why?"

"The underground group planned this all out. I was told to get to the border crossing on July 30th, where a couple would hide me in their car and get me over the border. Then, they'd drive me to Banff, where I'd pick up this train. They had all the tickets arranged for me. I think Greta planned my whole escape. I'm headed for Vancouver where the group has a job for me, working at the Hotel Elizabeth."

Now I'm really nervous as I've planned to go to the same hotel to meet Rob. I remember that I'd told Greta my travel plans just before leaving Vermont. I panic, wondering, *Why am supposed to meet this man called Will? Why is he so open about his situation? Who's told him what? Why did the porter somehow know to put him next to me?*

CHAPTER 14

My Knight

As the train churns up Roger's Pass, the rumble in the tunnels makes our conversation impossible. I relax into the rhythmic rocking of the car, blink at the strobe flashes of light and dark and turn my attention to the waterfalls frolicking down the steep-walled canyons. My nose enjoys the warm sunlight on the glass.

Occasionally, the train crawls by a mountain lake, so isolated that no roads go near. Reverently, I try to imagine hiking up one of the valleys, high into the snowfields and the overhanging clouds. I bask in the silence. Meeting Will seems too coincidental, It makes me paranoid about his presence, his choice of name that's so close to my skiing friend Bill's name, and his dilemma. The summer sun flares through the Vista Dome, heating my shoulders. To get more light, Will leans toward me, his red-checkered flannel shirt caressing my arm.

On the other side of the pass, we continue our conversation, eager to share more information in the fashion of two lonely hikers who've just found each other after soloing up a mountain trail.

"So, Bill … I mean Will, did you ever think about not deserting and simply accepting your deployment to Vietnam? You know, like my friend who was killed over there. Ironically, his name was close to yours." I look to see if he'll grow defensive or reveal some emotion.

His face reddens as he spits out, "That's a stupid question. Of course, I thought about it, but as I told you, during my leave, just before my assignment to Da Nang, I got involved with protesters. Once I learned the truth about the atrocities, the tortures, and the napalm devastation of the land, in all good conscience I couldn't be a part of that—no matter the cost to me."

He looks out the window at a crow flying alongside the train. Smacking his hand on the arm rest, he adds, "Vietnam is an immoral war." He stops again, glances around to see if others are listening, stares at me, and whispers, "So, I guess that makes all of us, you and me, and many American citizens, complicit in this immoral war. Yes, just like the citizens in Germany who didn't try to stop the Nazis … " He pauses to see my reaction before continuing, " … If you're not part of the solution, you're part of the problem."

I shiver, remembering Greta's anger about the war, and chastising myself for not questioning the role of civilians, like my father, who support the unjust war. To test Will, I ask, "How'd you learn about the actual events over there?"

"Through the SDS, you know, Students for a Democratic Society, the underground. I met a woman called Terry at a meeting in Washington. She showed me pages of documents about the harm we're doing, you know, to the South Vietnamese villages, to the children there. She described the corrupt leaders that our military has put into place there, such as President Thieu."

I gulp, realizing my meeting with Will might be part of someone's larger scheme. There are just too many coincidences. I decide to be very careful about what I say, not sure whether he's a setup by the FBI to learn more about my involvement with Greta, or whether he's a legitimate protester. I'm certainly not going to mention my relationship with Terry and Greta. At least not right now.

"So, what'd you learn?"

"Well, first, that the Vietnamese people do not want us there. That Ho Chi Minh, their leader, you know, and the North Vietnamese people think of us as both colonists and now invaders, criminals like the French whom they forced out of the country after Dien Bien Phu in 1954."

"So, what do the Vietnamese want?"

"Oh, you are a naïve one. For sure, all they want is to be able to control their own country, live in peace, and farm their land. And for this, they will fight to the last person. We'll never win this war … " and he tapped his chest, "because we can never win the hearts of the people."

Trying to sound innocent, I ask, "But don't we have more money, more weapons, and more bombs?" I'm thinking of my father's arguments for the war.

"Oh, my friend, look at history. No number of weapons can destroy the will of a determined people."

"Can't we outlast them?"

"Again, look at history. Impossible. Just remember your early lessons about our Revolutionary War. Remember how the American colonists outlasted a superior British army."

I nod, and he continues. "Now I see you understand. Already the will of many Americans for this war is gone. We, the young, are angry. The government has spent too much money, over 120 billion dollars, and over 46,000 American soldiers have died. And who knows how many North and South Vietnamese? Every family in America has been affected."

I lower my head, thinking about Henry David who could never return to his normal life after his war injury. I marvel at Will's command of the facts. "What about the fear of a communist Vietnam? My father thinks we have to stop the communists, or they will take over the whole Asian Peninsula."

"Far from it. That's old school, cold war thinking. I've heard that all Ho Chi Minh really wanted for his country was to be a democratic society, but the US wouldn't support him against the French colonists, so … he had to turn to the Chinese communists to get rid of the French invaders and now the Americans."

I am beginning to understand that the protest against the war is not just about my generation not wanting to die in another land. Certainly, it's not about truth, honor, or chivalry.

Will looks at me. "Ah, I see you're beginning to understand my argument. Let me give you more to think about. You've studied American literature, right?"

"Why, yes."

"Did you ever read *The Adventures of Huckleberry Finn* in school?"

"Of course, everyone does. I studied it during my junior year."

"Okay, now consider this. What if Huckleberry had decided to turn Jim in, you know, to the slave catchers when they got to Cairo, instead of protecting him?"

Confused at what he's saying, I chuckle. "Well, I guess there wouldn't have been much of a story."

"Not only that, but Huck would also have been collaborating in the great crime of slavery. At some time in life, each one of us must take a moral stand when we see injustice, cruelty, and corrupt governments." He looks at me and stiffens. "I'm making my stand. I'm going to work helping the draft dodgers in Canada. Just like Huck."

The conversation is starting to make my head spin. I'm thinking maybe I'm complicit if I don't do more to protest the war. Wanting to take a break, I pick up my knapsack, lay it over my knees and put my head on it. "Do you mind if I take a short nap? This information is way too much for me right now."

Will gently places his hand on my back and whispers in my ear, "I'm not sure what you know, so I might have told you too much." He rests his head back and closes his eyes. "Let's continue in an hour or so—okay?"

The rocking train puts me to sleep, but my day-mares of ghosts in American GI uniforms, of peasants lying in the mud, and of planes spraying napalm continue. I wake with a start, thinking I hear a bomb, but instead realize it's the train whistle screaming as it approaches a town.

Will, too, jerks his head up and jumps to his feet. When the train suddenly lurches and the car rocks, he falls forward. Trying to hold onto one of the bars on top of each seat, he's catapulted down the aisle, his legs flopping back as if an ocean wave has sucked them from under him. His head hits an Asian woman sitting two seats up the aisle, and he collapses into her lap.

I jump up to help him while the train continues slowing. The woman cradles Will's head. His knees strike the ground as he lies flattened on her lap, dazed.

I run to him and grab his arm. "Are you okay?" Then turning to the woman, "I'm so sorry, ma'am."

She looks up to me and in very broken English says, "He okay. But need porter."

Will shakes his head, pulls himself up, and announces, "No help. Please, Lia, don't call the porter." He becomes agitated. "Just, just get me back to my seat." He staggers back, pulling himself along the aisle like a drunkard, but stumbles.

I notice that a cut on his forehead has started bleeding and I give him my scarf to stop it. The rest of the passengers try not to look, but curiosity gets to them just as any voyeur would gawk at a car accident. One man in a Canadian military uniform gets out of his seat to help support Will's arm and leads him back to his seat.

Will aggressively shoves the soldier away and slides back into his chair, "I'm okay. Please don't call for help."

I crawl over him to my window seat, stammering, "Hey, you …you need some help. The cut's still bleeding." As I lean over to pull his collar away from the dripping blood, I spot a medal around his neck. Cupping it in my hand, I turn it over to see the image of a female Greek warrior, helmeted with her hair flowing beneath. On the back in small print, I read, "Go with God, Antigone."

He grabs my hand and squeezes it, "Please, don't tell anyone what you just saw." He yanks the medallion from my hand, "Just help me stop the bleeding. If aid comes, they may ask for my papers. I'm worried that I'll get caught and sent back to the US—understand?" He looks like a cornered cougar, eyes darting in every direction.

The panic in his face convinces me that he truly is a draft deserter. He hasn't come to spy on me, but only to save himself from fighting an immoral war. I now believe him. In contrast to Bill and to the knight in *The Canterbury Tales,* who both chose to fight for honor, Will, like Huckleberry, has chosen to decry, to defy his country's laws, to follow his moral conscience, and his dreams for a better country.

Also, he's chosen to sacrifice his American citizenship forever.

CHAPTER 15

Train Living

Will nudges me awake as the train slows for the town of Kamloops. "Hey, sleepyhead. It's getting time for dinner." His head wound has dried into a black scab, and he's changed his blood-stained flannel shirt for a blue turtleneck.

I rub my eyes, brush a wisp of hair from my cheek, and jest, "Oh, you've such a one-track mind."

He winks, thinks for a moment, and quips, "Is this any way to conduct yourself?"

I'm beginning to trust his company, so accepting his punning challenge, I continue the game, "Are you railing against me?"

Barely hesitating, he responds, "No, I just want to steer clear of any controversy." He frowns and puts his hands up. His dimpled cheeks burst into a wry grin.

"Oh, you've such freighted words." Proudly, I look around to see if anyone else is listening to our banter. I can't believe I've found someone who likes to play with words the way I do. The words become balls that we juggle in the air, but the responder must be quick, catch the idea, and return a quip or the game loses momentum. I continue, "Let's not break from this punning yet. I've coupled a few more ideas."

Searching for his next verbal spar, he stares out the window. "Umm, I guess I can bridge that one."

"Great, now you're definitely boxing me in."

"Sorry, I was hoping to elephant-style you."

I stop. "Now you've lost me. What's elephant-style?"

He stands up to stretch his legs, causing his sleeve to brush my face, while he steps into the aisle. "Hah, I win. Elephant-style is when all the cars in a train face forward, just the way elephants parade nose-to-tail in a circus."

Trying to get the final word in, I challenge him, "Let's not get off track."

Just then the porter walks past and announces that the dining car is open. Will leans over me and whispers, "How about I treat you to dinner tonight, okay? I've some extra money and could use a hot meal instead of the bread, cheese, and apples that we've been eating. Know what I mean?"

I cover my mouth and giggle, "Okay, as long as you don't try to signal me to do anything else."

Laughing, he offers me his calloused hand and says, "No, all I ask is that you tell me your story." He pauses, searching for a clever word, "How did you get to be railroaded onto this bullet capsule."

I blush, slide out past him, and announce, "Well said. I'll meet you in the dining car after I stop by the girls' room to wash up. If we leave our packs on the seat, no one will take our places." I grab my overnight bag containing my washcloth, soap, toothbrush, hairbrush, and makeup. Feeling giddy, I want to freshen up for my date on the train.

The bathroom is a four-by-four closet with a small toilet, a pull-down, stainless-steel sink, and a square mirror. I struggle to yank down my jeans, using the walls for balance, and then Houdini-style, I give myself a full-body scrub while splashing water from the twelve-inch metal washbowl. Looking into the mirror, I'm amazed at how tired I look. I actually have bags under my eyes from three days of not getting a full night's sleep. I brush on some eye shadow and powder my cheeks. I haven't felt so self-conscious in months. Living on a train makes my time in the mountain cabin seem like a luxury, just as I find skiing in sub-zero weather on an icy trail makes me appreciate all the sunny, powder days on the slopes. I've always welcomed the contrasts to find my center.

Walking down the windowless corridor requires a delicate balance much like in ski racing—fortunately, the hallways have railings. When I cross between the cars, a smell from the dank forest makes me sneeze and the deafening screech of the train wheels forces me to plug my ears with my fingers. Then the whiff of the engine smoke makes me gag. Now I know why Henry David Thoreau hated trains—trains that chugged right by his cabin on Walden Pond, trains that he said rode upon us, instead of our riding upon them. He preferred to walk everywhere.

Stopping in the next car, I gaze out the window into the forest, the virgin trees as tall as small hills. Looking at the world from this test-tube compartment takes away my full experience of nature. It's like looking at a postcard or at National Geographic pictures—beautiful, but sterile. I'm learning that to fully appreciate nature's beauty, I must have a total sensory immersion—not just in the sights but in the animal sounds, the tree smells, the ground texture, the air temperature, and even the taste of the water. Realizing this, I become excited about my upcoming adventure with my friend, Rob, in the Wind River Wilderness.

The dining car is four carriages away from our Vista Dome, so by the time I get to Will, my hair has again become a squirrel's nest.

He gets up, smirking, "Oh my gosh, you look like you just skied into a hurricane."

"Oh, thanks, you'll never understand how hard it is to clean up in a train bathroom. I'll be glad to get off this land missile." I fidget with the snarls before grabbing my brush and running it through the tangles.

He nods, and with feigned concern says, "Probably not, but you'll always look beautiful to me."

So as not to acknowledge his flirtation, I busy myself with my linen napkin, methodically folding it on my lap. Before taking up the menu, I ask, "So, what's my budget?"

I look beyond him to see all twenty dining tables set with linen, real glasses, and silver-plated flatware. A rose in a porcelain vase balances between us, so I focus on it to avoid his stare. For I moment I lose myself in its beauty—I touch its soft red petals, smooth as powder, and gently pick it up.

Smelling the center's sweet perfume, I'm back in my mother's rose garden in an instant, recalling how she loved to spend hours deadheading and trellising her favorites: her hybrid tea Irish elegance, the dainty Bess, and her double delight. My favorite was the rosa rugosa, a flower so wild that it could plant itself anywhere. She often called me RR, because she said I had the ability to transport myself anywhere and survive. At times, I really miss her and long for her advice.

"Hey, Lia. Why the silence? What're you thinking? At times you grow very aloof." He looks me straight in the eye, without blinking, "I wish our budget could be unlimited, but Greta only gave me fifty dollars for our trip. Let's try to keep our expenses below twenty."

I take a deep breath, now understanding that our meeting has been planned by Greta. She must have picked Will just for me: to sit by him, to play word games with him, to trust him, and finally, to have him convince me that I must join the protest movement. How devious. I'm amazed that he says "our" as if we're collaborating. I stutter in amazement, "I … I guess that leaves me one choice, a hamburger with a side salad. That's okay with me."

I start coughing and turn to see a rotund man behind me lighting a cigarette to accompany his meal. The smoke, sweet but musky, wafts in my face. Now choking, I question, "Uh, I'm not sure I can handle this smoke. It sure is nice to be in the Vista Dome where there's no smoking."

"Oh, sorry. This is the only table I could get. Near the smoking section. Let's change places because I'm used to smoke. Most of my army friends smoked to relieve the pressure of basic training. Most got addicted." He pauses and looks around, adding, "Now I hear that in Vietnam, our soldiers have turned to marijuana and even stronger stuff to deal with their fears."

For someone just out of college, Will seems wise beyond his years.

During the meal, I tell him about my life in Vermont with my father, and about my mother's death in a car crash. I also talk about my invitation to be on the US Ski Team, and about my training in Monmouth, California, and about my mentor and coach, Justin McElvey, and about my teammates, Wren, Becky, and Carla, and about my boyfriend, Bill Emerson, and his death in Vietnam. Then I go on to talk about my World Cup races in Europe, and about Tracy who was impregnated by the US Ski Team head coach, John Boast, and about my getting two predatory coaches fired. Finally, I tell him about breaking my ankle in Maribor, and about working in Washington, DC, where I met Terry and Greta. Then I tell him about my rehabilitation on Scrag Mountain while working as a fire warden.

He doesn't say a word during my monologue until I've finished. Very carefully, he asks, "So what happened to the coaches?"

Puzzled that this is his only question, as if he already knows my story, I mumble, "I'm … I'm not sure. For all I know, they were sent to other coaching positions. No one has told me anything."

He slaps his fist on the table and says, "Damn those bastards! They always get away with their abuse. Someone must stop such behavior." I put my fingers to my lips to quiet him, because the other diners are pointing at us.

The waiter comes over, asking, "Are you okay, Miss?" I wave him away.

Putting my hand on Will's, I try to reassure him "Hey, take it easy. I'm sure those coaches will be punished."

He looks around and leans toward me, "I'm so sorry, but I've had my fill with uncontrolled leadership, with the lies and deceit. Now I'm talking about President Nixon, Vice President Spiro Agnew, and Secretary of Defense Melvin Laird. They told the American people last December that the "Vietnamization" of the war was ahead of schedule and that we'd be pulling the 334,000 troops out by this summer. Lies! Lies!" His face grows as red as the rose on the table and his faint whiskers stand out like thorns.

"Wow, you sure know your facts," I say in awe.

"We must know. This is how we rally the protesters and keep the leaders honest." His anger grows until he looks like a bull preparing to charge.

He continues, sensing I need to know more. "Let me tell you about lies. For the last four years, the Nixon administration has been trying to work out a truce, meeting with the North Vietnamese at the Paris peace talks, but with no success." He scratches his head. "National Security Advisor, Henry Kissinger, keeps coming up with new proposals. At times the two sides even argue over stupid things like the configuration of the table where they will meet. They can't even agree on how to negotiate." He pauses and looks out the window. "Yup, stupid, arrogant men—the North Vietnamese know not to trust him or the entire Nixon administration."

"Is there any other way to stop this war?"

"Well, Congress tried this year. You know, for the first time this January, they called for an end to any war not voted on by Congress. It passed the War Powers' resolution, but Nixon vetoed it. Nothing happened." I notice some tears appear in his eyes. "You know that the US never officially declared Vietnam a war. Unfortunately, the president has ultimate power. Remember what someone, I think it was George Orwell, said: 'Power corrupts, and absolute power corrupts absolutely.' "

Now I know that I have a compatriot in my concerns and feel that I can trust him with the rest of my story. I tell him how I'll be going to Berkeley to help Terry and Greta with the antiwar movement, while starting my college courses.

He reaches out to hold my hand. "Lia, I already know all this. Greta and Terry have filled me in."

Angry, I challenge him, "Okay, so if I'm to trust you, you must tell me your real name."

"That could get us in trouble. If you know my real name, the authorities might force you to tell them. Remember, we'll be working as a team to disseminate the truth about the war." He reaches out to the rose in the center. "Anyway, to quote Juliet's question to Romeo: 'What's in a name? That which we call a rose by any other name would smell as sweet.' "

I conclude, "Oh, you're too much. Now you're quoting Shakespeare to dodge my question. I'm beginning to feel in over my head. So far, my life has followed a single path, predetermined by my passion for skiing. I'm scared now because for the first time ever, this December, I'll face a major decision: whether to go back to skiing for the Olympic team or stay in college."

A long silence follows. Will nods and asks, "You look confused. Are you sure you want to go back to the skiing—isn't that saying yes, to the dangers, the deceit, and the loneliness you told me about?" Rolling his brown eyes, he laughs, "Maybe your accident has already made your decision for you. Maybe your ankle won't be ready. Do you follow me?"

"Well, that's why I want to try college. I'll study, work out, and probably go to Monmouth at Thanksgiving to train with my friends again. My coach at

Monmouth has told my father that he's giving me some money for my college expenses, but with the stipulation that I'll go back to the team."

Will puts his hands up and tries to play devil's advocate. "Wait a minute—that sounds like a bribe! You also need to weigh all the good you can do if you stay at Berkeley and help with the antiwar movement. Maybe that's more important than being on the Olympic team." He picks up his knife. "Remember Huck Finn?"

I puzzle over this for a moment, as I've never really thought about my choices in this way—a decision for the common good instead of a decision for my own selfish needs. I used to feel certain that I'd go back to the team when my ankle healed.

Staring deeply into the rose, I realize that the beauty of this flower also lies in the complexity of its structure, intertwined petals that encircle each other—hiding the core, just as my relationship with Will is becoming more convoluted, layer upon layer of intrigue, and spying—all confusing me.

I pick up the rose and pluck off a few velvety petals. Just before putting it back into the vase, I prick myself.

CHAPTER 16

Hotel Vancouver

Greta, looking like a refugee, wrapped in a gray shawl and black pants, greets us at the Canadian National station in downtown Vancouver. She folds her hands together, bows, and then spreads her fingers to make the secret "A". Will does the same in greeting. Then, she holds out her hands to both of us as if she knew we'd be getting off the train together. I look up at Will to see if he's expecting her because I'm certainly not. He smiles and moves toward her.

Walking with us to the baggage claim, Greta announces, "Well, hello my two friends. I see you found each other, just as I asked the porter to help you."

I step back, shake my head, and demand, "Excuse me—did you just say that you'd planned our meeting?" I roll my eyes, "And that the porter was part of the plan?"

Greta looks surprised, "I would have thought that you'd have figured it out by now. The porter works for Antigone and, ja, I knew the train you were on. That's why I scheduled for Will to catch the same one in Banff. He knew what you looked like. And I knew that the porter would help him." She smirks, "I told Will to look in the Vista Dome for you, knowing you would probably be communing with nature. Anyway, now both of you will be working for me once you get situated."

She glances back and forth at each of us, looking for affirmation. Unsure, I just give her a blank stare, but Will nods in agreement. She continues demanding, "Right, Will, you'll be my liaison in Vancouver, and Lia, you'll be my new contact at the University at Berkeley. We need fresh bodies in the field because the FBI has begun to infiltrate our network." She looks around to see if anyone is watching. "You know, the FBI is worried that the protest movement is gaining momentum again. Ja?"

Nodding in agreement, Will puts down his pack, so he can retrieve his suitcase from the carousel. He then turns to me and says, "Don't look so surprised, Lia. I told you that I'd met Terry and Greta in Washington. The rest should have followed. You're Miss Sleuth, right?" He grabs my sweatshirt, laughs, and asks, "What does your bag look like? I'll help you with it."

"Oh, this is too confusing." I step toward the carousel. "Oops, there goes my backpack. It's the green Kelty hiking pack." Will reaches over me and effortlessly hoists my forty-pound bag to his shoulder.

Trying to understand just how Will and I might be working together, I turn to Greta. "You planned all of this, so am I a pawn in a game I don't know about?" I stamp my foot and slap my leg. "I'm not sure I want to be involved in so much subterfuge. After all, I'm just a small-town girl from Vermont who happens to have big dreams."

Greta looks concerned and temporizes, "Calm down. You're getting red in the face. You won't be doing anything illegal. And you won't be jeopardizing your chance for the Olympic team."

"Thanks," I say, taking my pack from Will. "I guess I feel better. I'm only helping you because I'm angry about my friend's death in Vietnam." Then, I whisper to myself, "It's such a stupid war."

A train whistle blasts, so I can't hear Greta's full reply, but I do hear her say, " ... your naiveté will be your cover."

Greta leads us out of the station where she is confronted by a tall, blond, Germanic-looking man. She steps back, putting her hands up in an effort to prevent him from getting close to our group.

The man steps around her and announces, "Excuse me, ma'am, but I've come to meet this young lady. She's a friend of mine."

I laugh, "Don't worry, Greta. He's not a spy. He's my friend, Rob. I'll be hiking with him. I met him in Grindelwald when I was in the World Cup race. Remember, he's been my fan and has supported my ski racing."

Will, holding his suitcase, steps forward, offers his hand, and winks, "You're a lucky guy. You get to spend two weeks in the mountains with my new friend."

The two step back and eye each other with daggers as they keep talking, but the whistling of a departing train drowns out the rest of their conversation. At one point, they look as if they are going to hit each other.

Greta beckons for us to follow her out to the sidewalk. Overhead, the green copper roof of the Hotel Vancouver, the tallest building in the city, spies on us. Once in the street, I'm overwhelmed by the honking cars and the surge of passengers pushing past me like civilians fleeing a bombed-out city. I'm reminded how much I detest cities.

Greta points to the hotel and starts to cross the street. A taxi slams on its brakes and a man yells out in French, "Arrêtez! Utilisé le passage pour piétons imbécile!" He gives her the middle finger. She stops, turns, and gives it back.

Inside the massive lobby, which is lit by crystal chandeliers that brighten the marble floors, I feel small, unimportant, and frightened. Looking up to the clerestory windows, I'm confused—nothing seems right. I'm left alone with Rob, because Greta and Will have moved to a small table in an alcove that's decorated with overstuffed velvet chairs. Greta waves, "Come over here, Lia. We need to make plans." She waves Rob away. "Can you come back in a half hour, bitte?"

Rob throws up his hands in disgust and scowls, "Um, okay, Greta. I'll go get some lunch so you can make plans. I'm not sure why." He grabs my backpack and challenges her, "I'll take this, since Lia will be coming with me." He spits the words out.

Greta doesn't move or say a word until Rob reaches the other side of the room, beyond sound and sight. I sit down with her and Will. She moves the artificial orchids in front of us and then turns to Will and me, covering the side of her mouth with her hand, and she whispers, "Note, you can never be too careful, ja? I've no idea who that man is. He could be working for the FBI. You must be on guard because the US government has spies everywhere."

At this point, I laugh, "C'mon. You make this seem like a spy versus spy from *Mad Magazine*. Rob's just a friend who's come to meet me and take me hiking before I go to Berkeley. He knows nothing about the SDS … about the student protests. He just wants me to return to ski racing." I look to Will for confirmation, but he indicates with his hands that he wants no part of this conversation.

Greta looks around to see if anyone is listening. "Okay, Lia, I'll trust your judgment on this one. For now, there is no need for you to know what I tell Will. Your roles will be totally separate. For you, Lia, after you get settled in Berkeley, go to the *Daily Californian*, the student newspaper. There you'll get your instructions. And Will, you'll come with me to the TV station on top of this building, where I've found you a job working in the media. In six months, you can apply for Canadian citizenship, ja?"

Guardedly, I ask, "Does this mean I can leave to go with Rob? He's waiting for me."

Greta hands Will an envelope, puts her head down, pulls her scarf over her head, and answers, "Of course. Will, why don't you walk Lia over to find Rob and say goodbye?"

Will pushes his chair back and leans over to me, so that I can see the scab on his forehead. "Come with me, 'cause I've a few things to tell you before you start your next adventure."

We head out the hotel door onto the sidewalk, making sure no one is watching us. I grab Will's arm for comfort. He pushes me away and stands directly in front of me like a parent about to scold a child. "Lia, we won't be able to communicate with each other for at least two months, while I get established here in Canada. I'm nervous that I'm being followed and that my phone calls will be monitored. The FBI knows that the draft deserters in Canada are encouraging the student protest movement. They can use us to track down the informers in America."

I step back nervously and smooth my white shirt collar. "Uh, okay, but who'll get in touch with me in Berkeley?"

"I don't know—maybe someone at the school newspaper. But I can assure you it won't be me unless … " he pauses, " … unless I get in trouble. If I do, that will mean that the authorities know about our meeting on the train, and they'll track you down. I'm safe here in Canada, because they can't extradite me, but you won't be safe in America." He turns to go back into the lobby and stops. "For this reason and this reason only, I would try to contact you … " He pauses and glances down, " … even help you escape to Canada if need be."

I push him back stating, "Wait a minute. Greta said I won't be doing anything illegal."

He stutters, "Um, of course, but ... but you'll have connections with other protesters in the underground news network. The FBI might want to interrogate you." He gropes for the appropriate words. "Remember, to be an agent of change, you need to feel unsafe."

He grabs my arm and leans over to kiss me on the cheek. He's put on fresh Old Spice cologne and his three-day growth of beard tickles my cheek. "Now go find Rob and have a safe trip in the mountains. Good luck in college." Reaching into his pocket, he finishes, "Oh, yes, Greta gave me this. It's your dad's money from Western Union." He hands me an envelope. "I hope you stay in Berkeley, aiding the protest movement, instead of returning to the ski team. Remember Huck," he says and laughs. "You do follow my train of thought."

Turning away from him, I hope he doesn't see me wiping a tear.

CHAPTER 17

Preparations

An impatient knocking wakes me. I take a second to realize that I'm sleeping in Rob's friend's house in Pinedale, Wyoming. After sixteen hours of driving from Canada to Wyoming in Rob's Austin Healey, after hours of no talking because we'd chosen to travel with the top down, after hours of enjoying the wind in my hair and the sun on my face, I'd collapsed asleep in a stranger's house, a rest with dreams of mountains, tundra, rocks, and glaciers—all soon to be mine.

In his deep bass voice, Rob announces, "Hey, Sunshine, your dad's on the phone. He wants to make sure everything is okay. I gave him this number before we left Canada." Rob, ever the gentleman, has always kept my father informed about his plans to meet me and take me hiking. As a gesture of respect, he even visited my Waitsfield home when I was in Washington, DC.

Feeling comforted by the fact that my dad is worried about my whereabouts, I slip on my jeans and run downstairs. Rob hands me the phone while I take a deep breath, "Hi, Dad, I'm in Pinedale, Wyoming. We had an uneventful trip."

I hear a pause before he responds, "I know, Lia. Rob has kept me in the loop. You know I'll worry about you until you get to Berkeley in three weeks." He clears his throat, "You do remember that I met Rob and I like him, but a single girl out with a single man, well … " He hesitates, "Well, what would the neighbors say?"

I laugh, considering that we have few neighbors in Vermont. "C'mon, Dad. I'm nineteen years old. I've been traveling the world. I know how to take care of myself. Besides, Rob is the most honest, knowledgeable man I know, other than McElvey, my coach at Monmouth."

"Okay, okay, I can't argue with you. Did you get the money in Vancouver?"

"Yup, thanks, I'll use it sparingly."

"Do you want me to send your clothes to Berkeley after you finish the hike? They can be waiting for you."

"Great idea, Dad. I can't even imagine what my hiking clothes will smell like after two weeks in the mountains." I look up at Rob who's holding his nose. "Can you send them to Aunt Susie's house in San Francisco?"

"Good plan. Will Rob drive you there after your adventure?"

"Yup, because he has to go to work at the Diablo Canyon power nuclear plant near there when we're finished."

"Okay, do call me as soon as you finish your hike. Oh, by the way, have you heard there's been a recent snowfall in the Wind Rivers?"

I look to Rob who's smiling confidently. "Not to worry, Dad, you've met Rob and know what an accomplished mountaineer he is. After all, he learned his survival skills in the navy."

"Well, that's what I worry about. The navy—really Lia. What does that have to do with the mountains?"

"C'mon, Dad. He told you on his last visit to you that he's already climbed both Gannett and Dinwoody Peaks in the Wind Rivers … , you know, when he was on leave."

"I know. And he does seem very self-assured, but you, on the other hand … "

"Dad, enough. If I can race down a mountain at seventy miles an hour, if I can out-ski avalanches, and even confront predatory coaches, I can handle anything."

"Do I need to remind you that 'Confidence is good, but overconfidence can sink a ship.' "

"Thanks, Dad, but I won't be on the ocean—I'll be in the mountains." I look at Rob who's running his fingers across his throat. "Oops, sorry, I must go now. Rob wants to start packing our gear."

"Oh, okay, call me when you're ready for me to send your clothes and books to San Francisco."

I cradle the receiver, waiting for him to say, "I love you." Nothing but silence follows and then a click.

Rob leads me into the living room where he's spread out our supplies. Rob, ever the engineer, knows how to plan, organize, and implement a project. When I see all the gear on the floor, I know that he's thought of everything for our trip: ropes, pots, pans, crampons, sleeping bags, pads, matches, a cookstove, and a tent—it looks like a L.L. Bean camper showroom.

He hands me my Kelty hiking pack, asking, "Are you okay? Uh, you look a little shaken after your talk with your dad."

"Oh, yes, I just wish Dad would show me more emotion, instead of always doubting my abilities."

"What do you mean?"

"I'll tell you later. So, what do we have to do with all these supplies now?" I ask, pointing to the mess in front of me. Picking up the ice ax, I demand, "And what is this for?"

"Well, we'll be climbing up the Dinwoody Glaciers to get over the Rockies. At 13,000 feet, there'll be snow and crevasses. We need to be prepared." He touches my hand, "Don't look so worried. I'll teach you how to use it and how to stop a fall when we get up into the snow, right?"

I take a deep sigh, thinking about the avalanche that I'd barely escaped in Grindelwald. When that happened, just with luck, I was able to dig out my teammate, Carla. "Okay, I trust you."

"Good, now unpack your bag so you can select which clothes to take. We'll put everything into waterproof bags. Take the minimum because we'll also need room for food for at least eight days."

"Wait a minute—eight days—I thought we would be out for two weeks?"

Rob picks up a fishing pole next to him and grins, "I plan to catch enough fish to supplement our meals. I hear there's great fishing in the Titcomb Lakes. Rumor has it that back in the 1800s, the cowboys stocked the lakes, so they'd have food when they went to round up their free-range cattle." He then shows me a can of Crisco and a box of cornmeal. "Some fish are two feet long, so we'll have plenty of protein. We'll cook them up in this batter."

I lay out a minimum amount of clothes: my ski parka, my hiking boots, sneakers, a wool hat, mittens, two pair of pants, three changes of underwear, three t-shirts, and six pair of socks. I like to wear two with my hiking boots to avoid blisters. For toiletries, I grab my hairbrush, shampoo, soap, deodorant, a toothbrush and toothpaste, and a box of Tampons.

Rob grabs my hand, scolding me, "Remember, each object adds weight. You won't need deodorant. We'll both smell. Forget the shampoo. We'll use the soap to wash our hair."

"Uh, okay. This is going to be primitive, but can I bring a book to read? You know that I love reading about John Muir's travels in the Sierras." When he nods, I also ask, "And I want to bring my journal and a pen."

He concedes, "Of course—I know you want to be a writer." He pauses, rubbing the blonde stubble on his chin, "But we'll share the toothpaste and soap, okay? I'll let you carry them. Just remember to put them in baggies. Everything gets wet and soggy." He points to my Tampons but says nothing.

Over in the corner, he shows me the food he's chosen, "Now that we've got the essentials, we can divvy up the food." He splits the twenty pounds of freeze-dried meals, saying, "It's important that we each carry some food in case the other gets lost, or … " He doesn't finish.

"Or what?" Something inside me tightens.

"Well, I guess I have to say it, or falls into a crevasse. We both must be able to go for help alone in case of trouble." He looks hard into my eyes, "Don't look surprised. You, Miss Brave One, know there are risks. You'll have your own survival pack, complete with matches, a compass, and a small map." He hands me a baggie with these and indicates that they need to be accessible in a side pouch.

Once our backpacks are loaded, we lean them against the couch. His red one stands at least a foot above my green one. Leaving the room, he returns with a scale. "Okay, hop on. I need to know how much weight you're carrying compared to me."

I get on the scale, and it reads one hundred ten pounds. I must've lost five pounds on the train ride. While I'm still balancing on the platform, he hands me my pack. My shoulders slump and I start to fall. He grabs me around the waist, saying, "Hold onto me until you feel comfortable."

I yell, "Darn, this is heavy! I feel like a turtle with an oversized shell." Looking down, I see the scale now reads one hundred sixty pounds. "Can I do this?"

Rob helps me step down, looking worried, "I think I'll carry your glacier gear until we get into the upper snows. By then, we'll have eaten enough food, so your pack will be lighter, and you can carry your own equipment, right?" He cautiously steps onto the scale, causing the needle to flip up to one hundred ninety pounds. I pull his pack over to him and he hoists it effortlessly onto his shoulders, saying, "Yup, just as I guessed—eighty-eight pounds of gear."

Laughing, I point toward the kitchen, "Maybe I need to put on some weight. How about some breakfast? It smells as if our host is cooking my favorite: bacon, eggs, and muffins. This could be our last big meal … " my voice quavers, " … for a while."

CHAPTER 18

Wilderness

After a three-hour drive from Pinedale to Dubois, Wyoming—a short trip in comparison to the next two-week hike back out over the Rockies—I take a deep breath, realizing that here at the trailhead, I'm really committed. We've already driven two miles up a dirt road, two miles into the mountains, five miles from the nearest town, and five miles from help.

Rob, sensing my concern, stops the car, jumps out, runs around to my side, and puts his arm around my shoulder. "Not to worry. There's a ranger station about a mile up the road. We'll check in there, tell him our route, and ask about any problems that might exist on our eighty-mile hike along Glacier Trail—right?" He pushes me back to see if there might be any reservation to what he had just said.

While Rob unloads our packs and locks the car, I wander to the nearest stream to fill my water bottle. In the shade of a pine, I dip my fingers in the cold water, listen to the breeze licking the trees, and close my eyes. The brook becomes a poem without words—once again I'm learning how to root myself in the landscape. I'd lost this on the train ride across Canada, where I'd become a disembodied observer with no senses other than sight—no smell, touch, taste, or hearing.

I hear a chipmunk chattering to my left and happily start reciting back to him John Muir's words:

> *Keep close to Nature's heart ... and break clear*
> *away, once in a while, and climb a mountain or*
> *spend a week in the woods. Wash your spirit clean.*

I've come on this journey to brush away the past, to highlight the present, and to straighten out my future plans. The whole dilemma swirls in my head, a giant knot that I need to untangle. I'm not sure why Rob offered to take me on this journey, but I know I'll find out.

"Hey, Miss Nature Girl, sometimes you get too absorbed in your thoughts. Time to get started, right? We've at least four hours of hiking ahead … of course, after our stop at the ranger station."

I don't dare tell him I'm communicating with a chipmunk.

He hoists my pack onto my back, helping me to adjust the waistband, as the tightness causes me to sway and stumble. The pack is top heavy, so I'll have to learn how to walk standing up straight or I'll tip over. He hands me the ice ax that'll become my third leg.

To hoist his pack, he sets it on a rock and then wriggles into the straps. With a few hunches of his shoulders, he adjusts the balance, reminding me of a fledgling flapping its wings before it jumps from its nest. He nods toward the trail and asks, "Ready?"

For the first mile, I'm so consumed with my footing and my balance that I don't talk. He seems to understand and says little except, "Let me know if you need to stop."

I can't even look up to see the surrounding peaks, the granite domes, and the overhanging pines. My eyes just search for the next footstep, the next rock, as if I'm walking on a balance beam, not sure to which side I'll fall.

Slowly, I find my rhythm in the luxurious simplicity. I allow myself to inhale the sweet smell of sage and pine, to hear the jays cawing at our invasion, to feel the hardness of the worn trail under my hiking boots, and to relish the warm sun caressing my head. Mountain light is unlike any other light—strong, pure, glistening, blinding—each step enhances my meditation.

Rounding a bend, Rob yells out, "Anyone there? Two hikers are coming up the trail." A small cabin with a wrap-around pine porch greets us. Rob turns to me and states, "Here's a rule for the mountains. When approaching a building, announce yourself. Otherwise, the occupants might think you're a bear or another form of attacker."

"What do you mean another form of attacker?"

"Oh, don't worry. Let's just say people and animals don't like surprises in the mountains."

I notice the horse corral is empty—just a few bales of hay lay spread in the trough as if the ranger had left with the animals before they'd finished eating. I point to the scene, asking, "Do you think the ranger's out on patrol? I don't see anyone around. It looks as if he left in a hurry."

"Probably. Remember, he's being paid to be out on the trails, right? He usually leaves the cabin open, so we can go in, sign the register, and write in the log, describing our route, as well as times of entry and probable exit."

Inside, the musty smell of unwashed wood floors, leather, and last night's hamburger choke me. As I adjust to the dim light, I sense that I'm being watched. Looking up, I recoil from a glint reflecting off a cougar's eyes, his teeth bared, and his paws outstretched, reaching for me. I scream, "Duck!"

Rob falls on the ground with his pack still on his back. He looks up into the plastic eyes of the big cat and starts a belly laugh. "Oh, my God. That's just a mounted animal."

I stamp my feet, snickering in embarrassment, and reach to pull him up. "Hey, you're the one who said that we should announce ourselves." I probe the corners to see if there are any other attackers. "So what kind of animals do we have to worry about here in the mountains?"

Rob sets his pack down, indicating that I should do the same. "Okay, my friend, now is as good a time as any to talk about the rules of the mountains." He pulls the topographic map from his pack and flattens it on the rough-hewn table. I drag a homemade chair over and sit.

Rob starts slowly. He caresses the map as if it's a newborn baby, "These mountains are different from your ancient Green Mountains. They're higher, more remote, alive, still in the process of being sculpted—right?" He points to the crest of the Rockies, "The highest is Gannett at 13,800 feet."

My finger traces the dotted route of the Glacier Trail, rubbing the waterproof surface, smooth as a polished glass. The legend tells me that one and a quarter inch equals one mile of walking.

Rob continues, "The animals here have encountered few humans, but, instinctively, they still try to avoid us."

"Ah, so what kind of animals?" I ask, remembering my days of hiking with my coach in the Sierra Nevadas.

"Well, first of all, there are grizzly bears. You can't outrun a bear and you can't climb a tree to get away. So, if we encounter a bear, you must throw your pack away because there's food in it. Then hunker down, curl up, and cover your head with your hands so that he just sees your back. Don't move. Just play dead. He'll paw you a few times and get bored. Bears don't like dead things."

I put my head down on the table, covering it with my hands, and chuckle, "Like this?"

He shakes his head to reprimand me. "Lia, this is no joke. We could also encounter cougars, rattlesnakes, bobcats, and moose."

"Moose! Do I have to worry about them, too?" I ask, thinking about the big, clumsy, antlered moose in Vermont.

"Where we'll see them is around the lakes, feeding in the grass. Just make sure not to get between a moose and her calf."

Looking back at the snarling creature on the wall, I continue, "Okay, but what about the others—the big cats?" Now I'm starting to worry more about the animals more than the dangers from avalanches and crevasses.

"You mean like the cougar? Remember, I said they're afraid of us. Just make a lot of noise. They don't think of us as food. We're more like predators. Noise will scare them off, right?"

Recalling how my California coach McElvey had shot a gun at an attacking bear, I ask, "Do we have any protection other than our knives?"

Rob reaches into his vest and pulls out a pistol. "Yup, I didn't want to scare you with this while we were packing, but I did bring a handgun, uh, from my navy days."

He lays the gun down and begins to run his finger along the map in front of us. "I want to show you our route in case you have to complete it by yourself …

in case I get hurt and you need to get help, okay?"

I touch the green spaces indicating vegetation, the white areas showing either smooth granite domes or glaciers, and I start tracing the small squiggly lines. "Are these the contour lines? When they get close together does that mean a cliff?"

"You got it. Do you can see the dotted line? That's our trail. The Glacier Trail. We'll cross the Wind River Range here between Gannett and Dinwoody Peaks. Notice that Bonney Pass is all white—a glacier. The blue circles indicate the many lakes in the high country. For example, here are the Dinwoody Lakes where we may find some trout."

Across everything is written in capital red letters, **W-I-L-D-E-R-N-E-S-S**. I'd never seen this on a map because we don't have any wilderness near my Vermont home, just national and state forests. I begin to think of the people who'd gone into the wilderness to find themselves: Jesus, Moses—even the Native Americans who called it a vision quest. I smooth my palm over the map, point to the letters, look up at Rob, and ask, "What does this mean?"

"Well, in 1964, President Johnson passed a Wilderness Act designating large, undeveloped, pristine tracts of land to be forever wild. Before that, we just had our national parks and forests, but this is a much stricter designation. In national forests, logging and mining, recreation, and grazing are allowed. Yes, in national parks there's more emphasis on keeping the land pristine. Only roads and lodges can be built there, for instance, in Yosemite Park. In contrast, in wilderness areas, there can be no new logging, mining, roads, lodges, or other commercial enterprises." He presses his hands together prayer-like. "Thank heavens, some wise people realized that the human spirit needs untouched places—places to go where there's no evidence of the modern life, no commercialism—a refuge where people can go to test their innate survival skills, you know, and transform themselves." His blue eyes stare deeply into mine to see if I'm getting the message.

Staring back, I add, "Oh I get it, like John Muir, Thoreau—my favorite writers." I stand up, declaring, "I'm ready. Let's go!"

"Great, but before we leave, I'd like to check outside to see if the ranger may be around somewhere. I've some questions for him." He carefully replaces his gun back into his shoulder harness.

After Rob leaves, I start wandering around the cabin. On the wall, I find a quote by another naturalist, Joseph Wood Krutch: "The wilderness and the idea of wilderness is one of the permanent homes of the human spirit." Behind the counter I find a photo of Gannett Peak and a quote by Henry David Thoreau from his essay *Walking:*

> *"Why should not we … have our natural preserves … in which the bear and the panther, and some even of the hunter race, may still exist, and not be 'civilized off the face of the earth.'—Our forests … not for idle sport or food, but for inspiration and our own true recreation."*

Rob returns, throwing his hands up in disgust, "No one around. I guess I'll just sign the register." He stomps over to the counter and fills in the information that the ranger will want. Grabbing a piece of paper next to the log, he reads it carefully and cringes before putting it down.

"What's that?" I ask, concerned.

"Ah, okay, it says that the ranger has gone out on the trail looking for a cougar, you know, somewhere near Arrow Mountain." He hesitates, weighing his words. "The cat attacked a hiker. The cougar appears not to be afraid of humans. It may be wounded, making it even more dangerous."

"Are we going near there?"

"Not really—we'll probably stay in the valley along Torrey Creek."

I look around the cabin one more time, trying to take in the details: an empty rifle cabinet, bear skins on the walls, snowshoes in a corner, ropes on the tables, saddles on sawhorses, boots stiff as soldiers near the door, cowboy hats on a rack, crampons, ice axes, and, in a corner, a backboard with a few blood stains on its pad. This place is well-stocked for emergencies, unlike my cabin in the Green Mountains.

Once again, I'm the stranger in a new land.

CHAPTER 19

The Crossing

I hear the thunder of water before I see the Torrey Creek Falls. Our trail, a mile beyond the ranger's cabin, drops into a river-carved canyon, curves along a cliff, and then stops at a bridge fifty feet above the water. However, creek is a misnomer. By New England standards, this is a narrow Niagara Falls, with at least three thirty-foot cataracts dropping into boulder-strewn pools where the water claws back on itself.

The warm day has exacerbated the glacial runoff—the roiling water creates a jet-engine roar so loud that I can't hear Rob. He signals for me to sit at the entrance to a narrow foot bridge, a wood-planked span strung along two guywires that are fastened to pines on both ends. He laughs, points to the shoulder-high cables, grabs them, and prances across, each step causing the foot bridge to sway and bounce. He stops in the middle, lets go and pretends to surf the rocking boardwalk the rest of the way. Safely at the other side, he beckons me on.

I step onto the bridge and hesitate, look down, and squeeze the wires with both hands as a cold races through my hands into my stomach. Now I'm forced to time my hand releases with each footstep, left to right. The bridge starts to sway so much that I lose my balance. One foot slips off a plank and I drop to my knees, still clinging to the wires. I freeze, looking down onto the top of a fifty-foot pine.

Rob yells, "Stay!" He drops his pack, steps back onto the bridge, and pulls himself over to me. He grabs a carabineer clip from his pocket and fastens my pack to the wire. Slowly, he helps me stand, while I avoid looking down into the dragon water. My pounding heart makes catching my breath impossible. Lifting my pack, he wrestles it from my shoulders. Once free of the weight, I feel more confident in crossing the rest of the bridge on my own. He follows me, making sure I'm on solid ground before he returns for my pack, unclips it, and carries it across, using one hand for the pack and one for the guy wire.

He scowls, then sighs. His broad, flat nose, which ends in a ski jump, turns red with frustration. "So, Miss Fearless, I guess I pushed you a little too hard to start. Let's go slowly. Let's assess any future dangers before we get to them." He nods, "And I'll be with you every step of the way. Okay?"

Catching my breath, I add, "You know, it's ironic. I love to be in the mountains, to jump off cliffs with my skis on, and yet without my skis, I'm afraid of heights. I guess you could say that without them I feel like a dodo bird." I laugh self-consciously.

"I understand, as I've experienced something similar. For me, ironically, my fear is drowning or suffocating. In the navy, I could spend three months feeling safe under the ocean, you know, in a nuclear submarine. On the surface, I could sail into hurricanes, and navigate with my sextant while in a lifeboat, and yet, in the back of my mind, I always feared drowning, or suffocating in a closed space. For me, I always worried that I'd sink like a fish without gills."

I snicker as I advise, "So let's try to avoid those situations."

"Wrong, to move ahead you must confront what you fear most. Confidence, strength, and courage are what you gain when you look fear in the face." His silence ensures that I've heard him before he stands up, brushes off his jeans, repositions his gun, and slings his pack on his broad shoulders. His sleeve pushes up his arm, revealing a bicep the size of a birch trunk. "Later on, let's talk more about what you really fear—of what you are really afraid, if you rejoin the US Ski Team."

An owl hoots as the sun slithers over Arrow Mountain. I caution, "Hey, we'd better get going if we're gonna settle in before dark." Jumping up, I grab my pack, and without help, I throw it on my back. I push my hands under the straps to lessen the weight on my hips.

Rob leads, stepping rhythmically up the trail to our first night's camp on the alluvial shores of Bomber Basin. Walking deliberately, I look up confidently into the rising peaks.

CHAPTER 20

Starry Night

Fortunately, the sun doesn't set until 8:00 pm, so we're certain that we can hike the three miles and still have enough light to set up camp and cook dinner. On the way, ever resourceful Rob explains the geography of the area.

He describes how the Wind River Range, a pristine place, is an immature land where glaciers are still kneading the bald domes, molding the rocky moraines, scouring the u-shaped valleys, burnishing the granite-walled canyons, and compressing the scree slopes. Of course, the real fingers of the sculptor are the snow-melt rivers that are birthed from the tarns—pools of water at the base of the glaciers.

Traversing high above the creek, we climb over granite, smooth as my knife blade. My boots slip on the gray rock, but luckily the wide trail prevents me from falling. Ironically, the roar of the river increases as we ascend, a kettle-drum sound bouncing up the canyon walls. My metronome steps begin to match Rob's, who shortens his stride for me. My ice-ax clinks on the stone, cymbal-like. My pack no longer sways but instead molds to my sweaty back as I step from one rounded rock to another.

Rob selects a flat area near Bomber Falls for our first night where the last of the sunlight paints a rosy glow over the peaks. He points to a spot next to a truck-size boulder for me to drop my pack. He makes no attempt to help me—I'm on my own now.

Pulling out his ice ax, he chips away at the hard ground, sometimes prying out a rock. I drag the sole of my boot to smooth the loose dirt until he shows me how to level the ground, using the side of my ax.

Our two-man tent, a bright red in contrast to the natural grays and greens of our surroundings, is six by eight feet and supported by a four-foot center pole with four metal arms. I stay inside, steadying the pole while he anchors the four ropes that extend out from the corners. To create a vestibule in the front, he stretches a flap over the door and ties the ends to two small pine trees. I watch carefully, knowing that he may ask me to execute this home-making endeavor sometime—all lessons in being self-sufficient. The process takes just ten minutes but seems much longer because I'm so tired.

"Well done, my friend," he laughs. "We have our moveable home. Now, carefully unroll your sleeping bag and pad and lay them inside. After dinner, we'll hang our packs from a tree, so the bears won't come around." He looks for my reaction. I try to appear nonchalant, although my heart pounds at the mention of wild animals. Continuing, he asserts, "Now, for dinner." He points in the direction of a small grove of lodgepole pines, commanding, "Gather some sticks and small branches so we can make a fire. We'll need our fuel when we get above the treeline—okay?" He begins smoothing the dirt in front of the tent and gathers some small stones to create a fire pit.

No one has camped here, so dry twigs are abundant. I stab myself a few times while gathering and snapping the sticks into burnable sizes. By my third trip, he has the fire crackling. I recall the question I was once asked in English class during our reading of *Lord of the Flies*: What are the necessary steps for survival? Answer: shelter, water, food, and fire. In fifteen minutes, we've established ourselves in the wilderness— safe, warm, and soon to be fed.

I return to the falls three times to get water for cooking and washing. On my last trip, out of Rob's sight, I shed my shirt and scrub my face and underarms. The water is too cold for a bath, plus I'm not comfortable fully undressing near him. I'm relieved to have survived the first day and handled one fear.

Lazing by the cascading pools, I begrudgingly replace my shirt before untying my hiking boots and struggling to remove them. My feet smell of sweat and wet wool. Finding a flat boulder, I settle into a rounded seat and slowly lower my toes into the icy water, testing its numbing caress. My ankle may become a problem on this long trip.

For an instant in the light of the rising crescent moon, I feel the presence of unknown spirits and wonder, *Who else has found solace in this ancient environment? Perhaps this wilderness has been home to many seeking answers.*

Returning to our campsite, I smell our first meal of freeze-dried fettuccine alfredo, and sliced bread. Rob not only has cooked, but he's also set a table complete with forks, knives, spoons, and toilet-paper napkins on a flat rock. Grinning, he stands and bows, pretending to pull out a chair for me. I sit bow-legged on the ground and delicately stretch a towel over my knees, miming that I'm at an upscale restaurant. I lift my water bottle as a toast.

He does the same, saying, "Now don't expect fresh bread for the whole trip. I sneaked a few loaves in my pack for the early part of our adventure, right?"

"Okay, I understand. Um, this sure looks good." I slurp the noodles, savoring the sweet white sauce before swallowing each one like a toothless child slurping the strands.

Although ravenous, I slow my eating so I can listen to the fire snapping and the wind singing in the pines.

My back grazes the granite wall behind me, causing some lichen to cling to my sweatshirt. Turning to brush it away, I notice a partially covered etching in the rock and announce, "Hey, it looks as if someone has already been here, even though you said we were the first."

Rob crawls over to the rock and scrapes away more gray, crusty lichen. "Incredible. You just uncovered a petroglyph."

"A what?"

"An Indian engraving on the rock." He lets his index finger trace the outline. "See, here is the head of a warrior, and here's his bow."

I stand up to get a closer look and notice that there's even some yellow pigment in the lines. "When do you think this was drawn? It looks as if he has spots all over his body."

"Not sure, but we do know that the Sheep Eater Indians were here between 1000 and 1874 AD." His gentle tone reveals that he loves to be my teacher/mentor.

"Why 1874? Can you tell me more about them? They must've been a rugged people to live here."

"I can't! I wish we'd stopped in the museum near Dubois to learn more. They were probably wiped out by the settlers as most Indians were." He shakes his head in disgust. "Whatever happened, they died out quickly and so did their culture."

"That scares me. Are we all so temporary on this earth that our whole culture can be wiped out so quickly?"

"Now, Miss Naiveté. You've studied history. Nothing stays the same."

"Well, yes and no. Look at the rocks, the glaciers, and the mountains around here. They have a sort of permanence."

"Time is a matter of perspective. These glaciers formed over thousands of years, sometimes moving only two feet a year. And the rocks, well, they were created even before the glaciers, over eons, through an accumulation of sedimentation and compression that began with the Great Lakes that once covered the earth. Then the mountains rose slowly, over millions of years, through a gradual upheaval of the earth. All this is in a continuous process of change, for sure." He pauses and scratches his lengthening chin hair. "Just look at what you'll learn when you get to college, right?"

Trying to outmatch him, I purse my lips and declare, "I agree with all this, but I'm convinced that there must be one thing that's permanent. One thing that we can count on to be the same forever. One thing that will guide us through our lives and the lives of all creatures."

Rob looks puzzled, mostly at my attempt to burst his bubble, "And what pray tell is that?"

I lie back, pointing to the clear night sky. The North Star has just come out and the Milky Way salts the darkness, similar to snowflakes in a snow globe. "Look up! That we can count on. It's the same North Star that directed the explorers, that guided the Indians. The same constellations that the Greeks and Romans named and that led the Magi to the Christ child." I smirk and wriggle my toes next to the warm fire, shivering from the cold breeze that drifts down the mountain. The trickling water behind me creates a soothing white noise.

Rob, ever the pragmatist, lets me bask a minute in my new certitude, waiting for a moment to one up me again. An owl starts to hoot. Rob decides to have the last say. "Oh, you Stargazer, you think you have the answers, but remember that we're all made from stardust. You know, we're just dead stars looking back at the sky. Even the stars will, in a trillion years, resolve into a black hole." He shakes his head, chuckling, "The only thing permanent is change."

Instead of being upset, I settle back next to the ancient drawing, my hands behind my snarled hair, and think how lucky I am to be alive, to have come from the stars, and to be a part of this starry night, even for a moment.

CHAPTER 21

The Initiation

Detonating hoofbeats wake me. I nudge Rob who's snoring next to me. "Hey, we've got visitors coming. Wake up!"

Rob crawls to his knees, grabs his gun beside the pillow, and unzips the door flap. The horse stops and a voice yells, "Ranger approaching."

Rob and I crawl out, but we can't see anything through the fog that enshrouds our campsite. He calls back toward the visitor, "We're here, over by the cliff."

Out of the mist prances a gorgeous golden mustang ridden by a tall, bulky man in a green parka and leather chaps. A white Stetson hat, with a hawk feather dancing behind, covers the rider's head, obscuring his face. The horse stamps the ground as it comes to a rest right in front of our smoking campfire. I cough from the blast of old embers, while Rob waves his hands to disperse the rising dust.

The ranger, pulling his rifle from its scabbard, dismounts with one deft swing of his leg, and extends his hand to Rob. "Howdy. I'm Jonathan Black Hawk from the US Forest Service. Welcome to the Wind Rivers."

Rob nods but proceeds cautiously, withholding his handshake, while he carefully replaces his own gun into the shoulder harness. "Can we help you?" Pointing to the horse, he steps back guardedly, cautioning, "Is this a usual greeting?" He laughs awkwardly as he tries to smooth his matted hair. I step behind him, not sure whether I want the stranger to see me. The man has no identifying patches.

The stranger apologizes, "Oh, sorry. I grabbed the wrong parka." He pauses and continues speaking very slowly, taking a breath after every few words. "I was in such a hurry … to find you … at the first light." He steps back toward his horse so as not to intimidate us further and nodding at me, takes off his hat to bow. "Pardon me, Miss. I didn't mean to scare you."

Every sentence ends in an upbeat note, as if he's asking a question. His face has as many creases as his hat. Dropping the reins, he says gently, "Easy, Bullet." The horse snorts like an old man clearing his throat, then lowers his muzzle in compliance.

Black Hawk moves over to a rock, replaces his hat, and sits. "Do you mind if I rest? Talk with you a minute? I saw your name registered in the cabin log. I had a feeling I could find you here near Bomber Falls. From the description you left of your route, you seem to know what you're doing and where you're going." He stretches out his legs, straightening them as if he's been riding for hours, his heeled boots digging into the ashen dirt. To ease the tension, he deliberately leans his rifle against the boulder and gives me a large, dimpled grin.

Rob grabs a few sticks, placing them one by one on the sleeping fire. Kneeling over the embers, he puffs into the smoke, igniting the pine. Carefully laying five larger sticks crosswise, he answers, "Yup, I've hiked before along the Glacier Trail. Summited Dinwoody once and, uh, climbed part way up Gannett, right?" He stops and squeezes his eyes as if trying to erase a bad memory. "Lia and I plan to either climb Dinwoody or Gannett, but that's depending on the weather. Have you heard of any incoming storms?" Rob takes a seat next to me on a boulder, so we both resemble upside-down toadstools.

The ranger lowers his eyes. "You might get a thunderstorm or two over the next three days. The temperatures should stay in the seventies, at least during the day. Do be careful of the snow-melt streams. They always quadruple, uh, during the first hot weather of the season." He thumps his fist on his jacket, "For sure, it's been a cold July. We even got a fresh snowfall."

Rob nods in agreement. "I've noticed how the rivers unexpectedly rise during the day and then slow to a faucet drip at night."

Black Hawk stands up and brushes off his tan chaps. "Well, I didn't come to warn you about the weather." He pauses and looks back down the trail. "I came, uh, to warn you about the mountain lion."

"Do you mean the cougar that you described in your note?" asks Rob with a nervous curiosity in his voice.

"Yes, sir, they are one and the same creature. This one must be young—very immature. He attacked a hiker two days ago. They usually avoid humans. We had to backboard the young man out. The cat mauled his leg. He couldn't walk. Luckily, his companion was able to run back to the ranger station, uh, for help." Looking from Rob to me, he adds, "Hiking in pairs, always the safest way to go. I'm not a fan of solo hikers. Not in these mountains. Too remote."

Rob reaches into his back pocket and pulls out his topo map. "Can you show me where this happened?"

Black Hawk steps forward and kneels, while helping to flatten the map on the dinner rock. "Okay, let's see. Here's Bomber Falls. Now look to the south. Up on Arrow Mountain just above the steepest cliff. Here was my last sighting of the cat. He appears to be heading west toward the Dinwoody Lakes. I tracked him yesterday and got a shot at him. I know I frightened him."

I gasp when I follow Black Hawk's hand. He's missing three fingers and has a scar running up his arm. Without thinking, I blurt, "What happened to your hand?"

Rob nudges me as if to say that my question is impolite, but Back Hawk winks. "Don't be embarrassed. I got into a fight with a grizzly. Guess who won?" He turns his head, takes off his hat, and turns to show me a scar that runs up the back of his head. "I'm proud of my wounds, young lady. This is the West, ya know."

Pulling out his pistol again, Rob probes, "So how should we handle this cat? All I have is a handgun."

"Just shoot in his direction. The animal should be wary now. He knows the danger of a gun. Don't try to outrun him. That's what the hiker did. The cat assumed he was prey. I'm headed west up the trail. I'll be ahead of you. If I get any sightings, I'll circle back to tell you." I like that he speaks with the clipped, definitive sentences of an outdoors man, a western cowboy. He reminds me of my Monmouth coach, Justin McElvey.

Rob and I absorb this information, allowing a silence to follow. No one knows what to say next. For some reason, Black Hawk isn't going to add any more information.

To break the awkwardness and out of curiosity, I turn and point to the petroglyph behind me. "Do you see what I uncovered last night?"

The ranger gasps and strides over to the etching. "What? How'd you discover this?" He lets his two good fingers run alongside the warrior's bow, slowly, in reverence.

Embarrassed, I stutter, "Uh, uh … I was just leaning against the rock, when the lichen fell off and I saw the yellow paint." I self-consciously run my fingers through my unbrushed hair. "I hope I didn't do anything wrong."

Black Hawk kneels in front of the rock. "Do you know what you just discovered?" His face grows flushed as if he's angry, remembering something from his past.

I crawl away on my knees, adding, "Not sure. Rob says it might be a petroglyph by the Shoshoni or Sheep Eater Tribes."

Black Hawk stands and struts back to his rock, lifts his head in pride, and asks, "Would you like to know more about what you discovered? This is amazing. To have found this drawing so high up on the mountain. All the known petroglyphs have been found in the valley, uh, near Dubois."

Rob, joining in the discussion, adds, "Of course. I was just telling Lia about the museum. What do you know about these Indians?"

Black Hawk begins, "This probably was done by one of my ancestors." After closing his eyes in reverence, he reaches inside his flannel shirt and pulls out a pendant. Holding it in the palm of his good hand, he continues, "See, here's an arrowhead. My grandfather gave it to me … many years ago."

I scrunch closer to the fire to feel the warmth and to hear his Indian twang better. He lowers his voice as if reciting a prayer. "My people, my people, settled here over one thousand years ago. They were called the Sheep Eaters. They lived off the Bighorn sheep that were bountiful in the area. I say bountiful because when white man came, you know, on the trains and covered wagons in the late 1800s, they hunted the Bighorn for sport." With dagger eyes, he looks at Rob and me.

"My tribe kept moving higher into these mountains, even during the winter, to follow their food." He lowers his voice, "They were peace-loving people. They didn't want to get entangled in the tribal wars on the plains. They survived in pole-and-hide huts—shelters called wickiups." He smiles with pride. "They made the strongest bows on earth from rams' horns. Bows that could send an arrow through the hide of a buffalo. When the soldiers came, they gave the other Plains Indians guns. This changed the simple lifestyle of all Indians and started warfare between many tribes. The Sheep Eaters kept moving back into the Wind Rivers, you know, to maintain their simple culture." He quiets and bows, "And their reverence for all living creatures."

Now engrossed in the tale, I encourage more, "So what happened to them?"

"You probably can guess. The white man not only brought weapons, but he also brought disease." He breathes deeply and shakes his head. "Didn't they teach you this in school?" He points to the etching in the rock. "Do you see the spots on the chest of the warrior?"

"Oh, that's what those are," I whisper.

"Do you know what causes spots, fever, and death?"

Thinking about my vaccine scar on my left arm, I answer, "Not sure. Maybe measles?"

"Close, but worse. One can survive the measles. But few can survive smallpox."

"Oh, yes. I think I had a smallpox vaccination, too."

Rob decides to add to the conversation. "You must have. We all got them in the fifties." Looking up at the high peak above, he continues, "Let's hope one day, smallpox and polio may be eradicated from the earth." He smiles back at me sarcastically, "So, Miss Know-It-All, in this case you must agree that change and extermination can be good. Right?"

I squirm, remembering last night's conversation about permanence. "Okay, I agree with you." But fearing Black Hawk's reaction to the word, 'extermination,' I ask, "Did anyone from your tribe survive?"

"Yes, one old woman who moved down into the valley to join the Shoshoni. She was my great-great-grandmother, as my grandfather told me. She told the story of how the army soldiers purposely sent one of their sick to our mountain tribe. Not knowing how bad the illness was, the Sheep Eater obeyed traditions, you know, that all people are equal. Yes, even when they are one's enemies. The elders took him in and tried to heal him. Instead, the soldier died. Then, the whole tribe came down with smallpox. No one knows why my one ancestor lived." He takes off his hat, smoothing back his long black hair as if to press the point that he's an Indian. "I'm told she was a shaman." He goes back to the petroglyph, kneels, and caresses the outline. "Maybe, young lady, there is a reason you discovered this painting. Maybe, my great-great-grandmother is trying to communicate with you."

Feeling that his next words might rock my beliefs, I stutter, "What … what are you saying?"

He folds his hands in prayer, "Well, don't you wonder why you, of all people, found this? I … I think, young lady, this could be an omen."

He hesitates, creating a moment of tension, like the silence between a lightning strike and the thunder, then stares into my eyes. I tremble. Black Hawk stands up, steps toward me, and raises his hand in blessing. "I … I sense, young lady, maybe it is your destiny to right the wrongs of the white man. To stop him from destroying nations. Of fighting *unjust* wars."

Rob frowns, puts his hand on my shoulder and shakes his head as if to say, "No, don't listen." A chill runs down my back. I wonder what Black Hawk knows about me.

The three of us trade a few more pleasantries before Black Hawk turns and announces he needs to be on his way. He nods to me, tips his broad-brimmed hat, and strides to his horse. With an effortless jump, he throws his leg over the saddle, jams his rifle into its sheath, reins the horse, and trots up the trail, yelling back, "Good luck, my friends. Abainth'i."

Rob doesn't say a word but shakes his head as he watches the gathering dust obscure the ranger. Turning back to stoke the fire, he announces, "Well, that's an interesting way to start our hike. I hope you aren't worried."

Not sure to what he's referring, I gasp, "What … what do you mean?"

Trying to ignore the prophecy, he changes the subject, "You know— the mountain lion."

Pleased that I don't have to affirm Black Hawk's prediction, I sigh, "Oh, yeah, I've never worried about wild animals before, but then again, I've never encountered a cougar. I've always thought that most animals are more afraid of humans than we are of them. At least that's what I've experienced in the Green Mountains."

Closing my eyes, I say prayerfully, "On the other hand, I'm appalled at how the settlers treated the natives. Ya know, Rob, this is exactly what we're doing in Vietnam right now. But instead of smallpox, we're napalming the people, destroying their crop fields, and killing their children."

Rob stands up, startled at my comparison. "Now, my friend, you shouldn't be worried about things beyond your control. To the point, I'm not sure where you're getting your information." He looks up to an overhanging cliff. "Anyway, we've come here to rid ourselves of all such concerns, to start anew, and to only think about the day's adventures, immersing ourselves in nature."

I laugh, looking back down the trail and trying to diffuse his frustration with me. "Hey, did Black Hawk remind you of anyone?"

"Not sure what you're getting at."

"This may sound juvenile, but I couldn't help but remember my love of the TV show, *The Lone Ranger*. Do you recall the show?"

"Funny you should say so. I had the same thought. A masked stranger in white clothes rides into camp to warn the innocent travelers about a danger—right?" He continues to build the fire. "I recall that the Lone Ranger lived by certain moral guidelines, including what Black Hawk said, that all men are created equal and, most importantly, that everyone has within himself the ability to make the world a better place, believing … " he picks up another stick and adds it to the flame, " … that nature puts the firewood here, but each of us must gather and light it."

We both look back down the trail, chuckle, and say in unison, "Hi-yo, Silver! Away!"

I look up to the overhanging cliff, realizing that this adventure is going to be more than about climbing a mountain and learning to survive on my own.

CHAPTER 22

The Climb

Striking camp is as methodical as setting it up. After our breakfast of granola, powdered milk, and coffee, I take our dishes to the stream, now a rill, scrub the bowls and utensils, and return to discover that Rob has been waiting for me to help him collapse the tent.

Working together, we fold the corners into each other, then roll the nylon into a tube, and stuff it into a twenty-four by four-inch bag. The poles disassemble and slide into their own pouches. Ingenious.

We douse the fire with our remaining water, scuff out all evidence of the fire pit, fill our water bottles, apportion some granola to put into our side pouches, and take a photo of the petroglyph. I remove my wet socks and camp sneakers and hang them over the outside of my pack, making myself a walking clothesline. Sliding into my tight boots becomes my morning's challenge. Already I have a red sore above the scar on my left ankle that aches under the boot's pressure. Plaintively, I ask, "Hey, Rob, what should I do with this blister that just formed?"

He grabs my foot, pulls down my sock, and pokes the limp pocket, "Not much. Just let it harden into a callous today. It'll hurt for a bit, especially when it bursts, but you'll learn to forget the pain." He smirks, "I'm sure you already know how to tolerate pain, you know, considering your broken ankle." He gently replaces my foot on the ground, "Mind over matter, Miss Risk Taker."

He's right. After a mile of hiking up Glacier Trail, I forget the throb and become enthralled by the scenery, the open meadows framed with aspen trees, the long narrow glacial lakes, and the granite-walled domes that morph into Greek monsters. My reverie turns their flanks into snouts, their ridges into dragon backs, their crags into wings, and occasionally their distant snow-laden peaks into standing waves. In turn, I become the wandering hero, the resolute warrior.

Best of all, every step on the narrow meadow path takes me further away from the recent trials of the ski team and the drama in Washington, DC, from the corrupt coaches and dishonest public leaders, the deaths in the Vietnam War, and the disillusionment of the survivors. I realize how obsessed I've been with the problems of others and haven't put enough thought into my own options.

For the first hour, Rob lets me set the pace, so I can adjust to the weight of my pack. He says little, although I know he's watching my every move. At times, I push my hands under the straps to take some of the pressure off my shoulders. For fun, I've even given my pack a name, Huckleberry, to help it become a part of me. Ever since I read *The Adventures of Huckleberry Finn* in ninth grade, I've wanted to have my own adventure, make my own moral choices, and create my own opportunity to change the world—to be like Huck, who by aiding his friend, Jim, defied the slave laws of his time. I've dreamed I could be just as brave one day.

But right now, I just want to bask in the luxurious simplicity of the present.

As the trail turns up into a series of switchbacks, Rob yells up to me, "Hey, let's stop for a minute and readjust. I think your pace has been a little too fast. You've no idea how much we'll start climbing soon."

He lowers his pack, continuing, "Just like in life, hiking is about pacing oneself. Even though you think you have the answers, or you think you're strong, you must be deliberate, slow down, and weigh your options."

I sigh, not liking being told what to do. He admonishes me, "Do I have to repeat myself?" He looks up into the bright sun, and tenting his eyes with one hand, he points, "Look ahead, the trail splits here and we need to decide which route is our best choice." Then, as if reading my mind, he adds, "Life is always about choices."

I sense there's an agenda here, but he doesn't continue. Wrestling out of my straps, I lower Huckleberry and start acting out in a playful voice:

> *I shall be telling this with a sigh, "Somewhere*
> *ages and ages hence" means someday, down the road,*
> *when I'm old and telling stories about my past, I'll*
> *sigh and say that I took the road less traveled by and*

> *that's what "made all the difference" in how my life
> turned out.*

Rob claps when I finish. "Oh, I see you know Frost, Miss New Englander. Well, even though I grew up in Colorado, and studied engineering at Annapolis, I still learned a little Frost, too, right?" He spoke as if challenging me,

> *Nature's first green is gold,*

> *Her hardest hue to hold...*

Uhhh ... he stammers, trying to find the next words, and concludes,

> *So dawn goes down to day.*

> *Nothing gold can stay.*

"And your point is?" I taunt him.

He pulls out his water bottle and granola. "Only to let you know that I, too, have done some reading and thereby hope you'll see me as your intellectual equal!" He points to a shady spot, indicating we should rest by a nearby boulder. Opening his granola bag, he starts munching, "I guess this is a good time for lunch and a talk."

"What, what do you mean?" All of a sudden, I'm uncomfortable.

"Lunch and a heart-to-heart. I have much to tell you about myself and why I've been following your career."

Shaken by the thought that he's purposely been stalking me, I move to a more distant boulder and grab my bag of granola. "Okay, shoot."

Rob begins telling me about his relationship with his former employer, Justin McElvey, who just happens to be my ski coach and mentor at Monmouth. After he'd left Annapolis and before he transitioned into active duty, he'd spent a winter working as a ski patroller at the California ski area, Monmouth. He and McElvey became friends and have stayed in touch.

After serving in the navy, he went to work for General Electric, helping to build nuclear power plants. Throughout this time, he'd stayed in touch with McElvey. At the same time that I was racing in Grindelwald, Rob was sent to work in Bern, Switzerland. Upon learning of this coincidence, Coach McElvey commanded Rob to find me, because he'd heard from my teammates that I was having doubts about my skiing career.

As he continues, I close my eyes and remember back to the time in Grindelwald when Rob took me aside to encourage me to focus on the Olympics. My head begins to ache as my thoughts jump to my last race in Maribor when Coach Boast attacked me sexually.

"Hey, you zoned out on me again. Why are you shaking?"

"Oh, just thinking about the past. You know, when Boast attacked me in Maribor. You do know about that?"

"Of course. McElvey told me, but don't worry! You and your teammates did the right thing, you know, turning both him and Coach Ryan into the authorities."

I lower my head in resignation, "Okay, so now tell me why you asked me to go hiking with you before I go to college."

"Well, I'm your biggest fan and want to help you make your next decision."

"Does McElvey have something do with this trip?"

"Ah … yes, and no?"

I grow angry, knowing I'm going to spend the next two weeks with him. I insist, "Now is the time for truth—shoot." Feeling deceived and controlled, as well as unsure of myself, I start to kick the scree around me.

"To be totally honest, you know that McElvey wants you to return to Monmouth and train for the Olympics. He understands that you're going to Berkeley for the fall semester and is excited for you. He senses how much you want to study and learn. In fact, he's the one who got the US Ski Team to give you some money for college expenses."

"And for that I'm totally grateful. But does he know how angry I am with the US Ski Team, with the authorities, with Nixon, and yes, and toward the

Vietnam War?" I say this in a huff, but then back down. "Oh, sorry, you just hit some sore spots."

"Not completely. McElvey only thinks that you're furious at him, because he encouraged your friend, Bill, to accept his army deployment and was subsequently killed in Vietnam. As your coach, he feels you need to move on, to focus on what you do best—skiing."

"Okay, but he does know about all of Coach Boast and Coach Ryan's lies?"

"Of course. Remember, he flew to Maribor right after you were hurt to make sure that Boast and Ryan were turned in to the authorities."

"Okay, so what happened to them?"

Rob takes a moment to find his words, "I'm not sure. No one has been talking." He pauses, as if holding back information. "However, McElvey reassures me that you don't need to worry about them—okay?"

I choose not to take the conversation further, and definitely do not want to tell him about my friendship with Greta and Terry or about my plan to work for the antiwar protest at Berkeley. Now it's clear that Rob has invited me on this hiking adventure to push McElvey's agenda.

I demur, "Okay, I respect what coach wants me to do. But do you know how disillusioned I am with the US Ski Team? With the corruption?" I cringe, remembering the lies of the coaches. And then I say it. "Do you know how much I fear meeting those coaches again?"

"A natural reaction, my friend, but you can't continue to carry this anger— especially if it's damaging your own future. McElvey feels that if you spend two weeks hiking and learning to trust yourself, plus get in shape, that you'll be more confident in your decisions. Then you can stand up for yourself."

"Fine, but how do you fit into this?"

"To tell you the truth, I want to be your friend and to help you make your own decision. Whatever you decide, college or Olympics, you'll have made the choice after much deliberation. Remember two paths diverged in a wood and … " A tear forms in his eye and he discretely tries to wipe it away. "Plus, I've got my own reasons for wanting to return to these mountains … ever since the accident."

Not sure whether to ask more about his reason for returning, I look up into the refracted light, toward the two trails, and point to the most difficult. "Let's climb to the top of Arrow Mountain. Each of us must conquer our own demons. We can talk later."

CHAPTER 23

The Confrontation

Switchback by switchback through the boulder garden, above the treeline, our trail gradually disappears, causing me to look ahead to find the path, often just marked by the next cairn—a pile of rocks left by former hikers. I'm so focused on retaining my balance that I can't let my mind wander. Placing my feet carefully so I don't step on the few yellow flowers that cling to the alpine cracks, I also try to avoid crushing the young grass that peeks from the fragile soil. A few innocent spruces struggle in the rocky crevices. My mind quiets to the point that I feel no separation—the plants, the rocks, and I are one.

Here at ten thousand feet, warmed by the afternoon light, I stop every fifteen steps, exhausted from lack of oxygen and dehydration. Finally resting in the shadow of a large boulder, I ask Rob, "Hey, do we have enough water to go over the top and back down to the Dinwoody Lakes or should we return the way we came? You know and take the lower route?"

He pauses behind me and looks down the scree slope that ends in a cliff, a five-hundred-foot drop into the river valley. "At this point, we're better off to go up and over. To return would take more time." Looking concerned, he adds, "Furthermore, we only have about four more hours of sun."

"So, should I ration my water?"

"Go ahead and drink it. Descending should be easier. Definitely, the water you drink now will set you up later. You should know that from your skiing, right?" His certitude helps me trust him, so I reach into my side pouch and grab my last water bottle. I slurp the water like a thirsty puppy.

He grabs my hand, almost spilling my bottle. "Hey, take it easy. Remember, do everything in moderation in the mountains." He nods, adding, "The mountains are supposed to be our refueling and recharging place, not our ... "

He's stopped by a loud screech. As quick as a cowboy in a duel, he draws his gun, looks to the overhanging boulder and yells, "Turn, but don't run!"

A small mountain lion leaps at me. My mind goes into slow motion, just the way it does on a racecourse when I am skiing in the zone. I can see the creature's outstretched paws, its snarling teeth, its yellow eyes. Turning and raising my hands to protect my face, I hear a shot and feel the impact of a body landing on my pack. Losing my balance, I fall forward, my head hitting so hard that sparks burst before my eyes. I begin a face-first slide down the scree toward the cliff, the cat still clutching my shoulder. Rocks and pebbles hit my mouth as I gather speed, all the while struggling to get my hands in front of my face. Suddenly, another body lands on top of both me and the cat. We're now a three-man bobsled, heading toward disaster. I can't breathe. My mind retreats into a fugue state—I'm in my body, yet out of it. Luckily, my fall starts to slow just before I hit a boulder. No one moves.

Finally, pushing up, I scream, "Help, I can't breathe!"

Rob slides off our pig pile and slips his hand under my face. "Don't move until I get the creature off your back. I want to make sure it's dead."

Another gunshot, not far from my ear, echoes throughout the valley. Numb, afraid to move, I slowly turn my face away from the dirt and gasp. The gunsmoke coats my lungs. Rob slides Huckleberry from my shoulders before he kneels next to my head and gently pokes my back, my arms, and my legs, "Do you have any pain anywhere? Can you move your legs?"

I pull my legs under and trying to sit up, I fall back into the boulder, gasping, "I can move everything, but I'm really dizzy."

Rob grabs a towel from the side of his pack, soaks it in water, and pats my forehead. "You may have a concussion, and definitely you have a cut above your eyebrow." At this, I feel a cool wetness, which slides down my cheek and see a growing red spot on my shirt.

Slowly, struggling to find my words, I ask, "How … badly … am … I, I hur … urt?"

"Not bad, just a small cut above your eye."

My pant leg begins to get wet and I wipe it. "But what about the blood on my leg?"

Rob grabs my knee and lifts it, realizing that the pooling blood is coming from the dead mountain lion that rests above me, its blood gushing from a severed neck artery. We both groan as only those do who have confronted their own mortality. Rob sighs, "Well, I guess it used up its nine lives." He jokes, "Lucky us, we still have eight to go."

Sarcastically, I answer, "I think I'm down to about three. I used up a lot when I was on the ski team." Propping myself on the boulder, I stand up, move each joint separately, and announce. "I think I'm okay—more shaken than hurt." Looking at the young mountain lion, I conclude, "Definitely, I'm better off than it is."

I stare into the animal's eyes that are clouding over and recall two years ago when I held my dying friend Damien's head and watched his eyes turn vacant. He had broken his neck while training for a downhill at Sugarloaf in Maine. A sadness, mixed with compassion, cramps my thoughts like a tourniquet around my brain. I know death. Crawling over to the creature, I kneel and reverently rub my hand along its tan fur, "Wow, this is still a baby. So skinny. Why do you think it attacked us?"

Rob, seizing a teachable moment, answers gently, "It must have lost its mother and grown hungry. Usually, a mother will train the cub as to what is prey and what should be avoided. It probably smelled some of the food in our packs." At this, I feel even greater empathy, because I know what it is to lose a mother and not to have female guidance and companionship while growing up. I pat the cub again and whisper, "I know what it is to be alone." I think to myself, *Never have I missed my mother more than at this moment.*

Rob stands up and asks, "You look troubled. Do you want to talk?

"Nope, just give me a minute to take all this in." Looking down into the valley, I'm aware of how close I came to going over the cliff with all of us on my back. Taking a deep breath, I demand, "Okay, so Mister-Know-It-All, how could we have avoided this confrontation?"

Rob wags his finger at me. "I think you know. We could have taken the river route to the Dinwoody Lakes. But that wouldn't have been in your nature. When we take risks and avoid the easy path, we must accept the consequences, right?" He looks up into the western horizon and points to the distant mountains. "But look, see what we've discovered. There ... do you see it behind the bald-granite dome?"

I look up to a transcendent, snow-covered massif, a jagged bejeweled castle, glistening white, higher than its neighbors, beckoning. "Is that Gannett Peak? Is that our goal?"

My heart expands.

CHAPTER 24

The Raw Joy of Wilderness

The next morning, a singing thrush wakes me. Turning toward Rob, I poke him, only to discover his sleeping bag is empty. My head throbs from lack of sleep. A storm had cracked and rumbled for over three hours during the night, plus, I couldn't get the image of the dead mountain lion out of my head. Rubbing the crust from my eyes, I peek out of the tent door into a blazing fire. Rob kneels, stirring a pot.

"Well good morning, sleepyhead." He laughs as a shaft of sun highlights his ruffled blond hair. "You must have had a tough night. You tossed and turned for hours." He carefully places a log on the fire. "I hope our discussion about the mountain lion last night didn't upset you."

"Ah, yuh, somewhat, but the storm also scared me. I don't want to talk about the baby lion anymore. I've accepted what you told me, that it couldn't have survived on its own." Reaching up to feel the scab above my eye, I breathe a sigh of relief that I hadn't been more seriously hurt. Changing the subject, I continue, "I woke at each clap of thunder and ducked when the lightning lit the tent. What a show of nature's power."

"Yes, but even so, I slept well. I knew we'd be safe while the storm moved on."

Marveling at his calmness, I answer, "Well, not something I could sleep through. Did you use earplugs or something?"

Rob shakes his head, saying, "Oh, you're so curious. To tell the truth, I'm partially deaf because of my five years under the sea, you know, working next to the nuclear turbines."

Pausing, not sure how to answer or whether to show sympathy, I change the subject. "Hey, thanks for starting breakfast. What's the plan for the day?"

He hands me a plate filled with sausage and grits, along with a small plastic jar. "And here's some maple syrup right from Vermont … for a topping."

"Thanks, you're too thoughtful." I smile and say, "On Scrag Mountain, I got used to doing everything for myself."

I settle against my lounging rock and slowly spoon in the hot cereal. With each bite, I envision the autumn sugar maple trees that line my Common Road in Waitsfield, their oranges, reds, and yellows, their gnarled bark and their embracing overstory. How I wish that I'd spent more time sitting under them, instead of running through them, always trying to improve my time, endurance, and agility. I'm already learning so much from this wilderness adventure—lessons that are so unlike my days of ski racing or my hikes up Scrag Mountain or my train ride across Canada. Ironically, the more vulnerable I feel, the more self-sufficient I grow and the more connected to nature I become.

"Hey, you're becoming morose again. What're you thinking?"

"Oh, just how much I miss home, but how much I'm learning on this trip. About the baby cougar."

"Do you want to share?"

"No, not yet. I'm still trying to find the words to express what's happening to me."

He nudges the fire with a stick and adds another log. "Well, to tell the truth, you asked what our plans are. I think we should lay over a day or two. That was a tough hike yesterday. I'd like to try some fishing and I think you need to get recentered." He points to my clothes and says, "To wash the blood from your jeans. To … to enjoy the sounds of silence." He starts singing *Hello, Darkness, My Old Friend* by Simon and Garfunkel. The lyrics carousel in my mind.

I get up, raise my hands, and to best him, quote Thoreau, "Time is but the stream I go a-fishing in."

Rob shakes his head at my grand gesture.

After breakfast, I walk to the lake to wash the dishes while he gathers his gear for a day of fishing at a distant cove. My bare feet are warmed by the sun's heat rising from my swimming rock. I pause, put the dishes down, and jump in fully clothed. Grabbing my soap cake, I scrub my jeans and tee shirt before shedding them and placing them up on the rock; then naked, I wash my shivering body and gnarled hair. As I lizard-skitter up the rock, the cold water flows between my buttocks. Smoothing out my jeans and tee shirt, I settle down, unclothed, next to them and pretend that they're my disembodied ego. With my eyes closed, immobile, I feel the sun drying my skin, my arm hairs tingling as the water evaporates. A slight breeze dries the wetness from my face. The sounds grow, one by one: the waves slapping against the granite, the peepers singing in the marsh, the jays cawing in the trees, the wind bouncing off the peaks, the fish jumping in the shallows—and even the grass stirring in the gentle breeze.

In a trance, I begin to imagine the sounds I can't hear, the unsounds of nature: the clouds billowing, pillowing, and then receding through the blue sky; the movement of the trout underwater; the trees growing to the sun, their leaves turning CO_2 into oxygen; the skimmers gliding in the shallows; the sunrays creating diamond ripples on the water; the mountain peak shadows moving up the valley; the grass growing from my rock; and the breeze caressing the hairs on my bare arms and body.

A trout, darting across the water, sends a chevron over the surface, waking me. While I listen to my own breath, I recite the beginning of Whitman's *Song of Myself:*

> *I celebrate myself, and sing myself,*
>
> *And what I assume you shall assume,*
>
> *For every atom belonging to me as good belongs to you*
>
> *I loafe and invite my soul,*
>
> *I lean and loafe at my ease observing a spear of grass.*

For the first time in years, I'm not worrying about the war, the ski team, the student protests, the need for goals, or for finding my place in the world. What lies behind me and what lies ahead of me are nothing compared to what lies within me. Resting here, my body carries an unknown wilderness, a sanctuary where all my sorrows dissolve in my joys, and in this inner wilderness are the answers to questions I haven't even learned to ask. I've become the disembodied self that lies next to me. I pat my clothes to make sure they're still there.

*   *   *   *

"Hey, wet hair!" A remote voice yells from the woods.

Grabbing my tee shirt, I slide it over my head even though it's still damp. "Ah, wait a minute. I've … I've got to get dressed."

"Okay. Wait 'til you see how many trout I've caught. We'll feast tonight."

I try to run my fingers through my tangled wet hair, but they just get caught. I must look a mess. Rob emerges from the edge of the forest, holding a string of fish in one hand and his fishing pole over the other shoulder. All he needs is a straw hat and he'd be Tom Sawyer.

He stops, not wanting to encroach on my private space, "Would you like to learn how to clean a fish? How to prepare it for dinner? I know this may be your first. Are you skittish?"

I nervously laugh, remembering the mountain lion's death and the two deaths I'd seen while training for the ski team, and answer, "I've seen dead things before. I'm okay."

On a boulder next to my swimming rock, he shows me how to hold the red speckled, scaleless brook trout, how to run my knife up its belly, and how to scoop out the intestines. His hands drip with blood, the rock grows red and then the water turns cloudy as he throws the entrails into the lake. Small fish nibble at the innards before the pieces sink. He points to the cannibalism. "See, we're just part of a cycle—predator, and prey. Nothing more. Just like what I told you about the baby mountain lion."

Boldly, I grab a ten-inch trout and feel the slimy skin as I turn it over, almost dropping it into the water. Its dorsal fin pricks my thumb. "I think you're testing me. I can do this." He hands me his extra knife.

It takes me the same amount of time to clean one fish as it would take him to clean eight.

*   *   *   *

Over dinner, nibbling carefully on the fresh white meat, picking at the bones, we start planning our assault on Gannett Peak. He seems to be more confident that I can take on new challenges, no matter how difficult, scary, or even life-threatening.

After dinner, I grab my journal and retreat to my bathing rock just as the sun sets over the Rockies, casting a pink glow on the lake. I can see deep into the clear water to the rounded boulders beneath. To ensure that this day, this solitary moment, can happen again and again, forever and ever, I scribble a poem.

Be Wilder

Be, being, decisions, friends

Promises broken, deceptive coaches

Boyfriends killed

Anger.

In the wild, without the being,

Confusion leaves

I become the grass

Bask in the silence.

I learn that to be in the wild

is to lose

Be

wilder

ment.

CHAPTER 25

Coincidence

"Do you know how to make God laugh?" asks Rob as I stir my coffee the next morning.

I put my spoon down, place another log on the fire, look into his freshly shaved face, and shrug my shoulders, questioning, "I didn't know we were going to get spiritual this morning. I thought we were going to make plans for our assault on Gannett Peak."

"You're right on both counts."

"Okay, so how do you make God laugh?"

"Tell him your plans." He chuckles, waiting to see if I get the point.

"Are you making fun of me because I'm always setting goals and making plans?" I stand up defiantly, then repeat angrily, "Are you mocking my desire to plan my life, to decide whether to go to college or go back to the ski team?"

"No, not mocking, mentoring."

"Okay, but I've already got a mentor—Coach McElvey."

"I know, but remember, he sent me to join you on this adventure. He knows you're in a personal crisis at the moment—right? He trusts me to help you out." He hands me a bowl of oatmeal, "Let's go back to the task at hand. A single focus is much easier to handle." He spreads out a map of the Glacier Trail on the rock, carefully smoothing the creases. "I think we should head toward Big Meadow today and set up base camp. From there we can practice glacier climbing on Dinwoody Peak."

I look at the tent, to the comfort and coziness that I'd found yesterday, to the peace that has finally cleansed my mind, and say, "I guess nothing gold can stay."

"What, what do you mean? Now you're making fun of me."

"Oh, only that I have truly found peace, you know, resting here by the lake. Now we must take off again." I close my eyes. "I was hoping that we might stay here a few days."

"Nope, we'll spend our time just about ten miles from here at a place called Wilson Meadows. There we'll establish ourselves for our assaults on Dinwoody and/or Gannett—weather permitting." He folds the map and lets out a groan, grabbing his back as he stands up.

Reluctantly, I begin breaking camp, feeling a sense of comfort that I know the routine. This is similar to when I was ski racing and the routines became a way to make life easier, helping me to weather the times when my plans were disrupted.

Departing camp, I look back to my bathing rock and notice that its reflection is ruffled and indistinct even though the water's surface appears to be smooth. I pat Huckleberry and whisper, *"Now you alone carry my notes, my memories of my one moment of true bliss. You are my raft."*

High on the ridge, I see an elk watching my movements. He's not bothered when I stop to point him out to Rob, who nods and says, "That's only the second elk I've ever seen. My first one was while hiking with Coach McElvey."

I step back and whistle. "Wow, that's the same for me. McElvey once showed me an elk when we were hiking above June Lake." A frown in Rob's brow tells me I'm putting too much into this coincidence.

CHAPTER 26

Big Meadow

Walking creates its own rhythm. Rob and I decide to tramp in silence, single file with me leading, one foot in front of the other, synchronizing our steps, enjoying the warm sun and gentle breeze on our backs.

As my pack lightens, so do my memories of the ski team nightmare. I've stopped stewing about what might have happened to the predatory coaches, to Wren's paralysis, and to Tracy's pregnancy.

The flat path through Big Meadow is worn, muddy, and straight. Created as an old lake bottom, it has no stones—just tall grass on each side. I feel like a sailor who's found a calm bay after escaping an angry sea. I'm amazed at how much wildlife lives in this strip—crickets, butterflies, blue jays, hawks, and crows. If we walk quietly, we can hear their calls to each other.

Rob definitely knows his flora and fauna and prides himself on being able to point out the wildflowers that line the treeless floor, including goldenrod, alpine arnica, cinquefoil, and mountain bluebells. He stops, so we can watch a bee crawl up the purple petal of an elephant-head flower to feed inside. He explains how the insect flaps its wings, coats its body with the fertile dust, and then grooms the pollen into its leg-pouches, a ritual known as buzz pollination. I close my eyes to hear the different pitches of the bee sounds. Like the bee, I'm filling my memory pouches with this beauty and these lessons.

Putting down Huckleberry, I squat, asking, "How do you know all this?"

He slowly lowers his pack and stretches out in front of me, resting his head on the nylon. "I guess this is as good a time as any to tell you a little more about me."

Relieved that I can relax and enjoy the smell of the sage, listen to the gurgling of a nameless stream, I stretch my legs, "Great, let's have lunch and you can tell me a story."

He opens his pack to pull out some GORP, a small granola bar, and two pieces of beef jerky. "Take your pick. Then let's fill our water bottles from this spring, as I'm not sure whether we'll run into any beaver dams above us. You know, they can pollute the water with Giardia." He grabs his stomach, mocking a cramp.

I add to the lunch selection with own my supply of GORP and chocolate. "It's only fair that we share." He takes a deep breath and looks up to the sun that is lifting the fog curtain from the snow-covered Rockies. "Remember, I told you I've been here before." His eyes water.

"Yup, you mentioned an accident, I think." I look toward the mountains, so he takes a moment. The noon sun turns the colors of the creek ahead into a golden thread.

"Yes, three years ago, in 1968, I came to the Wind Rivers with my best friend, Geoff—uh, during a break from the submarines. Geoff, always the romantic, had studied botany at Annapolis, while I majored in Engineering. We went into different branches of the navy after graduation—he to flight school and I into the nuclear subs … " His voice falters.

To encourage him, I ask, "Wow, sky, and sea. Were you that different in personalities?"

"Yes, he was always the romantic, like you. He loved the names of all the plants and trees. On the other hand, I just wanted to know how they could be useful." He pauses and laughs. "Just before this trip, Geoff had become engaged to his high school sweetheart. This would be his last bachelor trip."

"Okay, so what happened?"

"We followed the same route that we're walking now. Only it was about three weeks later in August—you know, when the weather becomes unpredictable. Snow can even fall." He pauses and looks me in the eyes. "Do you really want to know what happened?"

"Hey, we're friends. I'm listening. Your expression tells me that it's important to you." I twist to find a more comfortable position against my pack.

"Okay, I haven't told many about this." He picks a yellow cinquefoil next to him, turns it in his fingers, and continues, "Geoff and I had never climbed in the glaciers together. We had spent most of our free time rock climbing in the Appalachians. Foolishly, we were confident that the two experiences would be similar. First mistake in the mountains, overconfidence—right?"

I sigh, "It seems as if this is becoming a theme on this trip."

"I can't emphasize this enough. When hiking in the wilderness, like a carpenter, one must measure twice and cut once, right?"

"You lost me. What are you saying? You seem to be mixing metaphors."

"Well, with rock climbing, one has to know the route and be wary of rockfalls and weather."

I nod, still confused.

"On glaciers the problems grow exponentially. Not only do you have to worry about the route, rockfall, and weather, but also about crevasses and avalanches." He pauses, "Remember, plan twice, climb once, right?" He looks up into the face of a snow-covered peak, which throws back a blank stare. "We set out on a day like today, with blue sky after a storm had just passed. We had ropes, crampons, ice axes, ice screws, and lunch. Our campsite was up near Wilson Flats."

I lay my head back against Huckleberry because I'm sensing that Rob doesn't want to rush the story, that he has a message for me, or at least a lesson. He continues, "We left base camp just before dawn, using headlamps to find the trail. Geoff had picked out a route that took us up over the terminal moraine, across the glacier, and then up the eastern side of Gannett Peak. We wanted to stay near the cliffs because we worried about the crevasses that had opened over the summer. Oh, and we felt more comfortable near the rocks." He looks into my eyes, "You look concerned."

"I'm not sure this sounds like a good plan from the tone of your voice. Will we follow the same route if we climb Gannett?"

"Probably not. Two thirds of the way up, Geoff and I ran into a large bergschrund." He looks at me. "Do you know what that is?"

Despite my readings about climbing expeditions, I'd never heard the word.

All I can think of is a dachshund dog. "Not sure. Is it something long and skinny?"

"In a way. And very deep." He laughs. "A bergschrund is where the glacier separates from the mountain cliff. The sun warms the rocks, causing the snowpack to melt away. This creates a large gap like a crevasse."

"Oh, now it's clear to me. Remember, I told you I used to hike and ski Tuckerman's Ravine on Mt. Washington, but of course, always with my father. Well, at the top, the spring snow would separate from the rocks and create a hole so deep that if one fell in, one could tumble a hundred feet to the bottom." I gasp, realizing what he's telling me. "Oh no … what happened to you?"

He takes a deep breath, not sure whether to tell me the short or long version. "Okay, so we found ourselves on the rock wall and decided that we should lower ourselves back to the glacier, because the rocky overhang had become too unstable. I drove in a piton and belayed Geoff first. Once on the glacier floor, he planned to lower me. We were only five-hundred feet from the top when we lost our focus and caution. As Geoff stepped on the snow, I looked away and loosened my grip on the rope, feeling that he was safe. When I looked back down, he was gone."

In shock, I cover my mouth with my hand, "Oh no!"

"I can't begin to tell you the feeling of hopelessness and guilt I felt and still feel."

"You don't have to. I experienced the same feeling when I found my ski friend, Damien, lying against a birch tree with his skull split open. One instant he was with me and the next, he was gone. I felt anger, fear, panic. When I found him, I held his head and tried to bargain for his life."

"Oh, then you know how I felt when I climbed down and looked into the crevasse. Geoff had landed on a ledge, maybe fifty feet down. He wasn't moving."

"So, what did you do?" I shift uncomfortably

"I weighed my choices. To go for help or try to get him out." His blue eyes become vacant as if he were reliving the moment. "I decided to go for help, as I didn't know how to go down into the hole to bring him back. At this moment, I fully realized that we were in the wilderness, so that few people would be around." He shifts to a standing position and continues, "I yelled to Geoff that I was going for help, then climbed around the bergschrund, and glissaded down the glacier—not worrying whether there were any more crevasses. I just needed to get down." He ran one hand over the other, making snaking movements with his fingers. "I ran to our campsite, grabbed my pack, and took off down the Glacier Trail." He stops.

"Please tell me how this ended. I can handle it."

"Luckily, after three hours of running, I smelled smoke from a campfire and headed toward it. I found two climbers settled into their campsite back in the pines. When they saw me, drenched in sweat and mud, they grabbed their sleeping bags and covered me."

I pull my own arms around my body and begin to shake, as if reliving his fear. "So, what did you do then?"

"Well, we decided that it was too late to return to the glacier, you know, it was getting dark. The danger to us would be too great. We'd have to leave early in the morning."

"So, Geoff had to spend the night in the dark crevasse?" I close my eyes, trying to imagine what he must have felt … if anything.

"What else could I do? I couldn't risk my life and the lives of these two for one person. I studied moral dilemma at Annapolis. It is called the trolley problem. Have you heard of it?"

"Sounds familiar, but I'm not sure I've heard it called that. Is it when you are conducting a train and see a person standing on a track? You have a choice: you can divert the train to another track and possibly kill everyone on the train, or you can run over the one person. You, as the conductor, must make a moral choice."

"You understand. But I was lucky because I had a third choice. I could stay the night, not risk my new friends' lives, and perhaps still save Geoff in the morning."

I shake my head, wondering what Rob is trying to tell me. "Got it. So what happened? Do you want to go on?"

"Well, to make a long story short, we returned the next morning and found Geoff. He was still alive, but his left leg was severely mangled. My friends lowered me into the crevasse, and I tied a rope around him. They pulled us both out. Then, by making a drag sledge out of our frame packs, we lowered him down the glacier. We took him to the ranger's station. He spent a month in the Lander Hospital." He stops, swallows, and whispers, "Tragically, the doctors couldn't save his lower leg."

"Oh no! Why not?"

"Too much damage, you know, frostbite and gangrene. He lived, though, and is still my friend, but he never flew jets again. He left the navy and now is working for the CIA in Vietnam."

A shiver runs up my spine as I realize that we've been resting in the meadow for an hour. The sun is descending. I look for my watch and remember that I'd left it on the rock at the lake. I relax, thinking that I'd no need of Chronos time anymore, but suggest, "Maybe we should go. Can we still get to Wilson Flat before night?"

Swallowing hard, I get up, hoist Huckleberry, and accept that I've got some major choices to make in my own life. However, first I must face the challenge of climbing Gannett Peak.

CHAPTER 27

Plans

Following the meandering Dinwoody Creek, we pass the Ink Wells Trail, which veers north toward Dinwoody Peak, and begin rock-hopping across the creek. As the day comes to a close, we settle on a soft campsite at Wilson Flats, another dry lake bottom at 9,500 feet, where we can stomp out a tent site with a view of Gannett.

As Rob cooks up a meal of spaghetti, basil-tomato sauce, and bread, I lie back into the delicate grasses, the blades caressing the setting sun and air, cleansing every breath I take.

In awe, savoring the sweet taste, I congratulate him. "Hey, you've planned every meal, every stop. Do you ever just let a day take its natural course?" Waiting for his answer, I remember my endless days on Scrag Mountain when I could just let the day evolve with no worries and just one responsibility—to check every half-hour for forest fires.

Rob shakes his head, "Oh, you naïve one, you've so much to learn. To get where you want, you need to look ahead, or at least to anticipate the problems." Scraping his plate before dropping it into the pan of soapy water, he continues, "This is probably as good a time as any to talk to you about your choices."

I shiver, wondering about his agenda.

He adds, "Remember, I told you that Coach McElvey had asked me to take you on this trip? Well, he believes that I can teach you about self-sufficiency, but more than that, he wants me to help you learn to trust men. He asked me to teach you how to confront the disappointments on the ski team and to understand that the best way to overcome the trauma is to confront it and to return to the team. You know, he wants you to train with your friends and to try out for the '72 Olympics next year in Sapporo."

"Oh, no, I've been trying to forget that. I can't even think about facing Coach Boast again." For a moment, my knife turns into the razor blade that I used to fend off the coach's attack on me. Warm tomato sauce drips down my hand, like blood soaking me.

Rob grabs my shaking hand. "Easy, now. You can't change what happened. Believe me when I tell you that Boast will never coach again. McElvey told me that. Best of all, the ski team has asked McElvey to be an assistant Olympic coach." He waits to see my reaction.

I jump up and do a small dance. "Are you serious? I'd do anything for McElvey."

I quickly sit down again. "But what if I have to testify against Coach Boast? Can he or Coach Ryan hurt me?"

"Please calm down. Take a deep breath. Trust me. McElvey will make sure you have a good lawyer. Plus, your teammates will support you." He pats the air, reassuring me that I need not worry. "To the point, McElvey still believes that you have the potential to be the best racer in the world. Remember, in Maribor when you'd beaten all the racers by a second in the first run and would have won if you hadn't fallen at the bottom of the second run?"

My ankle throbs as I remember the compound fracture that I'd suffered in that race. "But … but I've been away from everyone for five months. I still have some healing to do. And I *really* want to study at Berkeley this fall. Do you think I can truly get back to racing form by January?" I'm afraid to tell him about my other motive, to help Greta and support the Vietnam resistance movement, especially because he mentioned that his friend, Geoff, now works for the CIA.

"Of course. McElvey thinks so, for sure. That's why he's supported you all this time, right? Trust him. He'll get all your equipment ready, you know, from the suppliers. Then, you can join the team at Monmouth over Thanksgiving. After your exams in December, perhaps you can fly to Europe and start training with the team in Chamonix? He has it all planned for you."

I close my eyes and take a deep breath, trying to erase the recurring memory of Coach Boast's attack in Maribor. It plays across my mind like a minor note on a flute—never to be forgotten, but from which I would learn much.

Rob stands up to assert himself and starts scolding me with a wag of his finger. "Now you know the reason I told you the story of Geoff and me. Now you understand why I've come back to the Wind Rivers. As we climb Gannett together, I'll learn to forgive myself for not saving Geoff, and you'll gain the confidence to confront your fears. Only by facing these challenges can you and I move on. McElvey knows that and he's smart, right?"

Sarcastically, I reiterate, "Right."

He pokes the fire, creating sparks that snap into the night sky, gems joining their light with the glow from the North Star. I'm overwhelmed by his cryptic purpose for this journey, but I'm also feeling my direction again.

CHAPTER 28

First Summit

Waking under the refracted pink glow of Gannett Glacier, I feel the mountains calling to me in a new way: not as a slope to ski down, but as a challenge to climb, a place to test myself, to confront my fears, and reach a goal.

Already I'm learning to live in the landscape, to open myself to the quiet lessons that nature offers me. I pull my sleeve up to check the time, and then laugh at my useless habit of checking Chronos time in the mountains. All I have is nature's time—Kairos time—in other words Divine time.

Rob is laying out all our climbing gear: crampons, ice axes, ropes, mountaineer goggles, carabiners, and harnesses. Rubbing my eyes, I ask, "Wow, so what's the plan for today?"

"I thought we'd do a test run. You know, before we attempt Gannett. How about a hike to the top of Dinwoody Peak?"

"But didn't we pass the trail to it two miles back?"

"Yup, but what's two miles in terms of hiking ten to twenty a day?"

"Got it. Will you show me how to use everything? I've never climbed on a glacier—only up short snow couloirs at Monmouth and in Switzerland."

"Well, Miss Mountaineer, today we'll change all that. Are you scared?"

I love how he changes my nickname, depending on our task. "No, not scared, just a little unsure of what to expect. I like to know what I'm doing."

Rob demonstrates each piece of climbing gear, how to tie the rope around me, how to affix the carabineer, how to work on belaying, and how to use both points of the ice ax—one to dig and the other to arrest a fall.

Handing me my goggles, he laughs. "You're turning the color of a penny.

These will protect your eyes from the glare off the snow—you know, higher up."

After a hot breakfast of freeze-dried scrambled eggs and toast, we each fill our day packs. My load is so light that I jump up like a fledgling ready to soar into the high country. My boots have dried out and my blister has hardened. Today I'm to become a real mountaineer like my heroes, Edmund Hillary, George Mallory, Jim Whittaker, and Willi Unsoeld.

*   *   *   *

After boulder-hopping over the terminal moraine, a tongue of rocks that mark the end of the glacier, and stepping onto the snow for the first time since my World Cup race in Maribor, I sense that I'm a different person—less self-centered, yet more self-assured, and the best, more at peace with myself. I fall to my knees, pick up a handful of the glacier's ice crystals, and bring them to my face. The cold water drips down my neck—a form of baptism.

Looking back at Rob who's silently watching me, I announce, "I think you and McElvey are right. This is the world I love."

The warming sun sparks off the peak, blinding me, forcing me to put on my bug-eyed goggles. The cornice at the top of Dinwoody casts a long shadow across the white glacier. "Hey Rob, do you see the overhang up there? How on earth can we climb that?"

He laughingly says, "One step at a time, like everything else you're doing and will do."

He helps me strap on my crampons. Struggling, I pull my harness over my blue ski team parka, knowing that once the sun reaches its full force, I'll have to unrope and take it off. Rob touches my gold and red US Ski Team sleeve patch and nods. "This is how I remember you—you know, in Grindelwald, a ski champion, and now soon to be a conqueror of mountains."

Giggling, I agree, "You're right. And I hope to learn what they have to teach me."

He puts me on belay with him in the lead. "Let's climb about a thousand feet before we practice a fall." As he points up, the sun highlights his chin stubble, making him become the consummate mountain man.

Rob must shorten his stride so I can walk in his steps. The snow starts to soften, causing my feet to sink in at times. I lose my balance and jab my ice ax into the snow. A magical blue light leaks from the snow. I'm glad I'm on belay with Rob. I sputter, "Hey … hey, can you please slow down? I'm having a hard time breathing."

I realize now that skiing down from 11,000 feet at Monmouth is very different from climbing up a 13,500-foot peak.

Rob leans against a large boulder that appears to be floating on top of the snow, like flotsam in a stream. He points up and asks, "Hey, how much do you know about glaciation?" I shake my head, still trying to catch my breath. He continues, "Well, you know that underneath us is the force that carves mountains and creates valleys. These mountains rose from the tectonic plates in the earth. As they smashed together, they pushed up the Rocky Mountains, perhaps eighty million years ago." He butts his knuckles against each other. "Now these glaciers, probably ten thousand years old, are trying to lower the plates. You know, geologic time is so different from our chronological time, it's so unbelievably slow."

"Now you're making me feel even smaller, more unimportant."

"Just a different perspective to help you understand that your choices probably will not change the course of the earth. To ski in the Olympics or to study at Berkeley becomes irrelevant to history— it's only relevant to you."

Confused as to why he's putting me into the story, I assert, "Maybe in the big picture, but in my small picture, I want to do what will help the most people." I still don't dare tell him about Greta and my option to stay at Berkeley to join the student protest movement.

Rob stands up and tells me to take off my belay. Unexpectedly, he raises his ice ax and places the flat end across his chest. He jumps into the air, lands on his back, and starts to slide down on his bum. While building speed, he rolls over onto his stomach, maneuvers his feet downhill, and pushes the pointed end into the snow-ice, making sure to cover the other end with his gloved hand, so it won't hurt his chest. The scraping sound of the ax on the ice reminds me of a car skidding to a violent stop. Snow wafts down on him when he finally arrests. He spits it out, calling up to me, "Do you see how I did it?"

"I think so." Fear and adrenaline begin coursing through my body.

"Okay, now you try it. Make sure when you roll over onto your stomach that you push the blunt end against your shoulder and also raise your feet behind you. You don't want your crampons to catch and break your leg."

I step away from the boulder, so I won't slide down on top of him. I carefully sit down and pick up my legs. Sliding, I gather speed. I panic. I'm headed for rocks two hundred feet below me. Rob yells when I glissade past him, "Roll over, damn it, roll over!"

I push the flat end of the ax into my shoulder and twist, throwing myself into the air. Fortunately, my shoulder hits the snow, so I can force the pointed ax end into the ice, while adding the weight of my body. Even so, I'm still sliding. In a final effort, I push my knees into the snow, causing my crampons to raise back like a sky jumper. To add pressure to the point, I force my stomach off the ground. In one hundred feet, I start to slow and finally stop just short of a rock.

Turning back up the hill, I yell to him, "I had trouble slowing myself. I don't think I weigh as much as you."

Rob bounds down to me, as awkward as a loon running across the water for a takeoff. He stops just above my snow-covered head. "Okay, Miss Snowman, maybe we should've tried this on a more gradual slope. Anyway, now you've learned the importance of the ice ax, right?"

*   *   *   *

We've made little headway toward the cornice, even though we've been hiking for three hours. The vastness of the snowfield makes distances hard to judge. My only perspective on how high we've climbed is the view across the valley to the pleated slopes of the Rockies. With every step, I can see more of their saw-toothed skyline, peaks melding into peaks like waves blasting against the shore. Meanwhile, ranks of clouds sail through the sky, scattering sun shadows across the snowy amphitheaters.

Kick, stomp, swing the ax, kick, stomp—our rhythm is methodical, slow, and deliberate. The snowfield grows steeper. My lips begin to burn from the hot sun and lack of water. Everything intensifies up here. Feeling as clumsy as a three-legged dog attempting to walk, I yell up to Rob, while yanking on the belay, "Hey, could we please take a break or at least slow down?" He points to the descending sun, "Okay, Miss Fitness, you know the rule about effort. When you feel like stopping, that's when you convince yourself you just started and can go on for twenty more minutes, right?"

I chuckle, remembering when I used to run up mountains and had to pretend, during the last one hundred yards, that I'd just begun. That is when I'd do the one hundred-step count to distract myself. I count: kick, stomp, swing the ax, *one,* kick, stomp, swing the ax, *two.* It works.

About five hundred feet below the cornice, Rob stops and points to his right. "Good job, Miss Mind-Over-Matter. Let's move off to the right, out of the shadow, so that we aren't directly beneath the overhang. You never know when a piece could break off."

Away from the overhang, I scrape out a shallow seat on the steep slope, using the adze end of my ice ax, while Rob is next to me, doing the same. A clump of snow breaks off and bounces down the slope, jumping higher as it gains more speed before its final leap into the air and over a cliff.

Resting, I take deep breaths to lower my heart rate. Carefully, Rob pulls out his contour map and flattens it on his knee. He begins to point out the surrounding peaks, "Mount Febbas, 13,468; East Sentinel, 12, 823; West Sentinel, 12,585; and the mighty Gannett at 13,835 feet." He squints, "Do you see the dark shadow below the summit on Gannett—you know, under the cliff?" I nod. "That's where Geoff fell into the bergschrund." He closes his eyes, trying to erase the memory. Turning, he points up to the north, "Do you see the gap between West and East Sentinel? That's Bonney Pass, where we'll cross the Rockies and head down to the Titcomb Lakes and Pinedale."

I shield my eyes, squint, and squirm. "Looks like a long trip on snow to me."

"You're right." He puts the map away, adding, "Maps don't show time, just space. Remember, I told you this winter has seen the heaviest snowpack in years. Normally, the route would be on scree and talus, all above timberline. So, Miss Skier, we're lucky. With the snow cover, we can slide down, using our boots as skis, and complete the route in half the time.

Climbing once again, we keep the belay on, forcing us to alternate our moves—one climbs while the other anchors with the ice ax. I hear a crack and look up to see a large chunk of snow, about the size of a semi-trailer truck, break from the cornice. As it barrels toward our foot tracks, the echo resounds throughout the valley, many voices warning me. Instinctively, I duck.

Rob laughs, "That's normal for this time of year. The snow is rotten underneath where the winds have undercut the lip. That's why we got up early."

We start up again, or I should say sideways, because we must go well beyond the cornice for our final approach to the top. Rob asks me to go ahead, continuing, "You should lead, because if you slip, I'm stronger and can stop your fall. For sure, you'd have a hard time holding me if I fell, especially when I gather speed."

The steps grow more arduous, because the sun has made the snow mashed-potato soft. We find ourselves post-holing up to our knees on every step. Rob has a more difficult time because he's almost twice my weight and, therefore, sinks farther down, even though he's following in my footsteps.

He stops at the bottom of a snow drift next to a rocky outcropping and looks down, poking with his ice ax. "Hey, stop. I want to show you something." I descend, making sure to re-step in each one of my footsteps until I reach him.

He points to a pale blue light seeping from the snow. "See that?" He uses his ice ax to break open the snow and I look down into a blue vastness of eternal winter. "Here is a bergschrund—you know, like the one I described to you on Gannett." He pauses, then pushes an ice ball into the gaping mouth, where it bounces down, echoing the sounds of a pinball jumping in an arcade.

"Wow, are we safe here?"

Rob points to his left and right. "As far as I can tell. From the angle of the rock, we're right on the edge, so if we move maybe a hundred more feet to the right, we should be able to climb safely to the ridge."

I step forward. "So how many centuries are we looking into here?" The different colors of blue descend into a black hole.

Rob laughs, "I think we're looking into a time before the creation of the United States, maybe even before the Middle Ages." He stops to see if I'm grasping the message. "Maybe even before the Greeks and the Romans. You do remember your World History, don't you?"

Out of the darkness comes a cracking sound because the ice is shifting. I jump back in fear and yell, "Let's go. I'm scared."

"Easy," assures Rob. "Remember, move slowly—prudence is best."

Once on top of the ridge, I begin climbing up the knife edge, but much more slowly because of my labored breaths. My heart hammers against my ribs. I make sure that my ice ax is set securely into the snow on each step. The slope off to my right is so precipitous that I know Rob could never stop me if I fell. As the cornice on my left grows more undercut with each step, I freeze. "Rob," I call out, "I can't do it. I'm scared. This is beyond anything I've ever done." I avoid looking down at him.

"So, my friend, this is what we've come for. This is your challenge. Can you convince yourself that you're safe? There are only forty more feet to the top. We can stop here and go down, or you can do forty more steps and conquer your fears. How do you want to remember this moment—safety or success?"

My mind overcomes my fear. I lift my right foot, kick, stomp, swing the ax ... *one, two*.

On top, standing in the embrace of white snow and blue sky, I swivel, looking in every direction, and let go of my ice ax to raise my hands. I've a sense of lightness—I'm falling up into the sky.

I realize how all-consuming my struggle has been. My two choices, entwined like two grappling hands, armwrestling, have suddenly released me, causing a space to open between them. Suddenly, I'm free to reimagine a new path. I've gone from the scared to the sacred, from a monkey mind to a Buddhist mind.

CHAPTER 29

Huckleberry

Back at Wilson Flats, we discover that the stream has tripled in size, caused by the extra snow melt from the summer sun. Since our tent and packs lie across the rampaging water too dangerous to cross, we decide to wait for the night's cooling air, hoping the flow will lessen. I'm exhausted and starving. All my creature comforts are inside Huckleberry, just across the way: food, dry clothes, and sleeping bag.

Rob refills his water bottle and settles against a large rock, splaying his tired legs. I can barely hear him over the torrent's white noise. "So, what are your thoughts about the hike?" He pauses, seeing my hesitation, "Let me put it another way. How did you find the confidence to get to the summit?"

Sitting across from him, I draw a circle in the sand. Then, I trace a smaller one inside it, and then one smaller. Finally, I put a pebble in the center. "Here's what I did. I stopped looking to the dropoff on my right and to the cornice on my left where the chunk broke off. I stopped looking ahead and definitely didn't look back at you. I stepped on my right foot, stomped twice to make sure it was secure, gripped my ice ax harder, tested my balance, and lifted my left foot." I kick one heel and then the other into the wet sand to demonstrate.

"I cleared my mind of any thoughts but the next step. My fears left me, my purpose became clear, and in forty steps, I was on the top with you, celebrating my first summit." I look at Rob who's nodding and smiling, not saying anything. I pick up the pebble and hold it up. "Finally at the top, I did a 360-turn and let my focus expand beyond the inner circle. I thought to myself, there's no fear I can't overcome with a deliberate, narrowed focus. I can do anything." As I speak, I notice that the waves in the roiling stream have diminished.

Rob puts his hands behind his head and looks to the sky. "You now understand how to handle any adversity, physical or mental—right? I mean, you're learning

143

the power of the mind, a force that has yet to be truly understood."

"Wow, so if I try not to let my monkey-mind blind me, maybe, just maybe, I can handle going back to the ski team. Then, by focusing on my training, I can make the Olympic team!" I half say, half ask.

Rob nods, reaching across to pat my knee with his oversized hand. "You're learning, my friend. How about we take a look at all the outer circles, as you call them. You know, that make up your monkey-mind?" He points to my large circle in the dirt. "I don't know how much you know about philosophy and decision making, but I'll tell you I'm an objectivist. I've read a lot of Ayn Rand, especially *Atlas Shrugged*. She says to look at the facts and just the facts. So tell me the facts—what are your fears?"

"I touch the outer circle. "Okay, my biggest fear is that I'll run into Coach Boast again. I can't face him and revisit all his lies, especially his assault on me."

He begins to erase my larger circle while saying, "Done. Coach Boast has been dismissed. Furthermore, your favorite Coach McElvey will be the assistant coach."

"Wow! Next, I'm also afraid that I won't be able to get back to my earlier form."

He erases the next outer circle. "Done. You know how to focus and work hard. I've seen that. All you need now is time on your skis." He reaches over and squeezes my thigh, "You're already stronger than you were this spring, right?

"Also, I'm worried about money. Who'll support me? I can't keep asking my father. After all, I'm nineteen and have declared my independence."

He erases the inner circle. "Done. McElvey and the ski team will support you."

I scratch my head, "Wow, that's good news." I relax against my rock, "So what's an objectionist? It sounds very negative."

Rob laughs, "No, silly, I said an 'objectivist.' " Slowly, he draws his own circle and writes 'reality'. "No, in fact it's just the opposite—it's someone who looks at just the facts and believes that reality is objective."

"I'm not sure what you're saying?" I trace my initials *LE* in the dirt.

"To the point, yes, each one of us has our own perspective on life. However, if we start with the physical facts, then we can come closer to agreeing with each other. For example, a mountain is just a high peak made of rocks, ice, and snow. If we can agree on this and ignore any subjective interpretations or emotional responses, then we can get closer to a truth."

"Do you mean that all my favorite writers were wrong, the ones who tried to put emotional and spiritual judgments on nature, to interpret nature? For instance, like Emerson who believed that from nature we can intuit universal truths."

"From my perspective, yes, I think that they were wrong. Just look at the facts. The sun is just a ball of gases. However, some like to interpret that it's either good, in that it sustains life, or bad, in that it's causes sunburn and cancer. But those are subjective responses, good and bad. On the other hand, to an objectivist, it's just a ball of gas. No universal truth. No spirit. No interpretations. Just look at the facts."

He then draws a smaller circle inside his circle. "If we accept this statement, then all we need for our understanding of the world is our own reason, which is an absolute. To the point, it's all we need in the world. We don't need other's interpretation, or worse, contradictions." He stops, "You look very confused."

"I point to his smaller circle, "Do you mean that we shouldn't listen to others or follow their beliefs?"

"In a way, yes, except when they agree with our purpose." He then draws a smaller circle and labels it 'selfishness'. And our highest purpose is to act only for our own selfishness—the pursuit of our own happiness."

I grimace, not wanting to accept this.

He shakes his head, "You look frustrated. Let me explain. Only if we attend to our own happiness, can we realize our highest potential."

I squirm and pull my knees into my chest. "But ... but what about helping others? I've been taught this all my life."

"Well, Miss Do-Gooder, here lies your problem. Selfishness does not mean

145

you exploit others for yourself. You must accept that others are living their lives according to their view of reality for their own happiness. I mean, just accept them—don't try to change them."

This makes sense to me in terms of my desire to make the ski team and I'm okay with wanting to pursue my dream of making the Olympics, but I decide to test him about other, more worldly decisions. "Okay, I can understand about limiting my focus right now to making the ski team. But what about other larger problems that are sucking my happiness?"

He looks quizzical. "What do you mean—larger issues?"

I pause, wondering if I should reveal my anger about the war in Vietnam and my friend's death as a soldier. "What about wanting to help change what I see as evil in the world?"

"What do you mean?"

I think he knows what I'm talking about, but he wants me to state it. "Well, right now, our country is involved in a war that I don't agree with. I had a friend killed in Vietnam and I'm angry. I want to join the student protest movement against the war when I get to Berkeley."

"First of all, you must decide whether the war is evil or just. I believe that this war is a just war, a defensive war in that America is trying to stop Communism from enveloping the Asian Peninsula, and worse, moving toward our country. You know, the domino effect. It's not an offensive war. We don't want to take over Vietnam. We just want to give the Vietnamese a chance to determine their own future—you know, as a democracy."

"But this sounds like altruism." I pull my knees tighter against my chest.

"Not really. Let me explain, right? First, I believe that Communism is exploitative and denies people the choice to live freely. Eventually, Russia wants to dominate us, the world. We must stop them. Secondly, if we can create a free society in Vietnam, then, selfishly, we can open trade with the whole Asian Peninsula. Right?"

"Um, at the cost of how many lives? I've heard that as many as 40,000 Americans have already died in the war. Did they die for selfish reasons?

Remember, these soldiers were drafted. They'd lost their ability to choose for themselves, to pursue their own happiness."

Rob stumbles, "You're jumping ahead of my reasoning. Each soldier has his own ability to decide what to do. Those who chose to go to war are following what they believe. Maybe they are looking forward to adventure or a chance to be a hero. In the end, they are doing it for themselves. I know."

"That's not what I've experienced with my friends."

He wags his finger at me and states, "Remember what I said, that in the end everyone acts out of self-interest. This self-interest gives their lives a purpose, helps their self-esteem." He watches for my reaction, then continues, "Case in point, why did you finish your climb to the top of Dinwoody Peak. I don't think it was out of altruism. No, you did it to give meaning to your life, to conquer your own fears."

I struggle to find a counter argument to his arrogance, even though his philosophy starts to sound logical. He's so smug. I look across to the stream, to my backpack, to Huckleberry. "Wait a minute, let me give you an example that contradicts your belief."

He brushes his hands together to get rid of the dirt and shifts his seat, puzzled by my defiance.

Feeling more confident, I speak slowly, "I'm looking at my backpack and thinking about how Huck Finn made a choice to defy the laws of the South, you remember, by not reporting the runaway slave, Jim. Do you recall the moment when he says, 'Well, I'll go to Hell, but I won't turn Jim in'? I don't think he was acting out of self-interest. I think Huck truly wanted to help Jim get free, so Jim could go on to buy his own family's freedom."

Rob slaps his knee. "You're wrong. I believe that Huck just acted selfishly, that all he wanted was Jim's company on the raft and to enjoy adventures with him. For example, when Jim was finally captured and locked in a cabin, Huck didn't do the easiest thing and just let him out. He, along with Tom Sawyer, made Jim do stupid things, like writing blood notes and digging holes. All for the fun of the adventure. And ironically, all at the risk of Jim's life."

I feel so inferior to Rob. I can't find any argument that would counter his belief in people's selfishness. Finally, I ask, "Do you believe in a God or a higher power?" I feel sure of myself again, thinking that surely, he would believe in some of the unselfish teachings of the Bible like humility, kindness, and love.

Rob starts laughing and then stops, "Are you kidding? If something can't be proven, such as the existence of a God, then it does not exist. Yes, even your Emersonian transcendental idea of an Oversoul is subjective. I can't accept it. I believe only in the facts and in the physical reality that we can see, such as that mountain up there. That mountain is not a symbol for a higher authority for a God—it's just a mountain." He looks up at the setting sun. "I try to get rid of all sentimental emotions, everything you call symbolism."

Disappointed, I drop my head. He's just taken all my beliefs and dumped them into a toilet. I want to see the world as more than just facts or data. "Okay, what about love? Do you believe you can love another and devote yourself to that person unselfishly?"

Rob gets up. "No! All love is selfish. Everyone wants to get something from someone else, such as money, self-esteem, security or, maybe, children."

I can find no common ground in this discussion, as if it's a hologram. Turn it one way and I see myself struggling up a mountain but turn it another way and I see myself having a divine, ecstatic experience. I prefer my way of seeing the world, of telling a story.

He picks up his pack and points to the stream. "I think we can cross now. Let's go set up the tent and I'll cook you a nice dinner of spaghetti. Then we can get to bed early. We need to plan our assault on Gannett." He looks up and states, "I'm worried that the sky is darkening. It might rain."

CHAPTER 30

Change of Plans

The storm rages, forcing us to hunker down in the tent for the morning. I spend my time with my knees propped up, resting against my daypack, writing. Rob only ventures out to grab some snack bars and water. At times the rain turns to sleet, beating so hard against the nylon roof that conversation is difficult.

I decide to compose a poem to capture my emotions on top of Dinwoody, a memory that I can use when I'm back in the real world, maybe floundering again, a statement to reassure me that I can conquer any obstacle and/or fear.

The Answer

The peaks, reaching, yearning

I, a belayed climber,

struggling, slipping, sliding.

Why?

Is there an answer on the top,

A reason that I want to conquer?

Kick, stomp, swing the ax

Fear?

Sun-time, ice-time, geologic-time.

Then, no time.

All

Is

One.

By noon, Rob decides that we're stuck until tomorrow. Plans for the assault on Gannett are on hold. We start to figure out how many days we'll need to walk out of the mountains and how much food we have left. He reassures me that we'll have enough food to last the trip, especially if he can catch some fish in the Titcomb Lakes on the western slope once we cross the Continental Divide. He helps me pass the time by reading aloud an essay that he'd brought with him.

I'm realizing that he's planned to share this letter all along and ask, "So what's this about?"

"The value of wilderness. Uh, I'd planned to read this to you after we'd conquered Gannett, but I'm guessing that adventure won't happen."

"Are you disappointed? I know you'd wanted to find some resolution to your tragedy with your friend, Geoff."

He lowers his head in resignation. "Not everything can be resolved as planned. I'll confront this later and accept the fact that I did the best for my friend at the time. The most important thing is to be able to forgive myself." He sighs and then asks, "You know, when you confront a fear, then it can't control you, right?"

I sit up, challenging him. "You always seem to be trying to teach me something."

Rob puts up his hands and says, "Relax! This isn't about me right now. I want to help you with the confusion in your mind. Before I read to you, do you want to try to explain what you felt on top of Dinwoody Peak?"

A clap of thunder echoes though the valley. I pause to find the right words, "Okay, although I'm not sure what it all means." I close my eyes, trying to recall the exact moment. "When I stood on top, I could look both east and west, to the past and the future, and to the ski races in Europe and to the potential of Berkeley. I felt that I was totally in control of my next decisions and that I could leave all the drama behind me. I was free, part of something bigger, a new person."

"Wonderful. Now you'll understand what Wallace Stegner was saying in this letter written in 1960 that I've brought. Stegner writes about the importance of preserving wilderness areas in America."

I rest my head on my sleeping bag and look up into the damp red nylon that bounces and ripples from the heavy rain and wind. I love the sound of his confident voice.

Rob begins reading, "*To David Pesonen at the Wildland Research Center at the University of California Berkeley.*"

"Oh, how cool. Maybe the Center is still there, and I can get involved when I get to Berkeley."

Rob rolls his eyes at me and says, "Please just listen," He continues reading, "*I believe that you are working on the wilderness portion of the … Commission's report.*" The rain drums out many words, but I can hear enough. His bass voice could be the harmony in a choir. Most of the time, it overrides the white noise of the storm. " *… What I want to speak for is not so much the wilderness uses, valuable as these are, but the wilderness idea, which is a resource in itself. Being an intangible and spiritual resource, it will seem mystical to the practical-minded …* "

I stop him, "Wait a minute, aren't you one of the practical-minded?"

"Well, yes and no. I don't try to imagine what's not there, but I can also appreciate the value of a place of peace and naturalness, one without technology or human intervention—a respite from all the worldly problems that our society has created. That's why Geoff and I came here for the first time. For me, the wilderness is all our common ground, a place that will never be destroyed by commercial interests." His voice fades off and he continues to read, but I can't hear every word. I try to read his lips.

"... *I want to speak for the wilderness idea as something that has helped form our character and that has certainly shaped our history as a people... What historians call the "American Dream." My mind wanders to my friend Henry David who sought the silence of the Green Mountains.*

"... *if we pollute the last clear air and dirty the last clean streams and push our paved roads through the last of the silence, so that never again will Americans be free in their own country from the noise, the exhausts, the stinks of human and automotive waste ...*"

Rob takes a break and asks, "Do you want to hear more? You look like you're daydreaming."

"Oh yes, sometimes my mind wanders, but I'm following the gist. I like what Stegner's saying."

Rob moves closer and continues reading.

"... *And so never again can we have the chance to see ourselves single, separate, vertical and individual in the world, but are part of the environment of trees and the rocks and soil, brother to the other animals, part of the natural world and competent to belong to it. Without any remaining wilderness, we are committed wholly, without chance for even momentary reflection and rest, to a headlong drive into our technological termite-life, the brave New World of a completely man-controlled environment ...*"

My mind wanders back to the train ride across Canada and the beauty that was disturbed by the clatter of the tracks and the blasts of the whistle. Now I know why I wasn't perfectly comfortable with it.

He continues, "... *the wilderness as opportunity and idea, the thing that has made an American different from and, until we forget it in the roar of our industrial cities, more fortunate than other men. For an American, insofar as he is new and different at all, is a civilized man who has renewed himself in the wild ...*"

I raise my hand for him to stop. "Wow, I'm having a hard time hearing everything you're reading, but I get the idea. What I experienced on the mountaintop is exactly what others have felt who had the courage to walk away from all creature comforts. But what about those who don't have this opportunity?"

"Good question. Let me jump ahead." He fumbles with the paper, and continues,

"… *Save a piece of country like that intact, and it does not matter in the slightest that only a few people every year will go into it. That is precisely its value. Roads would be a desecration, crowds would ruin it. But those, who haven't the strength or youth to go into it and live, can simply sit and look…they can simply contemplate the idea, take pleasure in the fact that such a timeless and uncontrolled part of the earth is still here.*"

I clap my hands in joy. "Hey, I get it. My thoughts while looking at Gannett Peak can last a lifetime." I laugh and caress Huckleberry behind me. "And for the first time, now I understand what Mark Twain was saying when he made Huckleberry Finn, after all his disappointment with man's inhumanity to man, decide to take off for the wild west … "

He holds up his hand to stop my enthusiasm. "Let me finish, please." He pulls out his last piece of paper, "… *These are some of the things the wilderness can do for us… we simply need that wild country available to us, even if we never do more than drive to its edge and look in. For it can be a means of reassuring ourselves of our sanity as creatures, a part of the geography of hope.*"

A burst of hail hits the tent, forcing the center pole to collapse onto me. As I push it back up, Rob grabs my hand to help and concludes, "Now do you understand why I have brought you here? Why McElvey wanted me to take you on this hike? I'll bet you didn't know that he's paid for everything in the hope that you'll sort out what you want to do next." He pauses and then ends in reverence, lowering his eyes, "And why I wanted to return with you."

I listen to the lessening rain, the laughter of the glacial stream, and relax. I'm beginning to feel optimistic again. Even proud to be an American.

CHAPTER 31

Crossing the Divide

I'm not sure whattime the hail, pinging like BB pellets, stopped in the night. I know Rob stayed up for a while, slapping the sagging tent sides, forcing the ice balls to slide, sizzling to the ground. I get a few hours of sleep before Rob wakes me, holding a cup of coffee. As he peeks in, an ice avalanche coats his wool hat.

Spitting out the shards, he announces, "Hey, sleepyhead, that was some storm, but I eventually heard you snoring. So, you must've gotten a little shuteye, right?"

"Yup, I do feel a little rested." Rubbing the crust from my eyes, I add, "I dreamed about jumping off the top of Dinwoody and flying west, free." To demonstrate, I spread my arms as I climb out of the ice-stiff tent. "Yes, free, and in my dream, my sleeves fanned like wings, so I could play in the thermals. Wouldn't it be fun to be an eagle?"

"Sounds as if you've overcome your fear of heights."

"Wow, I guess you're right. Not only that, but I also feel free of all fears, even fears of the unknown." I squint into the fog covering the mountains. "Yup, even what's on the other side of the Divide."

"Good, because that's where we're headed today. I've decided we need to pack up and head over Bonney Pass, you know, into the Titcomb Lakes. Okay?" He points to the tent that's white as an igloo. "See, the storm left a rime glaze everywhere, especially on the snow. Our best bet is to get over the glacier and back to bare ground by tonight. Plus, I did a tally, and well … " He shakes his head in concern, " … we're getting low on food." His voice drops as if he has more to say but doesn't want to worry me.

"Got it. I hope the clouds lift and we get some sun to soften our route, not to mention drying out."

It takes us very little time to finish our granola and pack our tent. Both of us feel the urgency, and for me, a strong desire to head back to civilization. I've grown self-assured, confident as a crusader returning home with the golden chalice.

Rob opens the plastic map and traces our route, showing me where we're going, just in case. I heft my pack that's grown heavier from all the rain. Rob asks me to dangle my crampons off the back, next to my ice ax.

We wade through the headwaters of the swollen Dinwoody Creek in our bare feet, our pant legs rolled up to our knees, our frozen toes struggling to find flat rocks, and stop on a log to lace on our hiking boots. I'm glad I don't have to start the trek with wet shoes. Finally, my blister has healed and, for sure, I don't want to irritate it by hiking with wet socks.

As we climb, the clouds thicken, obscuring our previous footsteps. The fog is so dense I can scoop it up with my mitten. Rob uses his compass to find our pathless route. Barely seeing two feet ahead, I just follow his holes: kick, step, swing the ax. I'm surprised that I'm not afraid. All I can hear is my labored breathing and the crunch of each step into the icy surface. The world becomes a monochromatic black and white—even Rob's red jacket looks gray. My mind starts to spin, not sensing up or down, as if I'm climbing inside a ping pong ball.

Every one hundred steps, he stops to take a bearing and search for any identifiable markings. In this total whiteout, my only sense of ascending is when each kick touches higher up and when the ax gropes above my shoulders. Occasionally, we tack around huge erratics, stone monuments on the glacier that's carrying them to their new resting place, slowly in ice-time.

Finally, he stops next to a cliff, stomps out an ice shelf for both of us, and announces, "It's time to strap on our crampons. From what I remember, the last three hundred feet is very steep. We may run into a few crevasses." He lowers his pack before helping me with mine. "We'll go on belay, also—just for good measure, right?"

The wet fog begins to soak my pants and jacket, adding to my discomfort. Impatiently, I ask, "Can we get going? I'm cold. Do you think the sun will come out today?"

"Not sure, but if we do get above the clouds at the top, we can get a sense of where we are and where we're headed. For sure, we'll have time for lunch in the sun and to warm up. According to the map, if we keep going up and a bit south, we'll find Bonney Pass." His voice falters.

The lacy clouds above begin to unfurl, exposing thin patches of blue sky, allowing for glimpses of the ridgeline. Rob lengthens his pace, forcing me to take two steps to his one. The snow has softened to corn, so we don't have to worry about sliding—our footholds remain permanent.

Just as I reach the top, the fog breaks. With the sun at my back, I point down to the fast-rising curtain and see a shadow of a person beckoning me, silhouetted in the mist.

Rob sees it, too. "Hey, that's the first time I've ever seen that phenomenon. It's called the Brocken spectre. And look, you've got a rainbow haloed around your head.

I flap my arms to make sure it's me, pronouncing, "This can only mean good luck."

Rob shakes his head, "I guess you'll never accept my objectivist way of thinking. To me, the spectre is just the magnified shadow behind your back, cast down by the sun into the water crystals that hover in the air. Nothing more, nothing less."

I goad him, "Maybe I don't want to see the world the way you do."

Before I can argue more, Gannett Peak ascends above the veil, close enough so that I can see the glacier that forms a cross on the summit. I have a brief moment of revelation similar to when I was walking on the icy pond near my home and would stare through a transparent sheet of black ice to see the silent depths. I squint and blink, hoping to camera-capture this image. To me, if ever there exists a wilderness, this peak says it all. It's beyond reach for me, but the idea of its divine head will always be part of my journey. In a way, I'm glad I didn't conquer it—I want to walk this earth, a foot in the physical and a foot in the spiritual. Instead, it'll remain my geography of hope.

CHAPTER 32

Way Out

We sit down and scooch over to the edge of the Continental Divide to peer into the smooth snowfield that extends down at least two thousand feet. The noon sun bounces off a chain of lakes, weaving a path toward the blue horizon. The air has an innocence, a transparency.

To my right and left, the serried peaks of the Continental Divide rend the sky, like pages in a book: to the east is all the turmoil of the US Ski Team and to the west is the new chapter of my life—college. I remember the last time, seven months ago, when I crossed the Divide heading to the World Cup races in Europe, when my heart held all the dreams of racing against the best in the world.

In ecstasy, I turn to Rob and ask, "Hey, I'm so happy we've done this. One day, when we're old, will you rejoin me here, you know, to help me remember this moment?"

Looking at me with puzzlement, he asks, "Why are you thinking so far into the future? We've still got at least three days of hiking before we get out?"

"I guess this is my way of saying thank you for what you've given me."

"No, you gave this to yourself by attempting something new, by pushing your limits." He pauses, not sure whether to add, but does, "You seemed very confused when you got off the train in Vancouver. Do you want to talk about it?" He picks up a piece of snow and sucks on it. "I'm still not sure about your new friends, Greta and Will. I question their motives."

"Hey, I don't appreciate your criticizing my friends. They've been a big help to me and will continue assisting me in Berkeley."

"I'm not sure they're a good influence on you." He pauses as if he wants to tell me more but changes the subject. "Okay, slide back. You're too close to the edge to stand up." My foot slips and he grabs my pack, cautioning, "Watch it." He stamps his crampons into the snow to secure his spot on the edge and hands me a cracker and some GORP. "I guess this is as good a time as any to tell you that Coach McElvey wants me to bring you back to Monmouth Mountain before I take you to Berkeley. He says that your friends Becky, Carla, and Stephanie, you know, from the ski team, are dry-land training there. He feels that it's time for you to reconnect with them. Okay?" He throws a snowball over the edge where it picks up speed, growing larger. "Your expression tells me you're concerned. Remember, he's been appointed the assistant coach for the Olympic team. You and your friends should be safe on the team."

"Okay, but I'm still not ready to get back on skis. You know that."

After a long silence he puts his hand up, indicating that I shouldn't follow him, as he inches toward the drop off. He grabs his ice ax and begins to chip away, causing frozen blocks to break off and tumble down like joyful kids bouncing on a trampoline. It doesn't take them long to drop out of sight. A skin of new snow snakes across the white sheen as the cutting wind freshens. I look behind me and see that our tracks have already been obliterated.

Beginning to unstrap his crampons, he commands, "Take yours off, too. You're going on the ride of your life. Okay?" He points to the opening he's created in the cornice. He adjusts his pack and then instructs me, "Now pull your pack up, so it'll ride higher on your back." He helps me shorten the shoulder straps. "Keep your glissade to a crawl so that you can stop at any moment. Use your feet as brakes. Keep your ice ax ready for a faster stop." He looks into my eyes, "Don't be afraid. Now I'm going to take you off the belay. Make sure I'm always in front of you."

I yell into the rising wind, "I'm not afraid anymore—remember?"

"Good. If you start going too fast, lean back onto your pack. It'll slow you. Are you ready? Let's stop every two hundred yards. You'll see, what took us five hours to climb, we'll cover in an hour, right?"

He disappears over the edge, laughing. I claw my way to the precipice, twist onto my butt, lift my feet, and let my jeans press into the snowpack. I become a six-year-old sliding down my first sled run, my knees up, dragging my heels to slow down, pressing my left and right feet to turn, and occasionally getting too close to Rob so that a crust of ice sprays up and wets my cheeks.

When he stops, I pull up behind him, dousing his already coated jacket with more fresh snow. An icy lump slides down my back, tickling my butt. Laughter jingles in my voice. "Wow! The best! This is the wildest ride I've ever had!"

We continue this controlled fall until we hit snow that's littered with dust and dirt and pebbles. I slide next to him, stop, and lie back, feet raised, like a puppy warming her belly in the spring sun. "If life could be this easy, just a free slide to the next adventure, I'd be on board."

Rob, shaking his head, disagrees. "No you wouldn't. You love the danger, the challenges, the unknown. You and I know that's what will build your character ... trust me." He stands up, claws the snow from his ten-day-old beard, takes off his woolen hat and shakes the snow onto my head. "Now you do the same."

I stand, a little unsteady from the sudden altitude drop, scrape the snow from my wet jeans, tighten the pack strap around my waist and announce eagerly, "I'm ready. What's next?"

Rob points down the sun-pocketed snowfield, "See Titcomb Lake at the bottom of the glacier? Let's run and boot-ski down to it." He pauses as our eyes trade concerns. "Being careful not to twist an ankle." He leaps forward with the moon-strides of Neil Armstrong, taking air with each step.

I follow, arms pinwheeling, hollering after each effortless step, confident that I can conquer anything now. Monmouth and Berkeley, here I come!

CHAPTER 33

Second Home

As we drive Rob's Austin Healey into the empty parking lot of Monmouth Mountain, I don't expect a reception because it's 6 pm on August 10th. Summer skiing and race training ended in July and most of the crew is on vacation until the first snows in October.

To my surprise, an assembly of friends of all ages, from my teammates to the chefs, the construction workers, and even the cafeteria crew, greet me outside the large timber-framed front door. Because the car's top is down, I hear their screams before I see each one. A sign reads, "Welcome Home, Lia." My teammates, Becky, Carla, and Stephanie, step forward singing our favorite song, *The Hills Are Alive with the Sound of Music*, just as we did when we were racing.

I look to Rob, who laughs. "I called McElvey from our last stop at June Mountain to ... to let him know when we'd be here." I tap his back as a thank you. He continues, "You sure are beloved here."

From the back of the crowd steps Coach McElvey, a muscular man in khaki pants and a collared shirt, his curly blonde hair swept back, and his face as tan as a lion's. Like a valet, he leans forward, opens my door, bows, helps me out, and embraces me with his bear hug. "Welcome home, Lia. We missed you at summer training." He steps back, still resting his hands on my shoulders, and looks me straight in the eye, "But what adventures you've had. Rob has told me everything." He looks at my ankle. "How are you healing?"

Not giving me a chance to answer, he continues, confident that he knows my every move over the summer. "When I spoke to your dad, he told me how hard you trained while you were in Washington and Vermont, and now while hiking in the Wind Rivers."

I burst into tears, realizing that all of them have been awaiting my recovery and return. "Oh, coach, thank you. I'm humbled. Yes, I'm feeling strong." I look around at the sunburnt, smiling faces. "I'm … I'm so happy."

Rob hefts my backpack and follows all of us into the base lodge. Inside, he grabs my arm and cautions, "Remember, we can only stay tonight. The admissions director at Berkeley expects you in two days. You must set yourself up for your courses, right? Plus, you'll need to find a place to live near campus."

Each step I take fills me with memories—the wax room where I first kissed Bill, the office where I cashed my father's checks, the ski schoolroom where Guy gave me photos of my training, the hall lockers were my teammates and I played hide-and-seek. Stepping up the stairs, I stop in front of the Olympic plaque. The circles, representing the five continents, are painted red, blue, yellow, black, and green in the colors of the many countries' national flags. Under the five rings, embossed in large letters, are the names of former Monmouth racers who had made previous Olympic teams. I bow, remembering that this was my dream when first coming to Monmouth.

In the great room, even though it's August, the fire is lit, and two chairs are pulled up in front. I gasp when I see a dark head silhouetted against the blazing fire. I recall my last night with Bill, sitting there when he told me he'd decided to go to Vietnam—for a moment time has rewound.

The darkened head turns toward me, but I'm still blinded by the fire. The person makes no effort to get up, so I walk around the chair, while my teammates move aside to give me space. A silence fills the room, as everyone is holding their breath.

A head turns and a shaky voice says, "Hi … my friend. Cool … welcome home." I look down and see Wren, her legs covered by a blanket. Making no effort to get up, she extends her hands to embrace me. "Give me some skin."

I lean forward, trying not to fall into her while I snuggle my teary face against her soft brown hair. I whisper into her ear, "Oh, my heavens. You're here." Immediately, I push back to see her thin face and darkened eyes. "Tell me. Oh, Wren … how are you?" The fire flickers on wet snail-tracks running down her cheeks.

There's a silence before Becky steps forward, saying in a mother-like tone,

"Okay, you two. We knew this would be emotional." Cautioning me, she continues, "You know that Wren's still recovering from her racing accident, but she wanted to come up from Los Angeles to see you. You know, she's still doing physical therapy, but, yes, she can walk with a walker now."

Wren nods, choking with tears. Through my sobs, my last images of her flash across my mind like a slide show, her legs akimbo, her head twisted, a toboggan carrying her away, then her head haloed in the hospital bed.

Becky moves behind Wren, clicking the safety on her wheelchair, and commands, "Okay, everyone, Stefan has dinner ready. Lia's favorite, chicken alfredo." She looks me up and down and exclaims, "And it looks as if you could use two helpings, plus all the dessert you could eat." She points to the cafeteria line.

I step in behind Becky, who's pushing Wren toward a walker, and grasp Becky's waist, leaning against her back. "Thanks for the warm welcome. I was nervous, ah, as to whether you … you all had missed me."

She turns and holds my shoulders. "Lia, we're a group of blood sisters. Our lives are forever entwined, because of our time together, you know, pursuing our passions."

I hear a small voice in front of me, giggling in response. "Far out. Yes, tracks of passion."

I see Wren standing, reaching for her walker for balance, and quip at her, "Hey, teammate, that sounds like the title of a book. Will you write it one day?"

Wren smiles with her gap-toothed, jack-o-lantern grin. "Lay it on me, but you first—only after you write your story. And that won't be for a while, because you've so much to do in the next year." I nod in agreement, affirming that these friends are the scaffolding I need to move ahead.

In the food line, Wren, struggling ahead of me, grabs a plate of noodles with one hand and puts it into the walker's basket to show me that she can be self-sufficient. She pushes forward, swaying with the awkwardness of a ninety-year-old woman.

My next stop is the salad bar where I pile my plate with every fresh vegetable

I can find—tomatoes, avocadoes, carrots, onions, mushrooms, and mounds of lettuce. Stefan's homemade bread awaits at the end of this station. I move to the dessert bar and grab some strudel, putting it on top of my salad. I hear Rob's voice from behind me. "Hold it, my Mountaineer Friend. I know we didn't eat much during our last three days of hiking. Remember, we just wanted to hike out as fast as we could." He puts his hand on my tray, touching the strudel. "No need for this. You haven't had any sweets for weeks. You'll get sick."

Disappointed and frustrated that he's patronizing me, I snap, "Okay, but remember, if one bites off more than one can chew, one will never go hungry." Blushing, embarrassed by my sassiness, I return the strudel.

I follow Becky to her table, where Stephanie, Carla, and Wren join us. Carla rolls Wren's empty wheelchair up next to me, saying, "Okay, Wren, you get the place of honor."

Wren pushes her walker aside, and like a climber on a steep face, she grabs the back of the chair and the table, and slowly eases herself around to sit down, her leg braces clicking against each other. I try to help her, but she pushes my hand away, admonishing me, "No, thank you. Hey, don't flip your wig. I want to show you how independent I am."

I laugh, saying, "My gosh, you sure have learned surfer-speak during your time in Los Angeles." The whole group relaxes in a belly laugh, a joy that knits us all together.

McElvey struts toward another table, pausing by us to say, "You, young competitors, teammates—sounds like you're having a fun time catching up." Then, sternly in his fatherly tone, he adds, "Lia, I'll talk to you later."

He ambles away to a place by the fire, his limp more pronounced than I remember, where he's joined by Rob who's apparently very comfortable starting a conversation with him. The two remain alone, as if conniving, but at times glancing back at me. The other workers head off to their familiar tables, some stopping by my table to welcome me home.

Awkwardly, Becky begins our discussion. "So, Lia, we hear you're going to Berkeley for the fall. Why don't you want to stay here with us?" The others nod in agreement.

I stammer, not wanting to hurt their feelings, "For … for two reasons. I do love being with all of you for sure, but you know, I've always wanted to try college. Also, my ankle isn't ready for ski boots yet. I still get some swelling at the incision."

Becky responds, "Okay, I get that. Last spring, we sure did miss you at the final races in Europe. You probably know that none of us did very well after your accident." She takes a moment, groping for the right words. "For sure, all of us were traumatized by the coaches."

"I'm sure." For a moment, I experience the old sense of dread and catch my breath. "So what have you heard about them?"

Carla shakes her head. "That's the strange part. Not a word. No one knows where they went. The US Ski Team administrators aren't talking."

I challenge Becky, "So exactly what did you tell the Chairman of the Board in Maribor?"

She stiffens her lip. "You know, we told the Chairman, David Solomon, about the coaches' abuses, especially Coach Boast's attack on you."

"Oh, good, and what's happened to Tracy?"

Becky continues, "First, Tracy ratted Coach Boast out by telling the Board how he got her pregnant. She also reported how he bribed her, you know, to be quiet, by offering her a position on the Olympic team." Becky hesitates, trying to find the right words. "Did you know that Tracy's talking about keeping the baby?"

I shake my head in confusion, "How can she keep the baby and ski in the Olympics? Why, she doesn't even have the points to make the team."

"Hey, stupid, guess what?" Becky shakes her head in frustration.

"What," I respond, growing angry at her toying with me.

Becky looks around at the other girls who already know what's coming, "He wants her to get an abortion!"

"A what? That's illegal! Not to mention dangerous."

Becky stands up and puts her hands to her waist, "Grow up Miss Naiveté."

Incredulous, yet relieved, I laugh. "Great, if she keeps the baby, then, just maybe she can file a paternity suit against him. Get lots of money." I stand up to be as tall as Becky, adding forcefully, "I'll testify against him and Coach Ryan."

Becky pushes me back down. "Be careful, Lia. Rumor has it that Coach Ryan has gone rogue."

Frightened, I ask, "What … what are you saying?"

Becky sits down and looks around at the other girls. "Just to let you know, he's angry—angry and accusing you of ruining his life, as well as Coach Boast's."

I clap my hands to silence her. "Yeah, ruining his life. What about all of us? Coaches Boast and Ryan deserve everything they get."

Becky grasps my shaking hand. "Okay, okay, you're right. But just to let you know, we've heard rumors that Coach Ryan, after being let go as assistant coach of the ski team, was immediately drafted into the army. Another rumor has it that he went AWOL—he may have joined the Weathermen."

Immediately, the memory of the riot in Washington, DC flashes across my mind, the image of the angry young Weatherman dressed in army fatigues, lashing out at me by the Lincoln Memorial.

I turn to Wren for affirmation, "We all know if you're never frightened or embarrassed or hurt, it means you never take chances."

Worried about how Wren might take my comment, I touch her shoulder. "So now tell me about you. You know I'm still mad at Coach Boast for putting the two bumps in the racecourse that made you break your back."

Wren drops her head. "My friend, I've … I've learned months ago to let my anger go. We all knew the risks we were taking. For sure, it's no use to live in the past. It takes from the present. I'm alive, learning to walk, and plan to go to college, yup. And this will blow your mind—I want to become a teacher, maybe even a writer!"

The image of Gannett Peak flashes through my mind, as I look through the window to the sun setting on Monmouth Mountain. I squint and blink. "I understand. How I understand. I'm also trying to let go of the past." Looking up to the high rafters I muse, "We all have so much to hope for."

Indicating that I should return to my seat, Becky brushes her dark hair away from her eyes and rests her hand on my arm, "You look upset. Please, oh please, promise that you'll come back here in December, you know, after your classes. I—we need your work ethic, your leadership here, so all of us can start training for the Olympic team—okay?"

Before I can answer, I feel a strong presence behind me. McElvey rests his hands on my shoulders, interjecting, "Well, actually Lia will be returning sooner than that. Rob promised me he can bring her back at Thanksgiving for a week of training on snow. He looks up toward the mountain. "That is, snow willing." He nods for me to follow him.

On my way out, the group starts humming the skiers' hymn:

In this white world that reaches the sky

I found a future for me.

McElvey directs me to the back porch, the exact place where Bill told me he would accept his deployment instead of going AWOL. I hesitate until Coach steps between me and the mountain. In his stern voice, he begins slowly, "Lia, Rob has told me all about your hike and your anger around Bill's death in Vietnam. He said that you blame me for encouraging him to serve."

I nod tearfully, stammering to find any words to answer, "But … but … "

He continues, "I can't explain everything to you tonight, because I must go to the summit. There's a problem with the top gondola … it needs to be fixed before morning." He looks me straight in the eyes, clenches his lips, and says sternly, "But I want you to know that Bill assured me, it was his choice."

"I … I understand. I don't exactly blame you. I'm just upset about the whole unjust war." I stop to see his reaction. "I've … I've been through a lot in these last months … anyway thanks for welcoming me back."

He raises his hand to stop me from saying more, "I just want to reiterate that you are the best skier I've ever sponsored, and I definitely want you to come back to train. Of all the racers, you deserve a place on the Olympic team in Sapporo."

Overwhelmed by his belief in me, I'm afraid to tell him that I'm thinking about staying in college and helping the anti-war movement, possibly forgoing my chance for the team.

He bends over and whispers in my ear, "I'm giving Rob a letter for you that will explain everything. I've got to go now, but you'll understand more after he gives you the letter." At a loss to say more, he gives me a tight hug and walks down toward the tractor sheds, his determined body disappearing into the shadow of the building.

CHAPTER 34

Yosemite

With the top down on our way to Berkeley, we drive over Tioga Pass, a bumpy road that rises steeply, its hairpin turns making a slalom course look simple. Rob and I have left Monmouth early to enjoy the sun rising on the ridges and flutes of the High Sierras. These above-timberline peaks, humped with more rocks than the moon, will become my powder fields in just three months.

At the top, Rob stops at the 9,943-foot pullout to look east across the flat desert, where only the cloud smudges identify the contours. The aquamarine water of Mono Lake offers the only color. He starts, "Okay, my friend, now we can talk." He looks around again. "I wanted to give you time to digest what McElvey told you before I asked you what you thought."

Angry at his intrusiveness, I bark, "Don't you already know?" Smoothing my wind-blown hair with both hands, I continue, "Didn't you two plan all this out. I'm growing upset that others seem to be planning my life."

Rob turns away so that I can see his rugged profile against the last remaining winter snow. His ski jump nose reminds me of Pinocchio's, an appendage that kept getting longer.

Not looking at him, I snap, "Well, as you know, he wants me to come back to skiing. He really believes that I've the most natural ability of any racer he's ever seen."

He laughs, "Yeah, that's for sure. That's what I've been trying to tell you. You need to believe in yourself and do what you love—what you do best. Forget the old coaches." Still not looking at me, he continues, "Trust me, I'll find out what happened to them, if that'll give you some reassurance, okay?" He licks his dry lips the way President Nixon does on TV when he's talking about the war.

"Good, as long as I don't have to worry about ever facing them again. Do you promise?"

"My word is as certain as the snows that will come this winter."

"Thanks, now about your telling McElvey about Greta, Will, and Terry. Why did you do that and what do you know about them?" I'm hoping that I can find out the true story, since he promised not to lie.

Playing ignorant to get me to say more, he grumbles, "I'm not sure what you mean to say. Can you be more specific?"

I know I've met my match regarding this interrogation. Not wanting to reveal more information, I ask, "Okay, back up—tell me why you told me you didn't like them."

"Ah, ah … ," he sputters.

"Remember, you can't lie," I smirk.

"Ah, well, first, I'd watched Greta at the train station in Vancouver before you got there She acted like a spy or someone guilty of something. She kept looking around and covering her face."

I laugh and ask, "So you think I'm caught up in a spy story?"

He doesn't answer, just continues, "And also, I'm not sure about your other friend, Will. He also had a worried look when he met Greta. He, too, covered his face with his hat. I guess you didn't see this. And what was the envelope that Greta gave Will to give to you?"

"Okay, Mr. Sleuth, where do you think that envelope came from? You sure have the keen eyes of an FBI agent."

Rob steps out of the car and stands tall in front of me, as if to assert his dominance. "I think it came from the anti-war movement. I think you've gotten into the wrong crowd, a group that may be using you for their purposes. Am I right?"

I shake my head, climb out of the car, and push him back, insisting, "Please don't try to control everything. I do have to figure things out for myself. Remember, you even told me that." In defiance, I raise my hands. "Enough! Furthermore, that … that money was money from my father. Just so you know!"

Climbing back into the car, feeling as if I've taken control, I conclude, "Even Huckleberry Finn had to make up his own mind, you know, whether to obey the immoral laws of the land or to free Jim."

Before I settle into my seat, Rob puts his foot to the accelerator to let me know he's unhappy with my new assertiveness. We speed down Tioga Pass as if we're glissading a snowfield. My shoulder slams into the passenger door every time the tires screech.

We descend into a valley fog where my only reference point becomes the trunks of redwood trees and, on my right, the Tuolumne River. Looking back up the valley, I imagine that I can see Half Dome and Bridal Veil Falls, remembering why John Muir and Ansel Adams revered this place. I wish that we'd have time to do some hiking. Traveling in a car is not much better than traveling in a train— there's little connection with the land.

We pull over next to a stone wall, which protects us from a precipice, a masterpiece constructed by the CCC in the thirties during the Depression. Over me towers the tallest red-barked tree I've ever seen, so high that the top disappears into the mist, its branches condensing the vapor and dropping the beads onto my cheek.

He says nothing, just looks up into the canopy and points to a sign: *Great Sequoia, 2,000 years.* His silence tells me that I need to observe, to learn something. He then hands me a letter. "Here's the letter that McElvey wants me to give you." He hands me a large white envelope. "He knows about your anger and decided to share this with you."

I take the envelope and slide my index finger under the flap. Inside I recognize Bill's handwriting, so I hold the letter up to my nose to try to smell his presence.

The letter begins:

APO 24

US Army

Vietnam

January 1, 1971

Dear Coach,

With all my heart, I thank you for the time you gave me to train at Monmouth. I know you tried to help me to get a spot on the US Ski Team. Unfortunately, Coach Boast had other skiers he wanted on the team. I have accepted my deployment and will be leaving for Vietnam in a week. If I don't return, please tell Lia that she was my first and only love and give her this poem.

I will serve my country with pride and want her to do the same on the US Olympic Team.

With eternal thanks,

Bill Emerson

Another folded paper falls into my lap. Rob looks down, surprised that there is more, and says, "Go ahead. Open it. I'm not sure what's in there."

I gently unfold the paper and read the typed poem aloud:

That we are still. To Lia,

Death is nothing at all,

I have only slipped into the next room

I am I and you are you

Whatever we were to each other,

Call me by my old familiar name,

Speak to me in the easy way you always used to

Put no difference into your tone,

Wear no forced air of solemnity or sorrow

Laugh as we always laughed

At the little jokes we enjoyed together.

Play, smile, think of me, pray for me.

Let my name be ever the household word that it always was,

Let it be spoken without effort,

Without the ghost of a shadow on it.

Life means all that it ever meant.

It is the same as it ever was,

There is absolute unbroken continuity.

Why should I be out of mind

Because I am out of sight?

I am waiting for you, for an interval,

Somewhere very near,

Just over the mountain.

All is well.

Henry Scott Holland

Staring back up the valley into the mist, I squint and blink. I imagine that I see the shadow of Bill striding along the Muir Trail, a rainbow halo encircling him, like the Brocken spectre. Walking next to him is a smaller person with a rucksack, floppy coat, staff, long beard, and large brimmed hat.

CHAPTER 35

San Francisco

My first sight of the Golden Gate Bridge convinces me that I'm in a new world, having only seen this iconic structure in *National Geographic*. Rob pulls the car over for a watery view just before we cross the Bay Bridge into the city, where I'll pick up my belongings at Aunt Susie's, my mother's sister. The fog slouches under the Golden Gate, consuming the water, the sky, and even the sun, resembling a jelly fish crawling out of the sea.

Once in the San Francisco hills, we're confused by the switchback streets, more lost than we ever were in the wilderness. We actually go the wrong way up Lombard Street, a path with more curves than a string of paper clips. Halfway up, a police car pulls us over. Rob doesn't flinch. He rolls down his window as I cover the side of my face with my hand.

The officer, checking out Rob's Colorado plates, tries to intimidate him, "Sir, I see you're a visitor, but this is no excuse for going the wrong way up a one-way street." Threateningly, he scans the inside of the car and glares at me. "Are you okay, Miss? You look a little bit, ah … "

Remembering my encounters with the police in Washington, DC, I panic before I can say, "Ah, yup. We've been camping for two weeks in the mountains. I'm just tired."

Turning back to Rob, he demands, "License and registration, sir."

Rob opens his wallet that's padded with hundred dollar bills. I gasp, not knowing he has so much money. He hands the license and some other papers to the officer who returns to his cruiser. While waiting, Rob turns to me. "Oh, yes, I see you're wondering about the money. McElvey gave me some starter money for you in case you want to rent an apartment near campus. You may have a problem getting college housing."

The officer marches back with Rob's papers, proclaiming, "Oh, so sorry, sir. You're free to go. No problem here." He then stands at attention and salutes Rob, saying, "We could use more of your kind here in the city. The students are starting to riot again."

Rob waits for the officer to stride back to his cruiser and shut off his blue lights before he asks, "Are you okay, my friend?"

Not sure what to say first, I stutter, "Wow ... wow, you seem to be very sure of yourself. Why'd the officer back off so quickly?"

Rob starts the car, turns around and says, "I'll tell you later. Let's just say, I've got connections."

He puts the top down as we continue to explore the city, hoping to see as much as we can before the fog obscures the buildings. Once on Haight Street, I gag when I see the long-haired hippies gathered on the street corners: girls bedecked with flower tiaras, long cotton skirts, and gaunt faces; guys covered with uncut hair, beards, bell-bottom pants, flowered shirts, or no shirts, torn military jackets, and frameless John Lennon glasses. Kids hang out the bay windows of the blue, red, and yellow Victorian row houses. Cigarette and pot smoke drift into our car. A sitar player, sitting cross-legged and wearing a Nehru shirt, strums a strange tune.

At the exact corner of Haight and Ashbury, we stop for a tipsy boy, who steps in front of our car, gives us the peace sign, and yells, "Hey man, you got any dope? Or at least some money, so I can get some." He laughs at the finger that Rob gives to him.

I nudge Rob, "Let's get out of here. I'm not comfortable with this scene. Remember, Coach McElvey hates marijuana more than anything. He'll kick a kid off his team, you know, if he's caught with it, just like he did to my friend, Brandy."

Rob spins the car around, barely avoiding the boy and his friends who are running to help him. Rob yells, "Go get a job or join the military." A bouquet of flowers, along with a fistful of pebbles, shower down on us as the protestors try to catch us.

*   *   *   *

Aunt Susie greets me at her Nob Hill house with a huge smile and a hug. Her coiffed gray hair smells of my mother's favorite perfume—Tabu. Pushing me back, she looks me up and down. "Oh my dear, I think we'd better get you cleaned up with some more appropriate clothes. You look like one of those darn hippies. My, have you grown." She turns to Rob, holds out a limp hand, and whispers, "And I've been so looking forward to meeting you. Many thanks for looking after my niece."

Rob, self-consciously straightening his t-shirt and taking off his baseball cap, bows. Both of us sense we've entered another world—one of money, decorum, and etiquette. I haven't seen Aunt Susie since my mother's funeral nine years ago. She leads us into a sunlit living room; large glass windows look out over the bay where the fog continues to crawl up the hillside, reaching with claw-like gossamer wisps. She asks us to sit, offering, "I'll get you some tea and cookies and let you enjoy this special moment—the fog is a miracle, one that happens every evening. Nature can be so predictable." I smirk at Rob, remembering all the unpredictable dangers we'd just encountered.

When she returns, I've a million questions running through my mind, mostly about my mother whose picture sits on the side table next to my picture. Aunt Susie never married, so she's lived vicariously through my family, that is, until my mother died and we lost touch.

I let her question me first, because I sense her nervousness about my travels with a single man. In a few minutes, when she seems to be more comfortable with Rob and trusts that he's truly a friend and gentleman, especially a navy man, as she eases up on her interrogation.

She turns to me and says, "Okay, my dear, I sense you'd like to ask me some questions. Let me show you to your rooms first and let you freshen up. Over dinner, I'll answer your concerns. After all, it's been a long time since we've seen each other."

I nod and self-consciously adjust my bagging jeans.

Over a dinner of beef bourguignon, I begin to ply her with questions that I've never dared to ask my father, questions that have haunted me about my mother's life. "Can you tell me about my mother's childhood and upbringing?

All I know is that she was born in Concord, Massachusetts. I think that's why she had so many books by Thoreau, Emerson, and Hawthorne. In fact, I think many were first editions, treasures that she wouldn't let me touch."

Aunt Susie takes a deep breath before answering, "Oh, that's where those books went! I always thought that she'd stolen them after our father died." She leans forward aggressively and then settles back to explain my mother's background. Their father, my grandfather, George Willard, had been a professor of American literature at Harvard. My grandmother, Bessie, had been a stay-at-home mom. My mother had been a tomboy, while Aunt Susie became a scholar. She went to teacher's college while Mother, a frustrated athlete, married my father, Stan Erickson, right after high school. I came along in 1952 to everyone's joy, but my mother was never able to accept her role as a housewife and child-keeper. My father, in his old-fashioned way, demanded that she not work outside the home, even though he made very little money as a teacher.

Aunt Susie gets up and changes seats to sit closer to me. She puts her hand on my knee and continues, "Do you know anything about alcoholism, my dear?" I shake my head.

"Okay, let me tell you. Your mother discovered alcohol, a drug that could take away her depression, as well as her sense of frustration. She always felt she had no control of … of her life, of her inherited money, of her sense of self-worth." She shakes her head, remembering. "She was always jealous of my independence."

I gulp to hold back the tears, recalling the nights when my mother would storm out of the house after dinner, threatening not to return, or worse, to commit suicide.

Aunt Susie explains how alcohol can change one's personality, makes them withhold affection, and cause depression and moodiness. For the first time, I'm beginning to understand my longing to hear the words, "I love you," from both my parents.

Aunt Susie looks away. "What I'm going to say next will be difficult for you, my dear, but you need to know." Pausing and turning back to me, she softens her voice, "My dear, you know that your mother died in a car accident. What you don't know is that we think she purposely drove off the side of the Appalachian

Gap, right at the top."

She waits for my reaction, so I pretend I've known this all along by nodding affirmatively.

She continues, "Your father shut down most of his emotions after that and never wanted to speak to me again. I honored this, as I understood how painful it must have been." She picks up my picture, the one of me when I was ten. "He also didn't want me to contact you. I've only been able to follow your successes through newspaper articles, you know, about your skiing." To emphasize her point, she stands up, "And I'm very proud of you."

Reaching down to help me to my feet, she gives me a smothering embrace. Confused, I look out the window to see the fog now licking at the glass, while the sunlight has turned an ashen gray.

CHAPTER 36

UC Berkeley

Finding the administrative offices at Berkeley requires reading the campus map like a trail map. I've never seen so many buildings hidden behind buildings with no connecting roads, just paths. Once we find Sather Gate, an ornate, curved, fairytale entrance, we follow the brick walkway to Sproul Plaza and Sproul Hall. Granite buildings sprout from the grounds without the warmth and familiarity of the mountains. I wonder if this is what I really want, but then I think about all the knowledge that lies hidden within them.

Being early, I have half an hour before my meeting with the Dean of Students, so I ask Rob to explore with me. He seems more comfortable with the complex campus, perhaps because of his years at the Naval Academy. We find Bancroft Library where I know I'll spend much time; Wheeler Hall, home of the English Department; the Botany Building; and the small Geography Quonset hut. On the path back to the Administrative Offices, I pick up a copy of *The Daily Californian*, the University newspaper, and check out their address on Hearst Avenue, a must-visit if I'm to follow Greta's instructions.

Rob leaves me at the Administrative Office to get his lunch at the Student Union, now confident that I can arrange my courses and, maybe, even my living situation. The Dean of Students, Mrs. Kelly, dressed in a masculine, two-piece navy-blue suit, her small head framed by a tight perm, greets me formally. Squinting, sizing me up and down, scrunching her pointed nose, remaining behind her desk, she sneers, "My, you do look just like I thought, uh, a skier, strong and tanned."

Taken aback, I acknowledge, "Well, I've been hiking in the Wind Rivers. I've been outside for two weeks." Embarrassed, I smooth the wrinkles in my tan slacks and straighten my white blouse, "Well, I guess I'm not so well-dressed for an interview."

"Not to worry. With the rioters here, the campus has become very informal." She opens a folder on her desk, begins to shuffle the papers, and challenges me, "So you'd like to come to Berkeley for the fall semester; that is, before you go back to the US Ski Team."

"Uh, I thought I was all set for the year. Didn't you receive my tuition payment from the ski team?"

She shuffles more papers. "Oh here it is. Yes, the coach sent five hundred dollars to cover your costs, but just for one semester." She paws more papers, "I guess he didn't send any money for room and board. I believe he thinks you can find your own housing since you may not be here long."

"Excuse me. What makes you think I may leave?"

She flips more papers, "It says here that you plan to go back to the team in December and try out for a place on the Olympic Team. I think it's in Sapporo."

Shaken that others have planned my future, I assert, "To tell the truth, I haven't decided whether I want to do that. Can you tell me who wrote that letter, please?"

She runs her finger to the bottom of the page and impatiently asserts, "It is signed by John Boast, Executive Director of the US Ski Team."

I gasp, put my head into my hands, and shake. "Oh no! I thought he'd been dismissed from the team." The horror of Maribor, his alcoholic breath, his unzipped pants, my slashing at him with my razor, all flash like a strobe light inside my brain.

Mrs. Kelly gets up and walks around her desk to place her hands on my shoulder. "Are you okay? Did I say something wrong?"

Gathering my breath and trying to erase my last image of Boast in my room in Maribor, I whisper, "I ... I'm okay. I just didn't know he was behind this."

"Well, young lady," she scowls, "you should be grateful to have such support."

I look behind her at her framed diplomas, especially her PhD in Education, and assert, "I'm not sure I want to go back to the team. Not after ... " I can't finish my sentence.

She moves back behind the desk and pulls out another piece of paper, saying calmly, "I'm confused. Anyway, to help you with your expenses, I also received a letter from a Greta Borst who has found a place for you to live, um, with a friend of hers, a Mrs. Rothstein. The woman has a daughter who needs to be attended to at night. Mrs. Rothstein has offered you room and board, if you will stay at the house in the evenings, taking care of her daughter, Sandra. She has to work at Bancroft Library."

Mrs. Kelly rubs her chin and looks me straight in the eyes, smiling, "The house is on Shasta Road. It's a beautiful location with a view over the bay to San Francisco and the Golden Gate Bridge. Ah, yes, you can walk across Hearst Avenue to campus from there. You'll not find a more beautiful view here in Berkeley." She glares at me, "You're a lucky girl."

Overwhelmed by all this news, I ask, "May I meet her this afternoon to see whether I like the situation?"

"No problem. "I'll have my secretary call her to see if you can go up after our meeting." She picks up her phone and ask her secretary to make the call.

"Thanks," I add, letting a wave of relief run though my body.

"Now young lady, what about your courses? You'll need to sign up for four. I recommend you get some of your freshman prerequisites out of the way. You'll need to take a foreign language, a science and an English course, and one other." She hands me a form to fill out.

Confidently, I declare, "I've decided to continue with my French studies. Can I take French 2, a botany course, and two English courses? Maybe American literature and Shakespeare?"

"All right, but you'll have to take a test for French 2. I can arrange that. I don't recommend two English courses, as that could be a heavy load." She squiggles her fingers on the desk. "You know, lots of writing."

"I know, but I've read Shakespeare every year in high school. Also, I want to be a writer, so I'm prepared for the hard work." I'm feeling very self-assured, proud of my writing ability.

Mrs. Kelly gets up, takes my completed form, and politely shakes my hand.

"Good luck, Lia. I'm impressed with your self-confidence. Please call me if you have any questions or concerns." She points to the door.

Rob is waiting for me in the annex with a sandwich and a huge grin on his ruddy, sun-burned complexion. "Well, it looks as if you once again have taken charge, my friend, right?"

"Uh, I'm not sure what you mean."

"Oh, the secretary gave me the name of a woman who'll give you room and board. I've orders to take you up to the house right now." Handing me a piece of paper with the note from Greta, he continues, "Apparently, Greta has made housing arrangements for you. You certainly have impressed many people."

"You seem a tad angry. You know that you and Coach McElvey don't have to make all the arrangements for me." I huff and continue, "I know you don't like Greta, but she's been very helpful to me, especially in Washington." I lift my shoulders to assert myself. "I think you know that."

Rob shrugs his shoulders, unwilling to respond. He squeezes my elbow. "No matter. Let's go up the hill to Mrs. Rothstein's house to see if you like the situation, right?"

Once again, in his Austin Healey maneuvering the steep hills, we find the large Tudor house perched on the side of a pine-covered slope. The stone walkway, laden with moss, barely looks used. The wooden sides of the house still drip with moisture from last night's fog. A strange smell wafts around the side of the house—an oily, pungent, wet-wool-sock odor that makes me sneeze. Rob laughs, "You'll get used to that odor. It's eucalyptus, a common tree in California."

The side door opens and a hunched, gray-haired woman waves to us. "Please, please come this way. I rarely have visitors and only use this door." She holds out her hand, but before I have time to shake it, she gives the "A" sign with her three fingers and then bows. "Welcome, Lia. Greta has told me all about you. Please come in. I'm Loretta."

She turns toward Rob. "And who might you be? Greta didn't tell me you had a boyfriend."

Rob backs up and bows, "Oh, I'm Lia's hiking friend and I guess you could say chauffeur, Rob. Anyway, I'm not staying—just helping her get set up."

The three of us walk into a large cathedral-ceilinged room with expansive views of the Bay and the Golden Gate Bridge. Heavy brocaded furniture fills the center; the walls are covered by shelves containing leather-bound books. Two large Tabriz rugs lie on the dark pine floors. Hanging on the chimney is an enormous triptych painting of the California coastline and surf with fanciful cypress trees clinging to the rocky hillsides. Mrs. Rothstein points to the painting, adding, "My late husband used to be the background artist for Walt Disney's movies. Do you like it?" She moves closer and states, "He did the designs for *Snow White*, *Dumbo*, and *Bambi* to name a few."

Before I can respond, a strange laugh/squeal comes from a side room and in walks a disheveled girl of about twenty-five, strands of dark hair covering her eyes and mouth. She giggles, puts her hands over her face, turns to her mom, and asks, "Oh, so ... so this is my new caretaker?" She giggles again and turns to me, revealing rotten teeth. "I think we'll be good friends." I step back from the odor of unwashed armpits and bad breath.

Mrs. Rothstein slides between the girl and me. "Oh, this is Sandra, my daughter. Please forgive her. She just woke up. She's been excited to meet you."

I start to speak, but Mrs. Rothstein holds up her hands, continuing, "Sandra has schizophrenia and often doesn't abide by all the social graces." She then turns to Sandra. "Please go back to your room and get dressed and comb your hair." Turning back to me, "I'm sure our guest will be happy to meet you then."

Mrs. Rothstein leads Rob and me out to a terrace overlooking the bay, where she has placed some cookies and iced tea. A glacier-blue swimming pool balances over the cliff. She offers me a snack, politely cajoling, "Let me explain my situation. I do hope this will work for you." Wistfully, she looks out to the Bay, "Sandra has been so excited that you'll be coming."

I look at Rob for support, saying, "Many thanks—so much has happened today that I feel overwhelmed. Greta never told me she was making these arrangements."

"Oh, I understand. This came about while you were hiking in the mountains. Greta has been my friend since our childhood in Dresden. I'm sure she told you about losing her parents in the Holocaust and how she and I were secretly adopted by the German family Borst."

"Ah, yes, she did." Not sure whether to say more about my time in Washington with Greta, I look at Rob who seems to be very interested in this story.

Mrs. Rothstein senses that I don't want to talk more, so she changes the subject. "Okay, let me explain my situation here. My daughter has been in and out of mental institutions—a horrible experience. I want her to be able to stay at home. She needs someone with her twenty-four hours a day, seven days a week." She smooths her wool skirt and waits for my response before she offers, "I can cover all daytimes, but I need time to work in the evening as a librarian, just four nights a week. This is where you'll come in. After your classes, in the evening from 6:00 until 10:00, I need you to give Sandra dinner and help her get to bed. She is very easy to work with."

I look out over the bay, shaken, "But I know nothing about schizophrenia."

"No problem. Did you ever do any babysitting when you were young?"

"Of course, I loved to take care of kids, especially eight- to eleven-year-olds."

"Okay, then, you know how to handle Sandra. She obeys every instruction like … like a child."

The French doors behind me open as if on cue and Sandra walks in with a Teddy bear. She hands it to me, smiling, "Here, you can hold my bear." She sits down and grabs a cookie.

Mrs. Rothstein grabs her hand and demands, "Now, dear, remember you must ask first."

Putting the cookie back, Sandra asks, "Mother, may I?"

"Of course, my dear, but then please go back to your room, so I can finish talking with Lia and Rob." Sandra stoops to reclaim her Teddy bear.

Mrs. Rothstein rises, gesturing, "Let me show you the separate apartment and the rest of the house. You can use anything you want and enjoy the pool and view."

While Rob stays behind, she leads me to a small bedroom off the kitchen that has a view, a library, and a kitchenette. On the bed I discover that the Teddy bear is already resting on the quilted spread. Feeling very welcomed, even excited to be a part of a family and at the same time able to help someone out, I remember my mother's name for me, Rosa Rugosa—one who can grow anywhere. Eagerly, I turn to Mrs. Rothstein and exclaim, "This is perfect. I'll take the job."

CHAPTER 37

My Days

Three days later, my class schedule arrives in the mail. By now, I've picked up my clothes at Aunt Susie's and settled into a routine at Mrs. Rothstein's. Rob, rushing to get to his job at the El Diablo power plant, left me with a quick hug and a promise to drive me to Monmouth during Thanksgiving break. I cried when he left, feeling deserted by a friend with whom I'd started to fall in love.

I work best with a routine, so each morning I pad sock-footed into the kitchen to smell Mrs. Rothstein's bacon and eggs and fresh coffee while she routinely asks me, in a motherly tone, "How'd you sleep?"

In the fashion of a self-absorbed teenager, I mumble something like, "Okay." Then I correct myself, grateful that someone cares and continue, "Thanks for asking and you?"

Before classes, I take a short two-mile run up Shasta Road and through the Berkeley Rose Garden, past the tennis courts. Later, during my mile walk down to campus, I memorize my French words. My Shakespeare class, nineteenth century literature class, and botany class are all lectures, so I'm becoming proficient at notetaking. After classes, I run five miles up to Grizzly Park, through the sagebrush, along the ridge, and down Centennial Drive. At the top, I relish the view east over the barren hills and reservoirs, but rue that I can't see my beloved High Sierras.

Some evenings Sandra and I take a swim in the pool as the fog blanket rolls in, its ruffled surface often glowing from the moon's tint. Sandra is easy to please; she loves to be alone, either watching her TV or playing with her dolls, allowing me, after dinner, to study from 6:00 to 11:00 pm.

After three weeks of this routine, I'm missing my mountain life, and especially Rob. I also long for the camaraderie I'd found on the ski team, where my teammates pushed me to work harder, and my coaches planned my schedules.

Finally settled in, I call for an appointment to meet the editor at *The Daily California*. Using Greta's name for introduction, I learn that he's expecting my call. Unfortunately, his off-campus office is a mile away on Bancroft Way.

The subterranean newspaper bunker resembles a war room. Desks, typewriters, and papers are strewn around, surrounded by articles pinned to the wall, along with a photo of President Nixon, defaced by a hen-scratched epithet, "Liar."

In the doorway, I'm confronted by a student dressed in a flowered shirt and torn jeans. She demands, "Excuse me, do you have an appointment? You know, we must be careful about who enters here."

I show her the letter I have from Greta, and she immediately moves closer and gives me the finger "A" sign, saying, "Cool."

I'm shocked when Greta comes out a side door. I barely recognize her. She's dressed as a hippy outfitted in a headband, baggy shirt, bell bottom pants, and sandals. Laughing, I exclaim, "Wow, in all my life I never expected to see you dressed like this!"

Blushing, she says nothing and beckons me into an office. After closing the door, she turns to give me a big hug. "How good to see you, my friend. I've worried about you for the three weeks … that … that you were lost in the mountains."

"Oh, not to worry. First, I wasn't lost. Second, Rob took good care of me. He's an expert mountain man, you know."

Waving her hand in dismissal, she answers, "Yes, I know all about him, but …" She hesitates and says, "I'm worried that he might work for the FBI."

"What! He never mentioned that! He told me he's a nuclear engineer and is going to help build a power plant at El Diablo."

"I'm not so sure he's to be trusted. Ja? Our protest group, Antigone, has been doing research on him." She looks at a poster of students protesting at the US Capitol. "I hope you didn't tell him about Terry and me, and your life in Washington, DC." Her voice snaps like broken glass.

"He knows you've helped me, but I haven't told him about your involvement with the protest movement. Give him a break. He just helped me, you know, to gain confidence by teaching me how to test myself in the mountains." Growing impatient with all the subterfuge, I raise my voice, "You probably know that he wants me to go back to the ski team after this semester."

"I know that, but I, on the other hand, need you here in Berkeley to help us, specifically with gathering and disseminating news about the war." She shakes her head. "Our group knows for sure that President Nixon and Secretary Laird are lying about America's involvement. Such deceit. Ja? They are trying to appease the American public by saying America is pulling out troops and getting close to a treaty."

She points at Nixon's picture on the wall. "Meanwhile, the US Army continues to bomb Cambodia, napalm the South Vietnamese villages, and spray Agent Orange over all the forests." She rubs her cheek, her voice trembling. "We … we are destroying the people and poisoning their beautiful land. Not to mention the psychological toll this war is taking on our own American troops."

She hesitates for a minute and then continues, "No one even knows if these chemicals will cause cancer and other lifelong problems later on." She raises her fist and cries, "Such war crimes against humanity!"

"Okay, but back up for a minute. Can you please explain to me what this secret group 'Antigone' is all about? You know, your secret sign and all."

"Calm down, please! Okay, sit down for a minute. I'll give you a short history lesson."

She senses that I crave any form of learning and pulls a chair up in front of me. "Maybe this will persuade you that our cause has a long history."

I stretch out my legs to rest my swelling ankle on my other foot and sigh. "Great, finally someone wants to play straight with me."

Greta continues, "Okay. Let's go back to the Greek times, about 460 BC. At that time, Sophocles wrote a play about a heroine, Antigone."

"Oh, so this is going to be a history lesson. I think I remember her name. So, what does this have to do with us now?"

"Relax, I told you once that history repeats itself." She stops and smiles ironically. "No, better to say history is bidirectional. From our perspective it's not certain whether we are becoming part of the past, or if the past is just reasserting itself in the present, or if we are all just in a vortex whirling and swirling. No past, present, or future—ja?"

"Okay."

"Well, Antigone was the daughter of Oedipus. She had a sister, Ismene, and two brothers, Polyneices and Eteocles. Antigone has become the archetype for all female activists and heroines."

""I'm not sure what you mean!" I puzzle, trying to remember my ninth-grade mythology studies.

"Okay, let me walk you through the whole story. Do you remember the myth about Oedipus, who blinded himself after he learned that he'd unknowingly killed his father and married his mother?"

"All gross! Of course, I remember that from my mythology readings."

"Good! Then when Oedipus exiled himself from Thebes, Antigone wandered with him, taking care of his needs."

"Hey, you're right, stories do repeat. This is just like the King Lear story, you know, when his daughter, Cordelia, defied the authorities and took care of him on the heath." My mind is swirling in confusion. "Okay, but … but what happened to Antigone, and what does this have to do with you and me today?"

"The two brothers Polyneices and Eteocles fought for control of Thebes. They were both killed. Antigone returned to Thebes to bury her brother, Polyneices, according to custom and religion, so that he could start his journey into the afterworld. Antigone was mad, because the Theban King Creon had ruled that Polyneices was a traitor to Thebes and anyone who buried him would be killed, while he had deemed that his brother, Eteocles, was a hero and should receive a noble funeral."

"So, what did Antigone do?" I gulp, fearing the answer. "Did she go against the law of the land?"

Looking directly into my eyes, she asserts, "Yes, stubborn and self-willed, she defied the king and declared that divine law, moral law, overruled manmade laws. So, she buried her brother."

"I'm beginning to see a pattern."

"You got it. Finally, in anger, Creon decreed that Antigone must be buried alive in a chamber."

"What? How cruel!" I pause, trying to absorb what she's telling me. "Okay, okay, now I get your point. Sometimes government decisions are wrong, and people must stand up against them, even at personal risk."

"Now you see."

"What a tragedy. So, what happened to her?"

Greta stumbles at this point. "Um, yes, it is tragic, because after Antigone was entombed, Creon recanted his decision to kill her and went to release her. But ... but she had already killed herself." She stands up, gives me the finger letter "A" and concludes, "So our protest movement has chosen her as our secret code. Don't look so shocked. Maybe, just maybe, one day the American government will recant and tell the people that this war in Vietnam is wrong, unjust. But instead of one life being lost, Americans will have lost thousands. Now that's a tragedy."

Like waves crashing on the shore, adrenaline and fear sweep through my body. "I get it, like Antigone, like Cordelia, we—I, have the power to make a difference. But ... but I'm scared ... it always seems to go badly for the heroines." Forgetting for a minute my dreams of college and the ski team, impulsively, I stand up and grab her hand. "Okay, so what do you want me to do?"

"Well, the FBI has infiltrated and identified most of the leaders of the protest movement here on campus. I'm counting on you to become our liaison between Terry in Saigon and others—brave ones who'll send the real story, the truth, back to Berkeley and the campus newspaper." She pounds her fist on her desk. "We must keep the protest movement going or Nixon will get away with his war crimes, his lies."

"And how will I do this? My days are already full."

She waves away my plea, as if batting a fly. "You have no idea how perfect you are to help us. No one will suspect you, because you are so innocent—you spend your mornings and afternoons running in the Berkeley Hills. We'll set up a contact place in the hills for you—you know, where you can receive the weekly reports and pictures from Vietnam. You can then bring them here to the newspaper. I'll make sure you get a small job working here as a weekend editor." She winks at me, "How would you like to edit the sports features? That should be a natural for you."

Once again, I'm overwhelmed with anger against the war, remembering Bill Emerson's death by friendly fire and my many friends who've been drafted. "Of course, I'll help. After all, you made the arrangement for me to live at Mrs. Rothstein's, who, by the way, acts like the mother I never knew."

A wave of relief crosses her face, "I was hoping for that. When I first met you, you ... you seemed lost, lacking the love that only a mother can give, ja? I knew Mrs. Rothstein would be perfect. I've never known a more caring person. She absolutely loves her daughter and tells me that you fit right into the family."

"Thanks. She certainly looks after my needs and even brings me library books for my papers on Shakespeare and Hawthorne. Better yet, she also proofreads my papers, sometimes giving me new ideas." I straighten my new blue and yellow U. Cal sweatshirt. "How lucky I am."

"Great. Also, I hope that here at the paper you'll become more involved with the other students and maybe even meet some boys." She laughs and says, "You know that the newspaper staff is a very friendly group."

I shake my head. "Sounds like you're planning my life. Tell me what I need to do." Before she answers, a dark-eyed, black-skinned, frizzy-haired boy saunters into our room and sits down. His nose and mouth are covered by a tie-dyed bandana. I cringe, rarely having been around an African American.

Greta steps forward. "Lia, relax. Meet Sam. He's the student editor and will walk you through your responsibilities. I have to leave now. I'm organizing a protest in San Francisco this coming Saturday. You're welcome to join me sometime." She gives me a gentle hug and whispers, "I trust you." Before leaving, she pulls her headband down to cover her nose and mouth.

Sam straightens his bandana and pulls some papers from a folder on his desk.

He carefully lays them out in order. He doesn't look at me, but just continues rearranging them. The silence is palpable, so I push my chair back, hoping to get his attention. He looks up, annoyed, and in a muffled voice says in a southern twang, "I'd no idea that y'ave such an amazing background, cool, a World Cup ski racer. Greta only told me that ya're a risk taker. An angry one at that."

"I'm not sure what you're reading." I pause, looking around the room as if assessing the dangers of a downhill course. "All I want is to help out with the antiwar movement, yup, while I'm here at Berkeley." I spot a black-and-white poster behind his desk: *Justice will not be served until those who are unaffected are as outraged as those who are. Ben Franklin.*

"I understand. Greta feels that y'all will be invaluable to our movement. Please, ah, excuse my facemask, but if ya're arrested, I don't want y'all to be able to identify me." He carefully picks up another folder, waving it in front of me. "But before I explain to ya what we're doing here at the campus paper, I've some questions for ya."

He hands me the folder with Rob Attelfellner's photo on the top. Under his name is a navy emblem and a stamp saying Classified and the date March 5, 1971. I open it and see that more than half the sentences have been redacted.

Sam demands, "Who's this?"

Feeling threatened, I flinch and say, "Ah, ah, he's a friend. Someone I met in Switzerland when I was on the World Cup Ski Team. Um, he's supported my skiing career, kept in touch when I got injured, and recently he took me hiking in the Wind River Wilderness." Staring at Rob's navy picture, handsome in his lieutenant's uniform, I continue, "He really believes I have the potential to win medals at the next Olympics in Sapporo."

Sam grabs the folder before I have time to read more. "Interesting choice of friend, since y'all profess to be so opposed to the war." He emphasizes the word "war" as if describing a dirty garbage dump. "How am I to trust y'all, ya know, with our sources, our facts, and our cause?"

Surprised, I don't answer him. He continues, "But, on the other hand, y'all come highly recommended by Greta. She tells me that she's followed y'all since your days in Europe and that she's worked with ya, y'know when she was arranging the protests in Washington." He stares at me as though interrogating a murder suspect. "I trust Greta's judgment. However, we've worked way too hard to have our organization infiltrated now. The students' antiwar movement has lost momentum, y'know, because the public actually believes President Nixon's lies, y'know, about pulling out troops and seeking a peaceful settlement." He backs away from me, slapping his hand on the table.

I grimace, realizing that he wants more information from me. "Wow, I'm ... I'm confused. Until Greta mentioned it, I didn't think that Rob might be with the FBI. I never talked to him about politics. As for Greta, she knows how angry I am about the war, even to the point that I might not go back to the ski team. I have to decide if the antiwar effort is more important to me than ... " I don't finish my thought because tears are choking me.

Sam pulls out another paper labelled US Ski Team. He reads it to me:

To the President, UC Berkeley.

This is a letter of introduction for Lia Erikson who has been a part of the US Ski Team for a year. Because of a serious injury, she has taken six months off from the team and chosen to go to college at Berkeley.

Enclosed is a check for $500 to cover her tuition for the first semester. After, she plans to return to the ski team and try out for the Olympic Team in December.

My regards,

John Boast Executive Director US Ski Team

Sam puts the letter down so that I can see it. He shakes his head. "It seems to me as if yer future has been decided." He pounds his fist on the table. "So how do y'all want to help us? And how can I trust ya?" He lets his eyes drop, "And do ya really plan on leaving after a semester?"

I jump up, face him, and slap my hands on the table. "How did you get this letter? I think I'm old enough to decide what I want to do. Right now, at this very moment, I want to take classes and help with the antiwar movement. I'm sick about this useless war, about our leaders who justify it for their own purposes.

Our generation, we kids, need to protest, to disrupt the leaders until they have no choice but to end the war or … " I snort, " … or until they're impeached."

Sam puts his hands up to calm me down. "Okay, okay. I feel yer frustration. I trust yer commitment. In fact, Greta gave me a list of some of yer friends who've been harmed by the war including…" He looks down and shuffles some papers. "… including 2nd Lieutenant Bill Emerson, KIA in January 1971; Private Henry David, PTSD suicide July 1971." He stops, letting me digest the fact that he knows a lot about me. "Do y'all want to talk about them?"

"No, ah, not now … their deaths are still too recent. What else do you know about me? Do you also know about my time on the ski team?"

Sam shuffles some more papers. "Oh yes, I've another letter from Greta telling me about yer friends, Becky, Stephanie, Carla, and Wren, and how y'all were molested by Coach John Boast and Coach Dan Ryan. And about how brave y'all were to turn them in to the authorities." He pauses for my reaction.

I cup my head in my hands. "Yeah, right. We turned them in. Little good that did, because now I see that Boast has just been promoted to head of the whole organization. I'm not sure what happened to Coach Ryan. I heard he got drafted. Do you really think I want to go back to that corrupt organization?"

Sam picks up the phone next to his desk and says, "Jane, I've got Lia here with me. Ya know, the skier who wants to help us on the paper … right … ya got it. The one staying with Mrs. Rothstein."

He listens, puts the phone down, and gets up. "Okay, Jane will go over your responsibilities for the weekend work." He puts out his hand, then pulls it back and reaches around to give me a big hug. "Welcome aboard, Lia! I could use someone with yer energy and commitment. I'll catch ya on a run in the Berkeley Hills." He hands me an envelope. "Please read this tonight … it's a project I'm working on."

He leaves without acknowledging my dropped-jaw look, while I wonder if I'm in over my head.

CHAPTER 38

Family

Running through campus, I let the excitement about becoming an editor, an activist, spur me on. The campanile bell strikes five, an exclamation point to my new adventure. I stop at the library to collect my reserve books on Emerson and randomly flip to a page, "Man cannot be happy and strong until he too lives with nature in the present, above time." Mrs. Rothstein was right when she said, "The books will chose you."

Out of breath when I return to the house, I'm greeted by Mrs. Rothstein, waiting outside like an impatient mother. "Lia, I'll be late for work. Please be better about your time."

I welcome her reprimand, knowing she cares. The smell of the chicken marsala dinner tells me she's not too angry. I apologize, "I'm sorry. I had to meet with the editor of *The Daily Californian*. And guess who was at the office."

Without pausing, she snickers, "Oh, you mean Greta and Sam." She shakes her head. "Don't look surprised … we all talk to each other."

Now I understand that I'm part of an extended family who cares, but who also has a mission for me. Hurrying past, I assure her, "Okay, I'm here and can take care of Sandra now. Oh, and by the way, you don't have to pick up the library books for my paper on Emerson. I just got them."

Mrs. Rothstein, unusually dressed in a black skirt and top, steps down the stairs. "Okay, and your dinner is ready. I'll see you at ten."

Inside, Sandra's watching the television while enjoying a fire in the living room. Fog has climbed up the windows and darkened the walls—a chill creeps in. Walter Cronkite gives his daily summary of the war in Vietnam. "Three hundred Vietcong killed, five Americans. And that's the way it is September 16, 1971."

Sandra cackles, "Stupid, stupid people." She begins to rock, tap her cheek frantically, and cry "na … na … na … ," in an effort to self-soothe.

I touch her shoulder to comfort her. "It's okay. We're going to end this war. I'd no idea that this news would upset you so."

She runs from the room, not waiting for me to dish out our meal. When I call to her, she returns with a glass-covered box and sets it on the table. She points to the plaque inside, next to a gold star and a triangular-folded American flag. The engraving reads:

To the family of Solomon Rothstein

Killed in Action

Vietnam September 16, 1970.

America thanks him for his service.

I touch the glass, reread the engraving, and look up into Sandra's tear-streaked face. I reach to give her a hug, but she pushes me back, still crying, "na … na … na … " Running into her room, she slams the door, leaving me alone to watch the fog claw at the window.

Alone, I spoon out my dinner and sit by the fire, opening the letter from Sam.

It reads: *The People's Peace Treaty, December 1970.*

CHAPTER 39

The People's Peace Treaty

Be it known that the American and Vietnamese peoples are not enemies. The war is carried out in the names of the people of the United States and South Vietnam but without our consent. It destroys the land and people of Vietnam. It drains America of its resources, its youth and its honor.

We hereby agree to end the war on the following terms, so that both peoples can live under the joy of independence and can devote themselves to building a society based on human equality and respect for the earth. In rejecting the war we also reject all forms of racism and discrimination against people based on color, class, sex, national origin, and ethnic grouping which form the basis of the war policies, past and present, of the United States government.

1. *The Americans agree to the immediate and total withdrawal of all U.S. forces from Vietnam.*

2. *The Vietnamese pledge that, as soon as the U.S. government publicly sets a date for total withdrawal, they will enter discussions to secure the release of all American prisoners, including pilots captured while bombing North Vietnam.*

3. *There will be an immediate cease-fire between U.S. forces and those led by the Provisional Revolutionary Government of South Vietnam.*

4. *They will enter discussions on the procedures to guarantee the safety of all withdrawing troops.*

5. *The Americans pledge to end the imposition of Thieu-Ky-Khiem on the people of South Vietnam in order to insure their*

right to self-determination and so that all political prisoners can be released.

6. *The Vietnamese pledge to form a provisional coalition government to organize democratic elections. All parties agree to respect the results of elections in which all South Vietnamese can participate freely without the presence of any foreign troops.*

7. *The South Vietnamese pledge to enter discussions of procedures to guarantee the safety and political freedom of those South Vietnamese who have collaborated with the U.S. or with the U.S.-supported regime.*

8. *The Americans and Vietnamese agree to respect the independence, peace and neutrality of Laos and Cambodia in accord with the 1954 and 1962 Geneva conventions, and not to interfere in the internal affairs of these two countries.*

9. *Upon these points of agreement, we pledge to end the war and resolve all other questions in the spirit of self-determination and mutual respect for the independence and political freedom of the people of Vietnam and the United States.*

By ratifying this agreement, we pledge to take whatever actions are appropriate to implement the terms of this Joint Treaty of Peace, and to insure its acceptance by the government of the United States.

South Vietnam National Student Union
South Vietnam Liberation Student Union
North Vietnam Student Union
National Student Association

Saigon, Hanoi and Paris, December 1970

Adopted by New University Conference and Chicago

Movement Meeting, January 8–10, 1971

> *Signed:*
>
> *Eugene McCarthy*
>
> *David Berrigan*
>
> *Noam Chomsky*
>
> *Rock Hudson*
>
> *Sam Erdenson*
>
> *Greta Borst*
>
> *University of California Berkeley, California September 1971*

CHAPTER 40

A Chance Meeting

The next morning, disturbed by last night's revelations, I take off early, embraced by the heavy fog. I lope through the Rose Garden, savoring the perfume from the ever-blooming flowers, even stopping at the rosa rugosa to say a prayer for my mother.

The thudding of a tennis ball against a backboard breaks my reverie—the pounding keeps beat with my heart. Through the bushes I spot a dark-skinned young man, hair covered by a baseball hat, dressed in an army fatigue jacket and baggy pants. He turns when he hears my breathing.

In an assured voice, he says, "I thought I'd find ya here."

Scared as if I've met a stalking mountain lion, I gasp, "Are … are you who I think you are?"

"Oh, ya have such perfect grammar. I knew I made a good choice to hire y'all for the newspaper."

Relieved, I sigh, "Oh, Sam. I was scared for a moment. I'm not comfortable encountering strangers in a city. I didn't recognize you without your mask."

He laughs and comments, "Oh such irony, Miss English student. Well, since we've been working together, I've learned I can trust y'all. Now ya can see exactly what I look like. I hope yer not disappointed."

"Uh, why should I be?"

"You know, I'm Black." He turns a three-sixty, so I can see all sides of him.

I laugh awkwardly. "To tell the truth, your skin color means nothing to me. It's what's in your heart."

He waves to dismiss my comment and changes the subject. "Did y'all happen to read the letter I gave ya?"

"Oh … yes, of course. I'd no idea that the students have gotten so organized. Could this People's Peace Treaty ever work?"

"Probably not in terms of the government's actions, but one of ya jobs will be to help disseminate its content to other campuses around the country. This can give hope that the students in Vietnam and America can work together, ya know, to end this horrible war. I love the quote by Carl Sandburg, 'What if they gave a war and nobody came?'"

"Good idea. I'm with you. I'll come in tomorrow to help." Grabbing a tennis ball, I throw it to him.

He hits it back to me. "Nice catch! Hey, before y'all leave, I have to show ya something. I just got these photos from one of our student spies in Vietnam, um, a friend who's been serving two years as an army photographer. Be prepared to be shocked."

He pulls an envelope from his inside pocket. One by one he hands me photos of soldiers, boys our age: two American GIs pushing a Viet Cong soldier out of a flying helicopter; an American soldier standing next to a tent with skulls hanging from the top post; a soldier with a necklace of ears draped around his neck; fields flattened by napalm; and children running naked from American troops, their innocent mouths open in soundless screams.

He then assesses me. "Shocking, right? These should help with the huge protest demonstrations that we're planning around the country in a month. I know that y'know about the incredible worldwide disillusionment with the war. Why even our soldiers in Vietnam are mutinying, sometimes even fragging their own officers." His voice builds to a frenzy, increasing like the buzzing in a beehive.

"What's fragging?"

"Oh, ya've so much to learn! Fragging is shooting their own officers in the back. That way the soldiers don't have to go out on patrol."

I take the photo of the soldier pushing the VC warrior out of the helicopter and study the GI behind him, a frightened boy who looks very much like my friend, Bill Emerson.

Backing away, I feel like I might vomit, but I choke out, "Okay, this is way too much information for me right now. Can I keep this photo? I think I recognize a soldier on the helicopter."

He grabs the picture and screams, "No way! I must keep this as proof of the atrocities. And ... " He hesitates, " ... to protect my source. Are ya okay? Ya'll look as if ya're going to faint."

Concerned, he grabs my arm, "I'm so sorry if ya know him. We've all lost friends in this blasted war. That's why I'm risking everything to help bring this nightmare to an end."

"May I ask what you're risking?"

"My scholarship at Berkeley for one. The possibility that I'll get drafted. Arrested. Imprisoned." He steps forward to emphasize his point, "Even my life. I've been threatened by people on campus, even by some of the security guards." He glares, "And what are y'all risking, my friend?"

I shake my head, not used to being challenged like this. I feel as though I'm on an emotional seesaw. "Well, for one, my chance to race in the Olympics." The mist drifting up the hill grows thicker. I tremble, reaching out into the heavy air, grasping for something I don't even know I want.

Sam reluctantly hands me the photo of the helicopter and Bill. "Here, ya need this more than I do. This will help ya remember why we're risking so much."

I toss the tennis ball back to him. "I'm with you."

He turns, hollering as he leaves, "Once ya get more information, I know that y'll commit to our cause, forgetting the Olympics." He picks up the tennis ball and throws it back at me, reminding me, "The only way for evil to triumph is for good people to do nothing. President John Kennedy."

CHAPTER 41

Studies

Mrs. Rothstein greets me at the door, holding two letters, and with concern in her voice, announces, "Well, my friend, I'm guessing that your friends have determined your Thanksgiving break. The weatherman says the snows have come to the Sierras, four feet, so I'll bet they want you to start training. Sandra and I'd hoped you'd share Thanksgiving with us—you know, like a family."

I glance around the room to the plush couch, to the family pictures on the side table, to the leather-bound books in the bookcase, to the warming fire. "Thanks for inviting me, but … but I promised them I'd return as soon as the first snow fell." I pause, smelling the bacon and eggs cooking. "You sure have treated me like a daughter. I'll just be gone a week."

To hold back the tears, I look away, out the window toward the Bay. My new life seems to be unraveling. Hugging the letters, I run to my apartment, almost tripping on the Oriental rug.

Settling into my fluffy white duvet, I pull out the first letter

Box 24

Monmouth, CA

November 15, 1971

Did you hear that Tracy had her baby and is suing Coach Boast for paternity? She wants us to testify against Boast and Ryan.

Also, you probably know that Boast is the Executive Director of the US Ski Team. So much for our reporting him. Instead of dismissing him, they promoted him.

We heard that Coach Dan Ryan was drafted.

Love, Becky, Carla, Stephanie

I reread the letter, looking for any sign of wavering. They really want me back. The second letter bears the official Monmouth seal, a large snowflake with a skier embossed over it.

Justin McElvey

President

Monmouth Mt

November 15, 1971

Dear Lia,

I trust that you are doing well at Berkeley. You must be thrilled to be studying with the best professors in the country. I know this has been your dream. But now it is time to rejoin the best skiers in the country. You are one of them. I will be coaching you here and on the ski team. As in the past, I will pay your expenses until you go to Europe.

I know you will qualify for the Olympics because you have the points, the work ethic, the skills, and the focus to take on the best in the world.

My best,

Coach Justin McElvey.

I clutch the letter to my heart and then reread it. I know I've no choice. He's supported me, believed in me, and coached me. How can I let him down?

I call Rob Attelfellner to confirm that, as he promised, he'll pick me up in five days.

Mrs. Rothstein walks into my room followed by Sandra, who peeks around her back, clutching her Teddy bear. Mrs. Rothstein closes her eyes and sighs. "So was I right? Do they want you back?" Her voice is hesitant, not wanting to hear my answer.

Unsure, as if I'm at the bottom of a mountain, trying to figure which way up, I take a deep breath. "Yup, and you know I have to go. I promised."

She reaches for my hand and squeezes it. "My dear. I understand. You are lucky to have such an opportunity."

Sandra's tiny body shrinks as she turns and runs from the room, her voice trailing in her self-soothing "Na … na … na.

I pick up on Mrs. Rothstein's encouragement, "Well, thinking of opportunity. I guess I'm lucky to have found you and Sandra. You know that you've been so helpful to me, giving me a home, a family, and helping me with my studies.

"You are most welcome, my dear. Likewise, you've brought much joy to our home."

Eager to change the subject, I brag, "By the way, I just got my papers back from my professors. Guess what?'

"What?"

"Well, remember the paper that you typed for me? You know, the one discussing Cordelia's defiance of her brothers in King Lear. Remember, I compared her rebellion against the state to Antigone's protests against King Creon."

"Why of course. I was so glad you researched Antigone, discovering why we named our protest group after her. Not to mention, you learned the power of women, as well."

"Well, I got an A."

""Wonderful!" She gives me the "A" sign with her fingers. "And don't forget this sign."

"I won't. My only concern is that both their rebellions ended tragically."

"I realize that. But we are hoping that we can change history with what we are doing. Already, President Nixon is trying to figure out a plan to end this dreadful war."

"I sure hope so! And now for some more good news! My botany professor loved my paper on Humboldt, Thoreau, Nature, and Protest. Thanks for getting me Humboldt's book *Cosmos,* as well as Thoreau's essay, "Civil Disobedience." Do you know how much fun it was combining my botany studies with my American literature course?"

"Ah, the advantages of being a librarian."

"Even better, did you know that *The Daily Californian* published my argument that we've no right to destroy the environment in Vietnam, you know, by napalming the villages. Thoreau would have protested, and we must continue to pressure Nixon in the same way."

"Well done, my friend. Your education is already giving you the new ability of expressing yourself, as well as a new self-confidence." She pauses. "No matter what you decide, I know college will be in your future."

"Thanks. Oh, did I tell you about yesterday's protest?"

"Nope. I haven't seen you for a while."

"Well, I'm a little nervous about my reputation at *The Daily Californian.* When I go to the protests at Sproul Hall during my lunch breaks, I think I'm being stalked by a creepy college security guard."

"What … what do you mean?"

"Well, this young officer in his oversized blue uniform always finds me. Yesterday, he heckled me, whispering, 'I know who you are. We don't want your kind here. I know what you did to my friend, Dan.'"

"That's not right. I can report him. And who, pray tell, is Dan?"

"Oh, don't you remember Dan Ryan? He was the other corrupt coach of the ski team, the one who took bribes and also molested us."

"Oh, right. Can you tell me anything more about this young guard?"

I pause, close my eyes, and try to visualize him. "Well, he has short brown hair, a snub nose. And, oh yes, he cracks his knuckles. The sound is like bullets ricocheting off a wall."

Mrs. Rothstein turns red in the face and leaves the room, saying, "I'll report him. You have the right to protest, to publish in the paper, and to listen to the speeches, as long as you remain peaceful. I think he's trying to provoke you or frighten you." She nods and says soothingly, "Try to stay focused. Remember, your exams are in two days."

Deeply concerned, I look out my window at the ghost moon, a thin pasteboard eggshell sliding under the Golden Gate Bridge. I close my eyes, trying to see, to understand.

CHAPTER 42

A New Courage

My exams are spread out, just one a day. For four days, I've foregone my runs in the hills, needing every free moment to study. Sam assures me that someone else can pick up the secret information.

Each exam feels like a ski race—my body tense but confident, my pencils sharp as my ski edges, my mind clear as the mountain air, and my focus narrowed to just the gate ahead. When I start writing my essays, I fall into the zone and my pen flows effortlessly. On the other hand, the multiple-choice questions, primarily in botany, feel random—it's like choosing which slalom gate to exclude in a race. It's a failing strategy.

On Friday after the last exam, I decide to celebrate with a run through Grizzly Park. I trot home to Mrs. Rothstein, who welcomes me, cradling a hot bowl of clam chowder in one hand and a new blue and yellow UC Berkeley vest in the other, saying, "Congrats, my dear New England daughter. I'm sure you aced each exam, just like you'll nail each racecourse. Well done." She looks back at Sandra hiding behind her, "We're both proud of you." I smile contentedly.

A memory of my mother disturbs my thoughts, a woman who could never find the words to congratulate me, instead always wanting more from me. The only way I could decipher her pride in me was to hide in a closet and listen to her brag to her friends. I hug Mrs. Rothstein, whispering, "Thanks, Mom."

Outside, tasting the fog's salty air, I lace my sneakers and lope up Shasta Road, adrenaline pumping through my body like a racehorse at the starting gate—free, strong, and confident.

Uphill, above the afternoon fog-prismed light, I revel in the sapphire sky. A breeze crests the ridge, lifting me into a wash of sun and wind. An explosion of brown hills, wave upon wave, stretches east toward my Sierras. The smell of

Dear Lia,

We just received four feet of snow and have started training. The powder is unbelievable, so Coach McElvey lets us free-ski all day. We miss you.

Remember, you promised to join us for training over Thanksgiving. Let us know when you'll be arriving, so we can have your bed ready. You'll be rooming with Carla.

sagebrush smell tickles my nose. My pace increases. My feet leave the ground as soon as they touch—I'm flying more than I'm walking. Pushed along by the wind, my long blond hair, flopping in front of my face, blinding me.

As the trail funnels around a boulder, a skinny hooded man steps out, his lower face covered by a checkered bandanna, his jaundiced eyes glaring like a cougar's. I skid to a stop, extend my arms to create space and blurt out, "Careful, you almost hit me! What do you want?"

Not moving, he cracks his knuckles and then clicks open a ten-inch switchblade. the sun glints off the metal, stunning me. He demands, "Shut up! Don't say a word. Just come with me." He points to an opening in the rocks. "Where's your backpack? I know what you're doing." The mental images of Coach Boast's assault in Maribor and the cougar's attack in the Wind Rivers freeze me.

Glancing around to see whether there's any help near, I judge the space between the rock and him. I gasp, "Let me think about it!" I try to stand tall, but my fear is spiking.

Taken aback, he threatens me by pushing the knife toward my stomach.

Surreptitiously, I fidget to find a small stone on the boulder's ledge, grasp it, throw it into his face, bolt around the flat slab, and head back down the hill. He grabs my vest, but I lower my arms, letting the cloth slip off like a molting snake. He trips but regains his footing. However, the delay puts me ten more paces ahead. He screams, "We don't like your kind!"

The trail that seemed so steep on the way up becomes a floating carpet. The pumping of my legs, the balancing of my feet, allow me to stay ahead of him. Heaving from exhaustion and fear, I don't dare look back. His panting tells me that he's closing on me.

I turn toward a paved road, hoping to find someone, or at least few cars. Observatory Road appears over the rise. I jump a ditch onto the pavement. My ankle buckles. I regain my balance. Hobbling like a wounded deer, I move into the middle of the road. A car careens over the knoll and, without slowing, swerves around me. The driver yells, "Hey hippie, stop dropping acid." Afraid to stop, adrenaline numbing my pain, I don't respond, I just keeping running.

My attacker's breathing gets more labored, louder. He's increased his pace.

While I'm still holding my place on the center yellow line, two cars approach from each direction. Not slowing, they pass me on either side, barely missing my shoulders with their mirrors. I whisper, "Shit," and try to wave them down. They honk in response and a passenger in one gives me the two-finger peace sign out a rear window.

Sweat blinds me, but I continue until I sense he's no longer behind me. Panicked, I veer off toward the Rose Garden instead of home, hoping to find Sam there. Also, I don't want my assailant to know where I live.

No Sam.

CHAPTER 43

Safety

Mrs. Rothstein lifts me from the concrete door stoop when she hears my cries. Her gray hair falls over my eyes as she pleads, "What happened to you?"

I stammer, "Please! Please, help me in and lock the door! Then I'll tell you."

I crawl to the couch bawling and carefully place my swollen ankle on the coffee table.

"My goodness, Lia, you're a mess!"

"I think I twisted my ankle." Pulling down my sock, I notice it's already turning black and blue. "Can you get some ice, please? Then, I'll explain everything."

In her absence, I hear someone move behind the couch, so I jerk upright. An arm reaches over to give me a hug—it's the first time Sandra has shown me real affection.

Mrs. Rothstein returns with the bag of ice. "Okay, now tell me what happened."

I describe the attack, blow-by-blow. Immediately, she puts up her hand. "We have to call the police."

She moves to the phone and dials a number she knows by heart. "There's been a knife attack. Please come to 14587 Shasta Road."

During the fifteen minutes before the police to come, she strokes my forehead, gets me more ice, and reassures me that my attacker won't be able to find me.

When the doorbell rings, she cautiously lets the police in. They force her aside, demanding, "Where's the blood? Who got stabbed?"

I burst into tears again, upset at their seeming lack of concern for me, and at the realization that I could have been stabbed. I moan, "No blood. But ... but I was attacked while running in the Berkeley Hills."

One officer takes off his cap and, kneeling in front of the couch, asks, "Okay, Miss. Can you tell us what happened? Can you describe the attacker?"

Feeling that I'd truly been in danger of my life, I stammer out the story once again. However, I forget to tell him about the knuckle cracking.

He asks, "Do you have any idea who this could be? Can you describe him?"

At this point, I describe the knuckle cracking, the yellow-stained eyes, and his praying-mantis skinny body. Suddenly remembering the security guard who had been threatening me, I declare, "He could be the security guard I know at the college—blond, about five foot, ten inches tall. I shake my head, trying to get the image of the knife blade out of my mind. "I really didn't see his face. He ... he was wearing a mask."

The other officer puts up his hand. "I doubt it. All security people at the college are carefully vetted. Okay, would you mind coming to the police station tomorrow to see whether you can identify him?" He moves toward the door and admonishes me, "You know, many people crack their knuckles."

I feel no reassurance from him. However, remembering that I'd be going to Monmouth tomorrow with Rob, I answer, "Okay, early in the morning works— I'm leaving for vacation tomorrow at noon."

CHAPTER 44

A New Confidence

Rob picks me up early, so we can get to the police station before our drive east over Donner Pass, a six-hour ride to Monmouth. He expresses concern but in a distant way, chiding, "So, do you think you might have done something to provoke the attack?"

"What? Are you saying it was my fault?"

"No, only from what I've heard, you've become quite the radical protester. Also, your articles about the war, about the napalm bombings in Vietnam, have radicalized the protesting students. I've been told that your faux stories and statistics have been picked up by the Associated Press." He stops at a light and stares at me. "You know what I mean—your data about the number of American deaths versus the Vietcong deaths, statistics that contradict everything the government reports on a daily basis." He slowly presses the gas pedal and turns to me, waiting for an answer. A car behind honks forcefully.

Not answering, I simply turn to stare out the window at the passing cars. Anger overwhelms me, and I blurt, "You don't believe me, but ... but I'm certain that everything I write is true."

He continues, "By the way, where do you get your information?"

Sensing that he's probing, I push back at him, "I should ask you the same. Where did you hear all this?"

He rubs his chin and licks his lips. "I have my sources." He waits for an answer, but I keep looking out the window. He acquiesces, "Okay, so someone sends me *The Daily Californian*. No big deal. In fact, I like your writing style— just not your so-called facts."

"Wow, now I'm a well-known writer, I guess." Still avoiding answering directly, I tease, "Anyway, to tell the truth, I'm not exactly sure where all the information is coming from. I'm told that the paper has access to reports from the returning soldiers. My editor, Sam, assures me that everything is the truth."

"I don't think you're telling me everything. How would you get so many startling statistics about deaths, so many pictures of the ruined villages?"

"Hey, I'm just helping out at *The Daily Californian.* Sam gives me the data, telling me that, like all true journalists, we corroborate our facts from at least three valid sources."

Getting ready to lie, I shift uncomfortably. "How do I know where he gets his information?" I hope that Rob doesn't know about my daily jogs into the hills to gather the information. In defiance, I turn to stare out at my last glimpse of the Golden Gate Bridge.

Frustrated, he slams his hands against the steering wheel. "I don't think you're telling me everything—blast it! I just drove past the police station. I'll let you out, find a parking place, and meet you inside."

The cement building has a narrow swinging door where an officious, pudgy secretary checks me in, asking for my driver's license and student ID. I feel like the criminal. She ushers me toward an interrogation room where the officer, who came to Mrs. Rothstein's house, is sitting. The blank room, barren as a jail cell, stinks of stale coffee.

I stare at my reflection in a large one-way window behind him. My straw hair protrudes in rat's-nest bunches and my eyes have dark bags below. A gray metal desk stands between me and the blue-clad officer. He doesn't stand, just indicates that I should sit across from him. I pull out a metal chair while he, licking his finger, shuffles some papers. He slowly returns to a picture of a few students protesting at Sproul Plaza. He grills me as if he already knows the answer. "Is this you with the red bandana over your nose and ski goggles?"

I barely recognize myself except for the blond hair, Bouton ski goggles, and bell-bottomed jeans. "I … I think so." I'm not sure where he got this picture.

"Good. Now do you see anyone in the photo who could've been your attacker?" His commanding voice makes me squirm.

I finger the colored photo, touching each face, but all I see are students, hippies wearing second-hand military jackets, and a few National Guardsmen. I shake my head and answer, "No." Then I look again at a dark half-face behind the students, a man wearing unkempt army fatigues, maybe an ex-soldier who has the dimpled chin of my ex-coach Dan Ryan. Not sure what to say, confused, scared, I hold my breath.

He pushes his chair back, questioning me more. "Once again, are you sure you don't recognize anyone?" He leans forward on his elbows. "You know that many of the returning soldiers are upset by the protest movement. They feel disrespected and unappreciated—even threatened by you students."

I'm beginning to feel as though I'm the villain needing to defend myself. He raises his voice. "Are you sure you were attacked in the hills? You could've been imagining it." He laughs, staring directly into my eyes. "By the way, do you take drugs?"

At this point, incensed, I stand up, push his folder back to him, and announce, "I've … I've never done drugs. I'm an athlete—a World Cup ski racer. How dare you accuse me of that?"

The officer puts his hand up to calm me down. "Easy, just asking."

Fed up, I push my chair toward him and storm out of the room. "I've had enough. I'm leaving for the mountains now. You can't help me."

A hollow pit grows in my stomach, an ache that won't resolve until I can come to grips with the coach's attack, the cougar's assault, the Berkeley predator, and now the possibility of my ex-coach being in the crowd. This fear wells up, an uncontrolled force, like a geyser waiting to erupt.

Hobbling down the narrow hallway, my taped ankle aching, I glance into another interrogation room where I see a black man, face covered by a baseball cap, staring at me. I stop and return to get a better look but lower my head when he puts his finger to his lips and waves me away. I realize that Sam has been brought in, for whatever reason I don't understand. He doesn't know that I was attacked yesterday. I nod discretely, giving him the "A" sign with my fingers.

Rob, pacing in the front room, wearing his ski parka, beckons me over and opens the outside door without saying a word. He can tell how upset I am.

Turning to the secretary as if he knows her, he announces, "Thanks. See you later." I'm taken aback by this statement.

Neither of us speaks until we drive onto the expressway toward Sacramento. Gently, he rests his hand on my knee, asking, "You look distraught. Let me know when you're ready to talk."

I put my head into my hands and start to sob. He turns on the radio to hear Bob Dylan singing, *This Land is Your Land*. Taking a deep breath, I join Rob in singing the words.

This land is your land and this land is my land

From California to the New York Island

From the redwood forest to the Gulf Stream waters

This land was made for you and me.

His voice reverberates throughout the Austin Healey. I close my eyes, imagining that I'm back in the Wind Rivers. Life in the mountains was so simple, a daily assurance that I could control my destiny. I'm wondering if I belong only in the mountains, especially Monmouth, an old sanctuary, where I can return to my former self, to my fun-loving, sports-loving, tree-hugging self.

As Dylan sings the last verse, Rob turns to me, "So, are you ready to talk?"

"Okay, first let me tell you about why I think I was attacked." He nods as if he knows. "You already know about my work on *The Daily Californian*. The reason I run in the hills daily is to pick up packages containing the information about the war. We don't want the authorities to know who's giving us this information, because these sources might even be arrested as spies."

I avoid telling him about Greta and Terry, still fearing that Rob might be an operative for the FBI, just as Greta had warned me. "I'm proud to be involved with the students' efforts to end the war. As you already know, I'm totally against the war. I'm furious at what it's doing to my friends, to my generation's trust in government, and finally to the Vietnamese people." I wipe a tear from my cheek, "My father always taught me to respect authority, but no longer. Boast's attack on me destroyed that belief."

I take a deep breath, happy to be telling him about my work. "No, now I won't be a puppet for other's beliefs. I believe that our President 'Tricky Dicky' is lying to us. I trust my sources and I'm proud that the Associated Press has picked up some of our information, especially about the bombings in Cambodia." Swallowing, I wait for his reaction. He bites his lip and lets me continue. "I'm worried that the attack on me is part of a conspiracy to discover how *The Daily Californian* is getting its information. You know, when I left the police station, I saw that my friend and editor, Sam, was being held in another interrogation room."

As we head up Donner Pass, Rob slams on the brakes and pulls over. "Lia, you don't even know who's making up these so-called facts. Facts can be pawns in anyone's arsenal."

I look at him and argue, "Well, what if I tell you that the facts are coming directly from sources in Vietnam, from the soldiers whose compatriots are dying over there, and from the war photographers who are witnessing the American crimes!"

"Do you want to tell me your sources? Who these people are? You seem to know all about them."

"Nope, I'm sworn to secrecy."

His face reddens. "Okay, then let's change the subject. Do you want to tell me about your courses?"

The car accelerates, forcing me to sit back in my seat. I gather my thoughts while looking out into the dense cloak of lodgepole pines. "Oh, yes, for sure. Let me tell you about the paper I just wrote about Alexander Von Humboldt. My botany professor introduced me to this explorer-poet-scientist." I challenge Rob to see if he recognizes the name.

"Humboldt ... oh, yes, you mean the man for whom the Humboldt Redwood Forest here in California is named."

"Yup, you got it. But remember, Humboldt traveled to the US in 1802. He's so revered by conservationists that he has more places named for him in this country than anyone else." Pleased with my new authority, I continue, "Why, he even met President Jefferson in 1802."

As we speed toward the top of the pass, the snow smudges grow larger. I laugh. "Hey, don't those white patches look like rugs hanging on the backs of animals?"

He slaps his hands against the steering wheel in frustration. "So there you go again. Turning everything into a simile, into something more than it is. Those are just patches of snow."

Feeling empowered now that I've the authority of scientists, professors, and writers, I challenge him," You know, Rob, I've learned from my reading that your Objectivist view of the world, relying only on facts or science, can be dull. Many brilliant thinkers, including Humboldt, have concluded that unless there's a larger vision, one that incorporates myth, tropes, and spirituality, there is no shared meaning in life."

He shakes his head and pauses, trying to absorb my new confidence, and asks, "Shared meaning?" He demurs, "Could you tell me what you mean by tropes?"

I know I've the upper hand and putting my head down in thought, I feel my words and argument starting to unspool like a roll of film. "Here is what Von Humboldt discovered—his ideas have become smelling salts to me. They've convinced me why you and I need many ways of understanding the world." I let my hand scan the horizon. "Science is only one way of looking at the world. Facts teach only the physical understanding, the chemical and physical reason for plants, animals, mountains, and us."

He laughs, rubbing his hand through his freshly cut blond hair, "Oh, good, now you understand why I became an engineer. To understand the physical world."

"Yes, and to create weapons, ships, napalm, and even the nuclear bomb."

"Easy there! I'm using science to help humans by using nuclear power to build electric plants that create reliable energy."

"Okay, but these can be dangerous weapons in the wrong hands." I clap my hands to quiet him. "Humboldt concluded that to fully give meaning to our lives, the world, and our human connection, we also need a deeper truth, a metaphor that we can share with each other and with other cultures. A trope is just that—a figurative expression that gives additional meaning to physical facts."

I stop to find the words I used in my research paper. "An eloquence that can describe the richness of reality. Science teaches only one or two ways of seeing, gives only the physics of our being. However, to see the beauty, we also need to express the subjective emotion and the spirit we feel." The words begin flowing as if I'm giving a lecture. "Art, poetry, and literature can bypass the intellectual understanding and transport us. For example, poetry transcends the intellect, the linear word, and takes us into our collective unconscious."

I sigh, pleased that for the first time, I feel empowered in challenging his narrow view of the world. I can use my research into all the great thinkers, from Plato, the mystic writers, Christian visionaries, to the scientists like Von Humboldt and Einstein and writers like Thoreau and Emerson.

Meekly, Rob nods and asks, "Go ahead, I'm listening. Tell me more."

Searching for the right metaphor, I continue, "Take, for example, a rainbow. To you, a rainbow is simply a collection of water droplets that create a prism that reflects the sun's rays, breaking them into different colors." He nods, acknowledging that I understand his way of thinking. "But to me, a rainbow can be a sign, you know, of luck, of beauty, and even of the mystery of the world. The colored arc always makes me feel happy. Throughout history, poets and prophets have expressed this in their works."

During the next three hours, as we traverse the Sierras, descend into Reno, and battle a snowstorm in the eastern Sierras, I describe the work of Von Humboldt, the new authority who has inspired not just me, but all the Transcendental writers whom I love. I tell him how college is finally giving me the words and the confidence to see the world in a cross-disciplinary fashion. I want him to understand what I love, make him love it too, and teach him how."

Rob doesn't interrupt.

CHAPTER 45

A Snowy Welcome

In the Monmouth parking lot, snow-mounded cars announce that we've arrived at the base lodge, where a few lights pierce the falling white veil. At 7:00 pm, everyone should be inside finishing dinner, so even the entrance isn't shoveled. If I hadn't lived here last winter, I'd think that I'd entered a ghost town or even that I'm the ghost. Stepping out of the car, I lift my head to feel the cold flakes on my tongue, superstitiously trying to interpret the swirling petals, like letters on a page.

Rob senses my anxiety, my fear that I won't be welcomed, that I'm an interloper. He reassures me, "Take a deep breath. Remember, we took two more hours than we'd planned to get here. Certainly, they wouldn't be waiting outside for you. Right?" He gently guides me toward the door. "Why don't you head in. I'll grab your bag and follow." His chuckle tells me he might have a secret.

Climbing the staircase to the first floor, I pass the multi-colored, wall-mounted wooden Olympic rings, a sculpture that'd been my last season's inspiration. Under the symbol are the names of Monmouth's Olympic heroes. A new quote is carved beneath, "*The journey is the goal.*" I stop, salute them, and whisper to myself, "I'm back. Your journey will be mine."

The lights are off in the main dining room, but the smell of Stefan's chicken alfredo draws me in. My stomach growls, reminding me that I haven't eaten since the morning. A roaring fire illuminates the hearth, the pine floors, and the two Adirondack chairs. Rob steps behind me and gives me a nudge. "Go ahead. I'm sure someone is here."

Out from the shadows stride my friends—Becky, Carla, and Stephanie, followed by Wren, struggling. An overhead light bursts on, then blinds me as it bounces off Wren's crutches. The group begins singing our song, *In this white world that reaches the sky / I found a future for me,* before I can say anything.

Joining in, I turn to Rob and smile, while he starts to harmonize in his strong bass voice. In song, I feel one with them.

When we're finished, I step toward Wren to hug her, being careful not to knock her over. Becky, Carla, and Stephanie enfold me in the all-smothering embrace of a mother bird spreading her wings over her nest. I kiss each one on the cheek and step back. "Love you all," I exclaim, and in the same breath add, "Together again, Wren-Becky-Carla-Stephanie-Lia."

From the back of the room, a cough announces a snow-covered man, his hair efflorescent, reminding me of the last time I saw my boyfriend, Bill Emerson, standing there. Coach Justin McElvey enters guardedly so as not to slip on the wet floor. His limp is accentuated while he brushes off his snow mantle and steps toward me. Placing his hands on my shoulders, he whispers, "Welcome back, my friend. You must have brought this storm, this good luck, this blessing." His short, wet, wavy hair drips onto my upturned cheek.

Spinning around to face Rob, I laugh. "See, I'm not the only one who turns the mundane into the transcendent." Rob frowns and puts his hand up to dismiss my remark.

Slowly stepping back to take a good look at my friends, I acknowledge each one. "Oh, Wren, look at you. You can walk. Your Peter Pan smile tells me all." Turning to Becky, I continue, "And you, you've changed your hair into a pixie cut. Cute. But you look as if you've lost weight. What's up?" Punching Carla's stomach, I observe, "And you, my friend, you look taller and stronger." Her squatty body belies my statement.

Stephanie, flipping her blond ponytail, retreats from the circle, so I grab her arm and pull her toward me. "And you—this year, you'll be coming to Europe with us. No more staying at home while we race in the World Cup."

McElvey, spreading his arms, forces his way into the middle of our nest. "And you, Lia, you'll lead us to great successes there and onward to the Olympics." He turns to Rob, who waves back in complicity, and he grins, "Many thanks for bringing her home to us."

Becky steps up. "And you, my friend, you look tired. Plus, you also need me to give you a haircut." She sweeps her hand over my gnarled bangs and continues,

"Okay, this can wait. Let's get supper. You know that we waited for you, Kiddo. Right now, we're famished. Stefan has made your favorite dinner—you know, complete with apple strudel." Wren, awkwardly hobbling from side to side like a wounded bird, takes her place at the front of the cafeteria line. I follow, trying to hide my limp—my ankle has swelled during the drive. McElvey grabs my shoulder and pulls me back. "Are you okay? You seem to have a problem."

"Oh coach, I just have a slight sprain. I can't talk about it now. I'll fill you in later."

He accepts this and dismisses himself in a tired voice saying, "Okay. I've got to go help the mountain crew tonight. We must groom the slopes for tomorrow's skiers. You know, we're short-staffed until Christmas time." He scowls, lowering his head. "This war has taken all young men who aren't in college." Smiling again, he pats my shoulder and beckons for Rob to follow him out. "And you, Rob, can you stay the week to help out?"

For an hour over dinner and dessert, my teammates grill me about Washington, DC, my time in the fire tower, my train ride across Canada, my hike in the Wind Rivers, my college courses, and my training. Keeping everything positive, I avoid any mention of the war, of friends such as Henry David and others who were wounded, of Bill who was killed, and of Greta and Terry. Rather, I cautiously describe my work for *The Daily Californian*, omitting my involvement in the protest movement.

I finish up, lacking the fortitude to explain the knife attack since I'm not ready for any psychological dredging. I change the subject and ask, "Okay, enough about me. Can you tell me what you all have been doing ... especially you, Wren?"

Wren swallows hard. "Our lives have been very uneventful compared to yours. You've really lived."

I scold her. "Uneventful? Wren, you've recovered from your accident and you're walking again. The rest of you have been training all summer for the Olympics. I'm not sure there's a comparison."

Kathy, in her assertive manner, holds up her hands. "Lia, you know what Wren means, to say the least. We've been doing what's expected of us. Training, you know, living in the racers' bubble, riding the hamster wheel. Just skiing, training, skiing, training. We've hardly heard about what's going on in the rest of the world." She looks at each of her teammates. "We're a little jealous of you. Tell us more about what's been going on in the real world."

So as not to go into all the subterfuge I've lived through, I turn the conversation back to them. "Not now. I'll tell you more later. For now, I just want to be part of your racers' bubble."

We return to my room where nothing has changed. The photo of my mom and dad is still on the dresser, Bill's army picture is on my bedstand, and my books nestle on my bureau. Carla's bed parallels mine, next to a picture of her mom, whom she had lost in Italy.

The four of us flop down on the blue shag rug, stretch out our legs, letting our toes touch, and chat. Wren carefully sits down on my bed. Becky gets up and helps lift her braced legs. As she gently places Wren's crutches next to me, I let my hand warm the cold metal.

CHAPTER 46

Coach's Talk

Before the others awake, I skip down to the ski room to check on my equipment. Next to my locker, lined up stiff like soldiers at attention, are four new pairs of 190cm Rossignol slalom skis, a pair of 195cm Atomic GS skis, and a longer pair of 213cm Head downhill skis—all waxed and mounted. They glisten with the rainbow colors of red, blue, and yellow. Coach McElvey, planning for me, ordered them from the companies, uncannily knowing my preference for shorter, more flexible skis.

Inside my locker, arranged in neat piles beneath my US Ski Team parka, nestle my hat, mittens, goggles, and snow pants. A paper note, embellished with doodles by Carla, Stephanie, Wren, and Becky, is taped on the door, "Welcome Home, Lia."

My worries of abandonment, of not belonging, melt away like an icicle in the sun.

After breakfast, McElvey allows us to join the ski patrol and take the milk run to the top, where we can play in the three feet of new powder—feathers from heaven. For six hours we chase each other over cliffs, around bowls, down couloirs, through snow pillows, up snow stashes, until we finally jump the top cornice, of course, after the ski patrol has blasted it. Like the Vermont barn swallows dive-bombing for insects, rising and falling with the currents, we cross each other's paths. At times, I hit a snow mound so big that I lose my balance and purposefully loft myself to reset my feet under me. My ski boot acts like a cast, so my ankle feels strong.

All our hearts are full of joy and laughter.

However, during my ride up the lift with Becky, I continue to struggle in the thin air, so she admonishes me, "Hey, Kiddo, you've some training to catch up on. Coach wants us to ski nonstop all day, you know, to help you get used to your skis and the altitude." Without mercy, she skates away from the lift and shoves off toward the pine forest on the north side where the trees are keeping the powder fluffy.

Like gliding on a cloud, I ski toward the largest lodgepole pine. Angling around the three-foot trunk, I look ahead, worried that these columns won't move if I hit them. The deep powder, blown into the couloirs, naturally slows me, while up-and-down unweighting allows my ski tips to rise above the wind-blown crust, forcing rhythmic turns. Often finding a dream line, I drop in and ride the sides of the slope. Not slowing or stopping, I bask in the adrenaline rush, a hormonal glow so different from the flight-fright rush I'd experienced in Berkeley.

Becky, mirroring my turns beside me, has to leave my line occasionally to avoid hooking a tree, but she always rejoins me below the barrier. It's as if we've done this together all our lives. The snow flows to both sides of us, opening like two adjacent pages of a book, while we write our own snow calligraphy.

Carla follows in my slipstream, because she's not brave enough to create her own line, at least not until she reaches the flats. On the smoother snow, she pulls up parallel with us and together we finish out the run, snaking perfect parallel "S" turns, moving simultaneously like the murmurations of swallows, intuitively sensing each other's movements. We stop at the bottom of the pitch, waiting for Stephanie who trails behind, and look back up into the blinding sun glaze that dazzles the slope with diamonds.

At the end, I hockey-stop near the base lodge. The others, following, pull up behind me, but their sudden halt makes them fall back into each other, like dominoes toppling on one another. In slow motion, I let myself collapse on top of them.

A yell from the balcony startles us, "Hey, girls. Wow! I got that run on tape." Laughing, Rob lowers his camera and slides it into a holster by his side. "You can see it later." His camera has a powerful lens with an eye that can see hundreds of yards up the slopes, equipment similar to those used by the FBI at the student protests.

At two o'clock, we finally break for lunch where our cook, Stefan, brushing the flour from his black-checkered pants, snags us., "Coach wants you in the ski room at three for a talk."

While we savor fresh salads and hamburgers, Wren joins us, taking the opportunity to describe her tedious rehab in Los Angeles. She doesn't complain as she discusses her back injury at T4, and her partially severed spinal cord. She has some feeling in her legs, which allows her to walk with braces. Her doctors are amazed at her tenacity and fully believe that she'll eventually regain enough strength to walk free of crutches. She brags about the college courses that she's taking at UCLA; her goal is to become an occupational therapist working with others who have spinal injuries. Completing the story, she confesses, "The worst part of this journey is remembering the future I'll never have." I stand up and put my arms around her shoulders, feeling the convulsions throughout her arms.

Becky motions me to sit down and joins in the sharing of our dreams. Tapping her long, slender fingers on the Formica table, she describes her wish of becoming a concert pianist when she's finished with the team. To support her desire, Coach McElvey has had a piano brought into the base lodge, so she can practice for three hours every night. Being the most musical of us, as well as the most focused, I know she'll achieve her dream.

Carla, throwing up her hands and sighing with frustration, blurts out, "So, is that why you're losing weight?" She looks at Becky, afraid to continue. "Is … is that why I hear you throwing up after dinner? You know, to fit into the tight dresses you'll have to wear in the future?" A loud gasp comes from all of us.

Turning to Becky, I ask, "Is that true? That's not any way to prepare for the Olympics. I've heard of gymnasts doing that. I think it's called bulimia. I really hope you're not doing that to yourself."

Becky sends eye-darts at me. "Enough of this. I'm my own boss and know what I'm doing." To diffuse the discussion, she turns to Carla. "So what do you want to do after the Olympics?"

In an effort to bring us together again, Carla adds, "Well, you all know what my dream is—after the Olympics, I hope to go to Italy to find my biologic family, especially my cousins. You remember that I was sent to an orphanage with my brother, Roberto, when my mother died after the war, you know, in 1948." She pauses, knowing that we sympathize with her quest to find her real family. "Toward this goal, I'm studying Italian. Then, one day I want to work with adopted orphans, especially kids who've lost their parents in war."

I can't refrain from blurting out, "Well, after this war, we'll have plenty of orphans!" I feel their stares—no one seems to know how to handle my anger.

To avoid discussing what I'd brought up, Carla interjects, "*Il modo più sicuro per realizzare i tuoi sogni noi viverli.*" While I shake my head in confusion, Becky and Carla, like a well-rehearsed chorus, translate, "The surest way to make your dreams come true is to live them."

Always reticent, Stephanie doesn't talk much about her dreams, because she knows that, as the coach's daughter, her job is to become an Olympian. Any post-racing dreams will have to be put on hold until her skiing career is over. With her head down, she acquiesces, "I just do what my dad wants me to do." She winces at the word 'dad.'

I chuckle nervously, trying to lighten the moment. "Of course, that's exactly what all of us are doing right now."

The group laughs together and I continue, "There—you see, laughter is the harmony that bonds us together."

I don't take my turn at revealing my dreams of becoming an investigative journalist, a writer who mines the truth while exposing demagogues and their lies. Instead, I reassure them, "You know, right now we're all preparing for our next life by learning so many important skills, you know, through our ski racing. Characteristics such as focus, self-discipline, ah … delayed gratification, adaptability, um … resilience, organization, and, best of all, self-confidence." Seeing their enthusiasm for my pep talk, I boast, "Why, I've already used these traits in my college courses and guess what? I'm getting straight 'A's."

Seeing their confusion, I wipe my mouth and reassure them, "But, for sure, I'm with you on this ski journey. Remember, life is partly what we make it, and partly what is made by the friends we choose. Now we have an immediate goal: to rejoin the US Ski Team and dominate at the Olympics." However, like a reoccurring drum beat in my mind, I recall my promise to Greta and Terry to work with them toward ending the war.

Wren excuses herself to go to the bathroom while the rest of us, comforted that we've bonded again through our honesty, wander down to the wax room, arm-in-arm.

Coach McElvey is waiting for us, sitting on the wax-bench, arms crossed.

"So, I've heard you made tracks down every trail you could find." He laughs, "And Lia, you were able to keep up, sometimes even lead, although you still don't have your mountain legs—awesome!" Becky pokes me.

We each find a stool and pull up in front of him, vying for the center spot. The metal scraping creates an eerie sound like crows heckling each other.

Scowling, Coach admonishes us, "Ah, so do you see, um … what you all just did? You tried to outdo each other, each trying to get to the closest position. That's the wrong attitude right now. At this time, you need to think about what constitutes a team, what it means to be in the Olympics, what it means to be an athlete representing your country."

Getting up from my stool when Wren hobbles in, I indicate that she can have mine. I grab her crutches and stand behind her, resting my hand on her shoulders. Her metal braces click against the stool legs. She leans her head back against my chest and says in a thin, weary voice, "Thanks, my friend."

Coach McElvey nods, "Lia, you seem to have some perspective. Why did you do what you just did?"

"Oh … uh, coach, during my travels this summer, I've realized how much I love being with all of you, how much I love the sport of skiing, and how much I want to be part of a team. In so many ways I've learned that we're not alone, that we're part of a bigger whole, of each other, of the mountains, and of nature." I smile contently, remembering my readings of Von Humboldt, of my epiphany while looking at Gannet Peak.

Coach praises me. "Wow, have you ever grown. Now let me add to this." He turns his head to look each of us in the eye. "Do you understand what it means to be an Olympian? Yes, you are all entering the highest level of achievement for an athlete—the honor of representing your country in the Olympics. You'll be training, honing your individual talents, reaching for personal bests, while also competing against one another."

He raises his hands to emphasize his point, reminding me of a conductor steadying his hands between movements in a symphony to halt the applause and let the silence speak. Continuing, he points at each of us, "Yet, you cannot do this alone; like the trees in the forest, you'll need each other's support and your coaches' protection." Again, he creates a mindful silence.

Standing, he concludes as if he'd overheard our lunch talk. "What lessons you learn, you'll carry into your future, interesting lives. But ... " He moves behind us to make his point, "... in the short term, right now, the goal is to become the best you can be, to be part of a team that will promote the sport, which, in turn will inspire the next generation. For all these reasons, you're not in competition with each other, but rather you're working with and for each other. Each run, each race, each success will take you, the individual, as well as the team, to new plateaus."

He steps back in front of us to see whether we are all focused and continues, raising his voice slowly and firmly, "From these plateaus, the next group of skiers can find new heights. You'll be attempting new techniques, adding new records, finding new individual successes, until finally the Europeans and the world will understand that the Americans are a force in the ski world." His blue eyes look directly at me, his voice rises with each pronouncement, "In many ways, you are all a part of a stream, building momentum to reach the final destination."

He takes one of my skis and flexes it, "Then, and only then, can you grow and become leaders—not just in skiing, but in other endeavors. If done right, you can use your triumphs, your resilience, your work ethic to make changes beyond sports. To make changes that you can only dream of now."

He nods to me as if he knows how involved I've been in the antiwar movement and, striding out of the room, concludes, "Think about this. I'll meet all of you in the conference room in fifteen minutes where we'll analyze Lia's new technique, the ones in Rob's movie.

My mind flashes back to the protests in Washington DC, to the student speeches at Sproul Plaza, to the struggles of Greta and Terry. No one moves; a silence builds in the room, our moment of unity.

As when I stood on the top of Dinwoody Peak, an idea comes to me: maybe I can use my ski racing platform as the vehicle to promote my objections to the Vietnam War.

My two worlds aren't mutually exclusive—instead, they're coming together.

CHAPTER 47

Training

During the next few days, I maintain an exact schedule: awake at 5:00 am to study, breakfast at 7:00, free skiing from 8:00 to 12:00, lunch, race training until 4:00, ski preparation and dry-land workouts until dinner, and finally, studying until 10:00 pm.

Each day I grow stronger on my skis and more confident in the gates. I'm working on a new technique whereby, before each gate, I unweight my downhill ski, transfer the weight to the upper ski, and then drive the inside edge into the hill, forcing it to become my downhill edge. I shift my weight, front to back, so that when I pull out of the turn, I gain speed, instead of losing it. My knees become shock absorbers, while my hips force an angulation against centrifugal force.

Coach McElvey suggests that the other girls try to emulate me, but they can't find the balance I've learned.

Frustrated, Becky asks me during the third day of training, "Lia, your times in the slalom are at least a second faster than mine. How are you doing it?" She stamps her ski on the packed snow, showing her frustration.

Carla and Stephanie gather around to hear my answer. I rest my poles under my armpits, and lean toward them, whispering as if I'm telling a state secret, "Sometimes it takes getting away from something to fully understand it. You know that I've been away from skiing for seven months, constantly rehabilitating my ankle. What you don't know is what I did during that time."

Coach McElvey skis over to us and joins the lineup to listen. I continue, amazed that he might want to learn from me. "First of all, I've strengthened my ankle through running, first in Washington by jogging up and down the Supreme Court steps. Second, I learned incredible balance while stutter-stepping down the rock-strewn streams of Scrag Mountain. I learned how to balance on one foot, shift my weight while in the air, and push off just as I landed. Here on skis, I do the same in my quick slalom turns, never too long on one edge. My thighs became powerful while hiking in the Wind Rivers—you know, carrying a fifty-pound pack up 11,000-foot mountains isn't easy. Finally, I discovered the body angulation during my afternoons running around the Berkeley Hills. The trails there zigzag in deep ruts, forcing me to use centrifugal force to balance."

Coach McElvey lifts his goggles, revealing his tanned crow's feet and the white owl-circles around his blue eyes. He steps forward. "Lia, you've always been a leader in terms of your focus and discipline. Now you're starting to develop new techniques that'll help all of us. I'll have Rob take more videos of your runs. Would you care to watch them tonight with us and share what you're learning?"

Surprised that he wants me to help the others, but also a little guarded in that I'll be showing others how to beat me, I respond, "Uh ... uh, I guess. I usually like to study after supper, but I could find an hour. I'm not sure that what I'm doing, others can do. After all, I'm just working on this myself."

He clicks his poles together in front of him to allay my doubts. "Remember what I told you in the wax room. You'll all be working together. You've obviously discovered a new technique that we can all use." He skates off, saying "Remember, like a tree in the forest." Stephanie follows, reproducing his turns for her turns.

Becky skis up to me and puts her arm around my parka. "I missed you this summer. Remember all the fun we had in Europe last winter?" I relax in her warmth as she continues, "Remember how we worked together as a team?"

Carla sidles up on the other side. "Me, too. And remember how together we forced Coach Boast out by reporting his scams and his sexual attacks."

I pull back, knock some snow off my skis, and protest, "Okay, now that you bring it up, I have to tell you my fears. I'm worried that Coach Boast still has control of the US Ski Team. Did you know that he's been promoted to Executive Director?' They nod. "But what you don't know is that he paid for my first semester at college, using the ski team funds." The group gasp is audible.

Both pull away from me and cover their mouths in shock. Becky quickly recovers. "What? How did he know where you were? Do you think he's trying to bribe you, to silence you again?"

I nod, agreeing. She continues, "However, have no fear. Coach McElvey promises that he'll be our Olympic coach and that Boast has no say-so when it comes to the team." She looks away, hoping I won't read her face. "And maybe he's relented, learned his lesson." She does a kick turn and faces the other way, as if to reinforce her point, "You know, people can change."

Shaking my head in amazement at her ignorance, I scold her. "Ha, I used to be as naïve as you. But I've learned that money rules. Once corrupted, always corrupted. I'm afraid that I'll have to confront him again." I hesitate, thinking about Coach Ryan, wondering what has happened to him, and ask, "Has anyone heard about Coach Ryan?"

Becky shakes her head. "Only that he was let go from the ski team, drafted, and went AWOL. I'll bet he's angry at all of us, especially you, Lia."

Carla stomps her skis to warm her toes. Her face turning red, she interjects, "I forgot to tell you all that Tracy Languile wrote to me. Uh, she's filed a paternity suit against Coach Boast. If she can prove that he's the father of her child, I'm sure that he'll be fired from the US Ski Team."

Horsing around, Becky and I fall to the snow and throw balls in each other's faces. Spitting out the wet flakes, I yell, "Right, and her case can stick as easily as this snow sticks to my face. Good luck with that!"

Carla flops on top of both of us. "Yeah, how about if we all step up and support her in her lawsuit. That's what she wants us to do. We did it once. We can tell the court our side of the story."

All three of us leap up, and I yell, "Now you're talking. One voice can become many, and many can change the world."

CHAPTER 48

Epiphany

The week of skiing and training flies by, convincing me how much I love the sport and that I must rejoin the US Ski Team. The mountains give me a respite from all my fears, an oasis in which to rebuild my confidence, hold a reunion with my friends, and solidify a trust with my coach.

In the past, I'd always longed for just such a sanctuary.

However, on this new journey back to the mountains, I've learned that there can be no final rest, no final escape. The mountains are neither a sanctuary nor a monastery, but instead a place just to refresh my dreams, set my goals, and continue toward making a difference. For me, there will be no ultimate sanctuary—just a break before the next challenge, toward the next goal.

The struggle is what counts. As Muir stated, paraphrasing Von Humboldt, "For going out, I found I was really going in."

I'll add to that, "For going in, I found my way out."

CHAPTER 49

Confessions

Saying goodbye to my teammates, even if temporarily, is hard. I've learned that with each departure, new paths are forged, but like sliding doors once entered, one can never go back. Although I'm eager to return to Berkeley to finish my studies, I also look forward to rejoining my friends in New York for our flight to Europe.

Coach McElvey assigns Becky the responsibility of bagging my skis, poles, and uniforms where they'll be awaiting me in New York. I choose to take my US Ski Team jacket and pants to Berkeley, as a reminder of the challenges ahead.

Rob generously agrees to drive me back to campus. In three weeks, he'll return from his work at the nuclear power plant to take me to the San Francisco Airport. The more time I spend with Rob, the more I trust him, even to the point of falling in love with him. He's been such a North Star for me at many critical times such as Grindelwald, Vancouver, the Wind Rivers, and Berkeley, always encouraging me to stay with my ski racing.

On the morning of my departure, my buddies walk me out to the car. I gaze up into the bright sun, the vast snow fields, the overhanging cornice, and whisper "Thank you," to the natural world of Monmouth, a place that has welcomed me like a loving grandparent.

Encircling me, my friends step forward individually to give me a small gift. Carla, joking, presents me with an Italian dictionary, saying, "Well, yeah, if you're going to join me in Europe on my family-quest, then you'll need to learn some groovy Italian words." She thrusts the book into my hands, adding, "*Ci vedimo a New York.*"

Wren, struggling with her tears, while being supported by her crutches, hobbles toward me to hand me a picture of the two of us skiing the cornice last year, resplendent in our blue Monmouth parkas. She wipes her face and places her wet hand on my cheek, saying, "Next year, if ... if all goes well, I'll be skiing with you again."

Becky, sensing that the moment is growing morbid, changes the tune by humming, "In this white world." After a verse, she hands me a photo of all of us, including my old boyfriend Bill, Coach McElvey, Stefan, and Fritz, the accountant. She rejoins the group, moving her hand in a circle. "It takes a team to make a champion. Catch you on the flip side."

Coach McElvey, pants greasy from his early morning work in the garage, strides forward holding an envelope. In a slow, commanding voice, he cautions me, "Don't let the protesters at Berkeley take you from your goal of joining us in New York. Uh ... we need you. Here's something to tide you over until we see you in three weeks." He nods to Rob, communicating a secret. Stephanie ducks behind her father, jealous of his attention to me.

I turn toward my friends, put on my US Ski Team parka, and reassure them, "I'm ready to do my best as a team member, to support each one of you. Let's take on Europe! I'll see you at JFK airport."

As Rob lifts my US Ski Team rucksack into the trunk of his car, I climb into the passenger seat, glance once more at Monmouth, and wave, tenting my eyes so as not to let the group see my tears.

Rob and I don't speak for ten minutes. He seems to understand the emotions that have flooded me. My mind is swamped with memories: parting with my boyfriend, Bill Emerson, here last January, just before he left for a war that would ultimately kill him; Wren giggling and laughing on the slopes; and my innocence when I first met Becky and Carla. Turning north onto Highway 395, he cautiously asks, "Do you want to talk now?"

"Give me a minute, please." To busy myself, I open the letter from Coach McElvey and four one-hundred-dollar bills drop into my lap. I unfold his letter and read quietly.

December 5, 1971

Lia,

I'm so glad you are returning to the team. I want you to know that I've spoken to the Chairman of the Board of the US Ski Team. Unilaterally, the Board has decided to relieve Coach Boast of his position as Executive Director of the Team until the lawsuit by Tracy Languile, which accuses him of fathering her child, is settled. You don't have to fear him anymore.

I don't know what has happened to his assistant Coach Dan Ryan, but be assured, I will be your coach in Europe and at the Olympics.

See you soon,

Coach McElvey

Looking straight ahead so that Rob can't see my tears, I gasp, "Did you know that Coach McElvey was doing this?"

"Yup." He keeps his eyes on the road and speeds up.

The slush of wet snow on the pavement makes conversation difficult, so I speak louder, "Have you been working with him?"

"Yup."

Squirming in my narrow leather seat, I sob, "It's all so emotional. I remember leaving here last December with my teammates on our way to the World Cup in Europe, you know, with all my hopes of becoming a great skier. So much has happened since then. I've … I've learned so much, met so many great people, and opened my mind to a world beyond ski racing. I pray that I can rediscover that sense of wonder and joy that I found here, you know, while skiing."

Rob hands me a handkerchief and scratches his chin, guarding his words. "Lia, you know I've followed you since I met you in Switzerland. I've met your father. I've been your liaison with Coach McElvey. I've even taught you about hiking, right?"

Confused, I squirm in my seat and mumble, "Uh … yeah."

Slowing, he pulls the car to the side of the road, turns to me, and looks me straight in my eyes. "What I haven't told you is that I'm in love with you. But … I've not wanted to distract you from your dreams … your mission."

Taking a deep sigh, I lean over and put my head on his flannel shirt, "Oh, Rob. And I think I've fallen in love with you but didn't want to complicate our friendship."

Rob kisses my cheek. "To complicate it even more, I promised McElvey that I'd be your guide and mentor while you rehab your ankle. He warned me that I had to keep our relationship platonic." He lets his finger run along my lips. "His only wish was that I protect you and keep you on the path to the Olympics." He then leans forward and kisses me, letting his wet lips sink into mine; the smell of his pine cologne relaxes me.

Surprised, then feeling a new and painful desire, I jerk back. "Oh, Rob, we can make this happen. You know that I've promised McElvey that I'll rejoin the team once I finish my classes." He leans forward again, kisses me, letting his tongue find my open mouth, and plays with my tongue. A warm rush of sexuality flows through my body, a tide of incoming emotions. He grabs my hand and places it on his crotch where I feel the hardening organ.

Sitting back, I gasp, "Wow, you sure are excited, but this will have to wait. You know that."

"Lia, I'll wait for you forever. I love everything about you and want you to achieve your dreams. Then, just then, maybe our lives can become one."

Giggling, I nod. "You've waited this long, so I know you can wait until after the Olympics. On second thought, maybe you can come to Japan to watch me."

"I'll try, but I've other work to do also." He looks to a distant mountain that disappears into a dark cloud.

Starting the car, he sighs, then continues, "But I've more to tell you. You'll not want to hear this." My mind races, wondering what could keep him from committing to me. He continues with the regret of someone who has done an unspeakable act. Swallowing hard, he stumbles, "Ah … ah, I'm not working at the nuclear power plant as I told you."

"Okay, that doesn't worry me. Do you do anything other than escort me everywhere?"

A long silence ensues, and he reaches into the glove compartment. He pulls out a plastic ID with his picture. He puts it in my hand, and I read:

FBI, U.S. Government, Rob Attelfellner, Federal Agent.

Shocked, I push him away and yell, "What's this? What are you telling me?"

His hands tighten on the steering wheel. "Hey, watch it. Well, while you were in Washington, DC, my agency let me know that they've been following Greta and Terry. Two of my fellow agents spotted you in Terry's apartment. They did a background check on you and learned about your ski racing and remembered that I'd met you in Grindelwald."

"Oh, my God, so you've been following me as a FBI agent?"

"Not exactly, because you've done nothing wrong. I told you the truth, that McElvey asked me to be your support. He has nothing to do with the FBI, okay? You know, he just wants to keep you from getting too involved with the protest movement and forgetting your role as a World Cup racer."

"Now I'm really confused. Are you working for the FBI or for McElvey?"

Rob shakes his head, lowers it, and pleads, "Both. But with you, I'm just trying to keep you on track with your racing, trying to keep you from getting involved with the wrong elements."

"Okay, so what are the wrong elements?" Frustrated, I slap the dashboard, "You know that I have a right to free speech. My friends, Greta and Terry, have helped me find a way to protest the war."

"Don't get all huffy. You have all the right in the world to protest. But if you get involved with subversion, stealing government secrets, and violent protests, then you'll hurt your chance of representing this county in skiing, right? Also, you could hurt your chance of getting scholarships, you know, to the university. Um, you could even get arrested."

Shaken, feeling deceived, I counter, "So far, everything I've done has been above board. Yes, I've protested nonviolently. Yes, I've written the truth for *The Daily Californian*, always using the facts, you know, the truth coming from the soldiers." I'm breathless with frustration.

"Slow down! I didn't say that you've broken the law. However, on the other hand, your friend, Terry, has. Did you know that she was an employee of the CIA in Vietnam and that she broke the rules when she brought back statistics and pictures from the war?"

Now I'm feeling boxed in, wondering how much he knows about Terry and of my helping her, and whether this makes me a criminal or a spy. Trying to avoid any questions from him, I ask, "Why do you say *was* ?"

"Oh, my friend. You haven't heard because you've been at Monmouth for a week." He shakes his head and fumbles for his words. That ... that ... Terry was killed in Saigon by a suicide bomber ... just a week ago. The police discovered covert papers, maps, and pictures in her briefcase."

My stomach turns over and I begin to choke, "Are ...are you sure? This is crazy."

"Yup, and now I want to protect you. When you return to Berkeley, I hope you'll just commit to your courses and stay away from the protest movement. You may have gotten in over your head. Plus, I ... I know that a violent group, the Weathermen, has infiltrated Berkeley. They want to cause mayhem."

I slap my knees to protest, "I've done nothing wrong. I'll finish my work for *The Daily Californian*, take my tests, write my papers, and then catch my flight to New York where I'll rejoin the team. You know as well as I do that this war is immoral and we need to end it."

Rob nods and swallows hard. "I agree with you that the war must end, but America can't afford to lose this war. I believe that we can't let mobs subvert the government."

When he says, "We … ," I wince.

He continues, "You know, President Nixon is trying to wind it down. Why, I'm sure you know that recently he recalled 45,000 troops. This leaves just 139,000 left in the country."

"Yes, 139,000 left to die. Well, if he really wants to end it, then he should just sign the peace treaty and pull all our troops out. Every day we stay there, every day we bomb innocent people, every day we destroy their lands, is a national tragedy—for us and for them. As John Kerry said, 'How do you ask a man to be the last man to die in Vietnam?' "

CHAPTER 50

Semester's End

When Rob pulls up to leave me at Mrs. Rothstein's, I lean into his car window and spout, "I'm still upset that you didn't share your story with me earlier!"

He waves me away. "I love you and thought I was doing the best for you, okay?"

Back at Berkeley, I have just one week to complete my papers for my Shakespeare, French, and American literature classes, and to take my final exams in each one. Fortunately, always thinking ahead, I'd worked on all these projects at Monmouth. I need only my typewriter to complete the drafts. Best of all, Mrs. Rothstein agrees to proofread my work and type the final copy.

Each night, I work on a different paper, so I don't feel overwhelmed, a lesson I learned from skiing—work on one technique at a time. The American literature paper is easy because of my research on Von Humboldt. I argue that his revolutionary thinking about the unity of the natural world influenced the transcendental writings of Thoreau and Emerson.

My Shakespeare paper proves to be more difficult, because I want to compare how the influence of Lady Macbeth and the witches in *Macbeth* is similar to the advice of Secretary Melvin Laird and National Security Advisor, Henry Kissinger, for President Nixon. They're all trying to manipulate their leader's *blind ambition*. My thesis is simple: if a leader doesn't have a moral compass, he can be subverted by extrinsic forces.

My French paper, written in my cursory French, is my simple attempt to weave the lessons that I'd learned while hiking in the Wind Rivers into some meaningful thoughts about life. It's one thing to formulate such existential thoughts, and another to express them in another language. My philosophy: We are all connected by thoughts and ideas that go beyond the five senses. We all have the power to create our own reality and purpose, and part of that purpose is to contribute to the greater good. I conclude that since all life comes from the same source, there can be no hierarchy. We, the animals, and the natural world are all equal. My professor had me read some of the writings of the French philosopher Henri Bergson and his concept of "élan vital." I struggle with French vocabulary and, unfortunately, Mrs. Rothstein can't help me. The worst part of this project is that I'm required to orally present my work to the class. I'm still afraid of public speaking.

Three days after returning, I stop in to see Sam at *The Daily Californian*. His dark curly hair hasn't been cut, adding to his generally haggard, defeated appearance. His office has been ransacked, his neat piles of paper thrown into a corner. The posters of Vietnam, Mario Savio, and the Free Speech movement are gone.

As I enter, he gets up to give me a hug. "Welcome back, my friend." He slumps back down and points for me to sit before continuing. "I'm so mad that all this happened." His hand sweeps around the room. "Let me start at the beginning. Remember when ya last saw me? I was at the police station … remember, being interrogated?"

I shift nervously and answer, "Yup." I play and replay the moment in my head.

"Well, those officers weren't policemen, they were FBI agents."

"Oh, my God! What did they want?"

"Let me back up. Did you hear that Terry was killed in Vietnam?"

I close my eyes and say a quick prayer. "Yup, by … uh...by a suicide bomber … " My composure unravels like a ball of yarn.

" … That's not what I was told," he interjects. "It may have been an inside job. And worse, they found papers with her. I think the CIA is tracking the trail of her helpers. That's why they raided my office." He glances around the room, looking for a spy camera, and turns back to me. "Ya may not be safe, Lia." He stands up and runs his hand along the wall. "By the way, how did ya learn about Terry? From Mrs. Rothstein?"

"Nope, from my friend, Rob, the one who took me to Monmouth."

"Who?"

My mind starts to race; I'm wondering which truth is real. *Who is who?* Fearing that Sam will think I'm a traitor, I don't tell him that Rob works for the FBI. "Oh, a friend who's supported my ski racing since I met him in Grindelwald."

"Okay, but I'm not sure how he knew about Terry. Do you think he knows about Greta? About how we're getting the information from Vietnam?" He stops and moves over to grab my shoulders and demands, "Who the hell is he anyway?"

Looking down at the floor, cupping my head in my hands, I sputter, "I'm … I'm not sure. It's all so confusing."

Sam slaps his hands on his desk. "Well, no matter. At some point we'll learn the truth. Anyway, we've a big job coming up next week, after ya finish your papers and exams. Uh, Greta wants us to organize a huge protest here on campus in conjunction with Don Luce's visit."

"Who?"

"Oh, Lia, ya've been so far removed from everything, back in ya're skier's bubble."

"Sorry, but before you go on, I have to tell you something about … about that bubble."

Sam sits down, shaking his head. "Go ahead."

"Well, you need to know that I've decided to rejoin the US Ski Team and go to Europe." I lift my shoulders to show my conviction.

Sam lowers his head in resignation. "But, c'mon, Lia, I thought ya were ready to move on. To take on a greater cause, a cause beyond the solipsism of the ski team." He stops to gauge my reaction to his criticism. "Remember what Joseph Campbell described in yer mythology studies?"

"I'm not sure what you're referring to. Does this have to do with Antigone?"

"Yup, in a way. She gave herself to something bigger than she was."

"Well, okay, but I've come to realize that I can do both. Yup, I can help the protest movement, as well as ski for the team."

"What? Ya're confusing me now." His strong black hand pounds the desk.

"Okay, I think I've a way to use my presence on the ski team as a means to influence others, especially if I go on to win medals at the Olympics. I can use my publicity to express my anger at the war."

He grabs a flier from his desk and pushes it toward me. "Okay, I'll accept that. Now ya're talking the skinny. And I ... I think I've just the right beginning for ya. Check this out."

I pick up the colored poster and turn it around. A handsome, smooth-skinned face stares at me. "Who's this?"

Sam shakes his head in disbelief. "Don Luce. Let me tell you what's been happening with the antiwar effort." He takes back the paper and hands me a map of Vietnam.

Pointing to the dark areas, he explains, "Here's the present situation. The Viet Cong now control all the areas along the borders with Cambodia and Laos. Remember that while Nixon is trying to appease the American public, ya know, by claiming he's negotiating a peace and pulling out troops, he's simultaneously increased the bombing inside Cambodia and Laos."

He glares into my eyes and continues. "He's also bombing the rice paddies in South Vietnam." He walks back to his desk and raises his voice. "We now know that he's moving the Vietnamese farmers out of their villages and into barbed-wire security camps, claiming it's for their protection. To say the least, he's bombing, mining, napalming, and destroying the land for generations." He snorts and states, "Nixon calls it Vietnamization."

I study the map again, asking, "So how can I help?"

Sam puts up his hand and walks to the door. As he opens it, a tall, dark-haired man with long sideburns strides in. Pulling his hands from his jeans, the stranger extends a greeting to me, "Hi, Lia, I'm Don Luce."

I stand up and respond confusedly, "Nice to meet you."

Don takes the map from Sam. "You don't know much about my anti-war movement, so let me explain." He indicates that we should sit down. "Well, I'm on a tour of this country to educate the American people through photographs, films, and lectures about the culture of the Vietnamese. My goal is to show all Americans that basically the Vietnamese are just like us … that they have the same problems, desires, loves, and needs as we have."

Feeling intimidated, I look to Sam who puts up his hand. "Just listen, Lia."

Don continues, "If I do that, then I can convince them that bombing the villages and moving the people into 'strategic hamlets' and off their farms is counterproductive." He pulls his chair closer to mine. "After all, Lia, I know about small towns, especially in Vehmawnt, just like you do. Yes, I grew up on a farm in Calais, Vermont." He pauses to see my reaction. His accent becomes heavier, drawling his 'R's' to 'H's" and dropping his "G's". "How would you like anothah country to come in and bomb your lovely fawmin village of Waitsfield, Vehmawnt."

I throw up my hands. "Of course, I wouldn't. I'd fight and fight and fight, until I had no more resources."

Don continues, "Well, this is what Nixon's new policy of Vietnamization is doing to the South Vietnamese. It's ludicrous. He's a madman."

Scratching my head, I respond, "I see your point, but how can I help?"

Sam pulls his chair closer to me. "Let me take over here, Don. So, Lia, Don's campaign that he calls the Mobile Education Project is coming to Sproul Plaza on December 15th, the day before ya leave for Europe."

I shift uncomfortably. "I'm still confused."

Sam speaks more confidently. "Well, I … you know that you've become a popular writer for *The Daily Californian*. Yup, and while you were gone, I received numerous letters asking for more articles and editorials from you. As a result, I thought you might want to write an article introducing Don Luce and announcing his rally."

"No problem," I respond, "but, you know, I still have to finish my coursework."

Sam nods to Don, dismissing him. "Okay, I know ya've much to do. Greta is waiting to meet ya. I'll explain all the details to Lia."

Don gets up, bows, squeezes my hand, and looks at the map once more. "We've much to do and I'm counting on you." He turns to go, stops, and then looks back at me with a grin on his face. "In fact, uh, I'd like you, yes you, Lia, to introduce me at the rally. Okay?"

I look at Sam and back at Don. My voice shakes as I respond. "You know, I'm a writer, not ... not a speaker. In fact, uh ... you know that I'm afraid of public speaking."

Don continues, "Sam has told me your plans, how you want to rejoin the Olympic team. Because of your celebrity status, I think you're just the right person to inspire the students. And ... it's time to learn how to use your platform to influence others. As a future leader, you'll be called on to do a lot of public speaking."

I sigh, recognizing that this challenge will become my own personal Gannet Peak.

CHAPTER 51

The Last Fear

Exams are over. Straight A's. Another hurdle completed. I've shown myself that I can accomplish anything if I set my mind to it. Yet, my doubts remain about my upcoming speech on the steps of Sproul Hall.

Writing the article about Don Luce's rally proves easy because I'm so committed to his cause. In fact, I've learned that his one-man campaign around the Midwest is changing conservative, hard-working Americans' views about the war. Nixon, continuing to propagate his lies, rants that Don's photographs are destroying his credibility, not just in the US but around the world. Just one image of a burned child running naked from napalm or a family hugging behind barbed wire can eradicate the administration's falsehoods as quickly as a hurricane can wipe out flimsily built houses. Nixon calls Luce, "A bomb to the heart of America."

Giving a speech, on the other hand, torments me. It's so much easier for me to express myself through my writing and my skiing. But then I remember Coach McElvey's talk—how, through his words, he encouraged each of us to work together, striving for something greater than ourselves. For sure, he inspired me to rejoin my friends on the team.

On the morning of December 15th, the crowd starts forming early, because a Bob Dylan-look-alike has agreed to warm them up for Don Luce. Surrounding the plaza, mounted on large, plywood boards, are images from Vietnam: a young girl, naked, running for her life out of her village; prisoners in Tiger cages, their backs bearing torture stripes; bomb craters filled with bloated, dead water buffaloes; burned-out thatched-roof villages; parents carrying dead children; a teary mother burying her daughter; and a slumped old man hobbling from his village past his ancestors' graves.

The one that stops me on my way to the steps of Sproul Plaza is a poster of two young GIs in front of an army tent, each wearing a necklace of dried ears around their shoulders, all hauntingly observed by a skull staring down from the tent pole. My only thought is, *What have we done?*

Outside the rally gathering, six Vietnamese students are cooking a traditional dinner called 'thit ga.' As I cross the plaza through the crowd of two hundred, a delicious curry aroma follows me. I turn when I hear a young man, dressed in army fatigues and a yellow bandana, yelling at these students, "Fucking gooks!" He throws a paint-soaked rag at a photo that displays a Buddhist monk sitting cross-legged, self-immolating. Beneath the image are the words, "Remember brother, remember, man is not your enemy."

Recognizing the angry man, I yell, "Stop. I know you." He turns, spits, and then disappears into the crowd." Now shaken, I look for Rob. He's agreed to meet me on the Sproul Hall steps. Pushing his way through a line of National Guardsmen, he finds me, grabs my arm, and scolds, "What do you think you're doing? Chasing a Weatherman? Don't try to provoke anyone, Lia. Crowds can be very unpredictable!"

"But ... but Rob, I think I saw the man who attacked me. Oh, my God, he looks like Coach Ryan from the ski team. What would he be doing in army fatigues?"

"Relax. You'll be well protected up here and I'll be nearby. I also know that the FBI has many agents dispersed in the crowd, as well as National Guardsmen. You and Don Luce have all the right in the world to speak. Just remember the courage of Mario Savio and the Free Speech Movement. These steps are for all to exercise their right to protest."

I pull my speech from my pocket, tuck my tie-dyed shirt into my bell-bottoms, and tighten my head scarf around my ponytail.

Once I'm up on stage, Sam grabs my arm and leads me away from Rob, saying, "I still don't trust him. Stay by my side, please. To start things off, I'll say a few words about Don Luce's past in Vietnam and then ya can introduce him. The editorial you wrote about his eleven-year career in Vietnam as an International Voluntary Service member has made my introduction easy. Then ya'll follow me. I know ya'll do yer part to inspire the students to listen to him."

He puts his hand on my shoulder, laughing. "My brave one, remember the words of Eleanor Roosevelt, "Every day do something that scares ya." I give him a thumbs up, even as my heart roars in my chest.

The folk singer finishes with a revised version of Dylan's archetypal song, *Their*

Land Is Their Land from the Gulf of Tonkin to the Mekong River. He asks for the crowd to join him once more in the final verse.

As Sam steps up to the microphone, I hear the cheers, "Sam! Sam!" I can't hear everything he says, because a policeman beside me is talking on his walky-talky. He seems to be directing his fellow officers toward a commotion near me. A group of Weathermen is engaging with the Vietnamese students.

Sam nods to me and turns to the microphone. "And now let me introduce yer favorite reporter, Lia Erickson. She has a few words for ya'all before she heads to Europe where she'll rejoin the US Ski Team, yes, and we hope they will be the *Olympic* ski team. Please give her a warm welcome!"

As the crowd starts applauding, I leap up three steps to the microphone, my ankle stronger than ever. Sam grabs my hand and raises our arms over our heads. Leaning toward me, he whispers, "Take a few deep breaths before ya start. The crowd is getting restless, and the silence will quiet them."

The sun reflects off the campanile, blinding me. I breathe deeply, tent my eyes, look up into the white marble, and think of Gannet Peak. I picture myself at the start of a race—a race I know I can win if I make each turn with conviction, each glide smoother, each bump a transition into the next gate. A wind picks up behind me like the wind from the top of Dinwoody Peak. The wind speaks the truth from Bill Emerson, from Henry David, and from Terry. My mind caroms—the crowd quiets in anticipation.

I feign a camera-ready smile. "Thank you, Sam. And thank you all for coming to support Don Luce. I'm grateful to you, to the Berkeley professors, and to the administration for giving me the opportunity to speak here today." I look to my left and see Rob inching closer. He's concerned.

My hands begin to shake, making it difficult for me to read my written speech. "As I … I wrote in my editorial, I've chosen to return to the US Ski Team, you know, instead of remaining here with you, um, to protest the war." A sudden gust blows the paper from my hand, so I start speaking from my heart.

"This has been a soul-searching decision. But I feel that I can help your cause, our cause, America's cause—yes, America's cause, if I go to Europe and tell the young people there, the press, and the World Cup racers about your/our commitment to ending this war. To assure them that we'll not give up our protests … we'll not cease our battle … until the war is ended." I pause to listen to an extended applause of affirmation. Gaining confidence, I yell, "For sure, if there is *no sanctuary* for the Vietnamese, there can be *no sanctuary* here."

A cheer arises from the back, "Tell 'em, Lia! Tell 'em, Lia!"

Taken aback by the power of my words to excite the crowd, I pause until the chanting stops. Then I begin reverentially, "Now I'm honored to introduce Don Luce, a man who has dedicated his life to the Vietnamese people, to their desire to be free of all foreign invaders, whether it be the Chinese … the French … or now the Americans."

Don, standing tall next to me, waves briefly to the crowd.

"Please check out his photographs at the back of the plaza. They're pictures of individual lives, of families, of children, of mothers, of fathers and of villages. All the values that I know we, as Americans, believe in … . Answer me, do these pictures represent American values?"

A chant repeats from the crowd, "No! Stop the war! No, stop the war!" I look into the crowd, a cloth quilt as colorful as the flags on a slalom course. I stop to remember my notes; but instead, as easily as the next turn in a racecourse, my words begin to flow.

Speaking louder and more confidently, I continue, "This war … this Vietnam tragedy, has become an American tragedy. Raise your hands if you know someone who's died or been wounded in Vietnam." A forest of hands, like the tops of trees, starts to move and sway in the gentle breeze. I look to Sam who's clapping his hands.

"To honor them … to honor those still to die … to honor the wounded … and to honor those retuning, wounded in their souls, please keep the protest going. War doesn't determine who's right—just who's left. It doesn't make a difference who wins the war to someone who's dead." I pause to encourage a rhythmic clapping and raise my hand to quiet the crowd. "How can we save American family values when we destroy these family values?"

The crowd grows restless and begins yelling, "One, two, three, four, we don't want your effing war." Realizing I've created an emotional avalanche, I hold up my hands, but before I can quiet them, someone wearing a yellow bandana jumps up the steps toward me. A knife blade flashes in the sun, his yellow, drug-ridden, weaponized eyes cut into my heart. He screams, "This is for Coach Boast. You ruined both my life and his." His knife slices my cheek and blood runs into my mouth. I spit.

Rob throws himself at the attacker; both of them tumble down the steps. Sam grabs my arm and pulls me back toward the barrier behind us, "Time to go, Lia. Now ya know the true power of words."

Once safely inside Sproul Hall, I fall into Sam's arms. "What have I done?"

Greta steps from a side door. "It's okay, Lia. Don will quiet them. He has a soothing voice and he's spoken to crowds for three years. You did well, my friend."

"But … but what about Rob?"

She reassures me, "I'll check on him. I saw him get up after the National Guardsmen handcuffed the attacker." Her voice turns softer, "Right now, you need to go home and pack up. I'll meet you in the morning to take you to the airport." She hesitates before finishing. "By the way, your attacker was Dan Ryan. He told the police he's angry at you for ruining his life, you know, by reporting him and Coach Boast to the authorities. He disguised himself as a Weatherman so he could maneuver unrecognized through the crowd."

"Okay." I sigh, adding submissively, "I'm ready to do whatever Coach McElvey and Rob want me to do." Heaving a big sigh, I exclaim, "Wow, I just overcame my last fear, you know—public speaking!" Then, laughing, I continue, "Now I know, yes, words can inspire me to the mountaintop, but I alone must act to get there. I'm ready for my next challenge."

Greta and Sam are smiling as they guide me out the back door where a soft wind lifts the blood-spattered hair from my eyes.

A READER'S GUIDE

Lia Erickson, a 19-year-old aspiring Olympic ski racer injured in a World Cup race in Maribor, Yugoslavia, has returned to the United States to rehabilitate her ankle, overcome the trauma inflicted by two predatory coaches, and decide whether protesting the Vietnam War in 1971 is more important than returning to the US Ski Team.

During her months of self-doubt, she travels from the US capital to her home in Waitsfield, Vermont, to Monmouth ski area, and to the University of California at Berkeley. She confronts numerous dangers throughout her journey while climbing in the Wind Rivers Wilderness, studying in college, and protesting in Washington, DC.

Questions and Topics for Discussion

1. Where is Lia Erickson in the first chapter and why is she there? What major decisions does she face?

2. Most elite athletes, when injured, experience self-doubt about their abilities during their rehabilitation. How is Lia handling her loss of self-confidence?

3. When returning to Vermont, in what way does she gain a sense of comfort, as well as confidence?

4. Throughout the novel, the Vietnam War is a theme. What does Lia learn about the war when she is home?

5. Post-traumatic stress disease (PTSD) affects many characters in the novel. Identify and describe how this illness changes some of these characters' lives.

6. Nature has always been Lia's sanctuary, yet through the hardships and dangers in the Wind Rivers Mountains, she gains personal insight. Why do some people learn most during their times of struggle?

7. Although a contrary character, Rob Attlefellner aids Lia in her journey

toward self-awareness. Explain how he helps her.

8. Cities frighten Lia; yet by putting herself in unfamiliar settings such as Berkeley, she acquires new talents and confidence. Why?

9. Why does Lia return to the mountains at Thanksgiving and how does her reunion with her teammates help her decision?

10. Terry and Greta are strong female role models. Are they positive influences and how do they affect Lia's choices?

11. In working through self-doubt, an athlete needs supportive mentors, both younger and older. Identify some of Lia's mentors.

12. The transcendental writers such as Emerson and Thoreau found solace in nature. What does Lia learn from their writings and how does she use their ideas during her time of exploring?

13. Identify the characters who are either physically or spiritually wounded by the Vietnam War. Discuss how Lia's interactions with these characters affect her choices.

14. Lia has numerous fears that she must overcome. Identify some of these fears and how she conquers them.

15. Do you agree with the choice that Lia finally makes?

CPSIA information can be obtained
at www.ICGtesting.com
Printed in the USA
JSHW030306050822
28919JS00002B/9